PRIEST
IN A SUITCASE

P.J. MONTGOMERY

For my wife.

CONTENTS

To Dr Ann Moore,
for reading each chapter and offering advice
and encouragement to carry on.

CHAPTER ONE

Father James Fenwick folded the altar cloth carefully. He put the unused communion hosts and the altar wine back into the tabernacle and locked it carefully. As he did so he noted the last few parishioners walking out of the church. There were never more than a few these days, it was a depressing sight; that had reflected the declining numbers for the last year or so.

Father Fenwick had been moved to St Matthew's parish fifteen months ago. It was considered at the time by the bishop that a younger, more outgoing member of the clergy might encourage parishioners to return to church, particularly those with youth on their side. Father Fenwick was only thirty years of age himself. However, this hadn't been the case and the overall numbers who attended mass had continued to decline.

Father Fenwick thought about this for a few moments. He had never really considered becoming a priest when he was younger. He had wanted to become a motor mechanic, or join the army, because he was an active youth, who loved sport, particularly running. His father, who was an Irishman by birth had wished to have a priest in the family, as was an expectation that was held by many Irish families.

"Dad," he had explained. "I don't fancy being a priest, I'd rather join the army, or be a motor mechanic."

"Ah son," his father had replied. "It's a dream for an Irish family to have a priest in it, so it is."

This is the way the conversation continued for many months. James had just completed his 'A' levels, and was expected to do well, so his father had aspirations for him eventually becoming a Bishop, Archbishop, or even the Pope.

He was a few weeks off his 18th birthday, so his father had decided that he should enter a seminary shortly after his birthday, rather than joining the army, embarking on an apprenticeship, or entering university.

So, here he was at the present time. A Roman Catholic priest, attached to St Matthew's Roman Catholic Church, pounding the pavements of Liverpool in his spare time.

*

After a few moments, Father Fenwick moved into the vestry to disrobe. He changed into a bright red tracksuit, white socks, and training shoes. On the back of the tracksuit was the logo, 'Liverpool FC'. He was a keen fan of the football club, but didn't attend the matches so much nowadays. He decided that he would jog about three miles on this particular day; he had decided this whilst presenting his sermon to the sparse congregation.

Father Fenwick felt quite alone while he jogged, and he relished this, because it helped him to ease the stresses of his role as a priest. Because St Matthew's was a small parish, he was on his own a great deal. He shared the presbytery with Father Frederick, who was in his eighties and the housekeeper, Mrs Davies, who did not live in the presbytery. So, Father Fenwick only had Father Frederick for company for most of the time, and due to the age gap, they didn't have much in common, apart from their ecclesiastical role.

Roman Catholic priests were not allowed to get married, so any relationship with a female would be regarded as a friendly relationship, with no reproductive activity. Father Fenwick wished that this could be different, because he had an eye for the female form, but sexual encounters were not an option for priests. Father Fenwick would not do anything that would compromise his vow of celibacy, however.

After five minutes of jogging, he started increasing his speed while he imagined all sorts of possible scenarios, that would be feasible for him if he wasn't a priest. Fr Fenwick was quite a good athlete, he had competed on occasions for a local running club. He didn't fancy joining a gym, because the thought of changing in the dressing room and showering after his workout with other men, in close proximity, was not a prospect that he relished.

*

On this particular day, however, the going seemed rather more of an effort than usual. He was puffing and blowing much more. His right calf was painful, and he felt a sharp pain at the back of his knee. This was not what he needed right now, as any interruption to his training regime would not be very welcome. He needed to keep running in order to keep his mind active, and to ward off the anxiety which plagued him constantly.

As he ran, he kept an eye on his stopwatch. Six and a half minutes for a mile, that was not too bad considering his aches and pains. A further half mile to the presbytery and he could look forward to a hot shower.

He was so busy concentrating on his pace that he didn't notice the attractive young woman that he was passing.

"Keep your knees-up Father," she shouted.

Father Fenwick slowed and turned around to see who it was. He continued jogging on the spot, to avoid losing his momentum. He was confronted by one of his parishioners, Julie Bingham. She was twenty-two years of age, and someone whom Father Fenwick had always found very attractive.

"Oh, hello, Julie," he said, slightly out of puff. "How are you today?"

"Oh, not too bad, Father," she replied. "I'm just on my way to work, and I'm running a bit late."

Julie worked in the local corner shop. She hated working there, which was a pity, because she was a bright girl and was well capable of finding employment more suited to her capabilities.

"Right then, you'd better be on your way Julie, I hope that I see you at mass on Sunday."

"You will Father, I'll see you there," she said, presenting him with a huge smile, and a wink.

*

Father Fenwick was glad to continue with his run, he didn't fancy cooling down too much, and so he sprinted off briskly, as if to catch up on lost time. As he did so, he was aware that Julie had left him with a hint of her perfume in the air. Mm, he thought to himself. That's nice, and he savoured the delightful aroma as he continued with his run.

CHAPTER TWO

Some five minutes later, Father Fenwick reached the presbytery. He felt quite elated, although he wasn't sure whether it was the result of his workout, or the whiff of Julie's perfume. One thing that he was sure about, was the amount of perspiration that was dripping off him. He really did need a shower now. He stood in the hallway for a few moments, to reflect on his run and to get his breath back.

There was a sudden creaking sound, and the door of the lounge opened suddenly. Mrs Davies, the housekeeper stood there.

"Oh, hello, Father, you're back," she said. "Bishop Larkin is here to see you, and he doesn't appear to be in a very good mood."

"Oh no," blurted Father Fenwick. "I remember now that he wanted to see me, but I had forgotten all about it. I suppose that I'd better go in right away."

"I don't think that's a very good idea, to see him in that state," remarked Mrs Davies. "You look as though you've been dragged through a duck pond."

However, the matter was resolved suddenly. The bishop appeared at the door behind Mrs Davies.

"Ah, at last Father Fenwick, I've been waiting here for over an hour, and you eventually grace me with your presence, looking like you've been dragged out of a lagoon."

"Yes," replied Father Fenwick. "Sorry about that. I thought that I would do a little bit of training after morning mass, it saves me using the car as well."

"Hmm," replied the bishop. "No matter, I want to have a word with you, it won't take long."

They both sat down at the table. Father Fenwick wondered what Bishop Larkin wanted to talk to him about.

"You've been here for just over a year now Father Fenwick, and I note that the congregation hasn't increased very much. However, this is not the reason why I wish to have this discussion with you."

Father Fenwick sighed. It wasn't his fault that the congregation had not increased. After all, they were not trying to sell a new line in washing powder.

"The archbishop has been in contact with me," continued the bishop. "Have you heard about the new estate that has been built in rural Cheshire? It's called *New Pastures.*"

Father Fenwick had heard that there was a new estate that had been built, not far from Chester. It was designed for the overspill from Liverpool, to move people out to a new, more modern, cleaner environment. Out of the dreary houses of yesteryear, a better way of life, the so-called experts called it. There would still be the same problems of poverty and crime, nothing much would change. He wondered what this had to do with him though.

"Well," Bishop Larkin added, "I have been advised by the archbishop that he is looking for a young, outgoing, forward thinking priest to establish a new parish, and he asked me if I could recommend anyone, so naturally I thought of you."

Father Fenwick's heart sank. Just what he didn't need, a further move, where expectations would be high. It was hard enough trying to increase parishioners at St Matthew's, but a new community would be a lot of hard work. He would be on his own and would have to search out who were Catholics and encourage them to become involved in the new parish. It would be a challenge, but in his present state of mind, he felt that he didn't need a challenge.

"You would be right there at the start," the bishop said. "A new parish, just think of that. Naturally, there is no church there at the present time, but hopefully, we can arrange for one to be built in the future. However, because it is a new town, the council have a duty to provide such facilities. They would need to build a school, so a church could be part of that."

"Where will the presbytery be?" Asked Father Fenwick.

"Oh, that is taken care of," replied the bishop. "We have arranged for you to move into one of the newly built homes on the estate. You will be living right in the middle of your flock, so to speak. It will be furnished, quite sparsely of course, as befits a member of the clergy."

No expense spared, thought Father Fenwick, no surprise there.

"You won't be supplied with a car, of course," advised the bishop. "The car will remain here. You'll be able to get around quite easily on the estate, I'm sure. In fact, you'll be able to run around, and attract parishioners as you do so."

Father Fenwick noted the sarcasm in the bishop's tone, but the thought of running in the countryside, instead of on inner city pavements, washed over him like a breath of fresh air. He would also be on his own, to run the new parish as he thought fit. No Father Frederick to constantly check on him and interfere with his methods of working. The very thought of this new placement suddenly began to appeal to him.

"Father Frederick is getting on a bit now, so he would not have the energy and foresight to get a new parish off the ground, he will be much better remaining here at St Matthew's, and will need the car for transport around this parish," advised the bishop. "You will continue to receive a stipend as you do now, but as this is a new venture, the diocese may be able to add to the basic amount, to get you started, because you will need extra items of furniture for the presbytery."

The basic income for a catholic priest is very low, so in order to top the allowance up, a priest may rely on donations from his family and parishioners. Father Fenwick could approach his father for a little financial assistance to help him out, but assistance from the parishioners would not be an option from the outset.

"Right," concluded Bishop Larkin. "That's done, I'll be in touch to let you know when you will be able to move, I expect good things from you Father Fenwick, good luck."

The bishop left with a flourish, leaving Father Fenwick to contemplate on his new life. He went up the stairs to have his shower, at last, his sweat had now dried on him. He had a great deal to think about. Maybe it would turn out all right in the end.

CHAPTER THREE

Father Frederick buttered his second slice of toast, cut it in half and took a bite. He looked rather thoughtful as he chewed.

"They don't make teeth like they used to," he said. "I used to be able to chew a house brick, but now I struggle with a piece of half-done toast."

"Mrs Davies does the best that she can," replied Father Fenwick. "But I admit that the toast would do just as well as a sponge."

Father Frederick looked pensively at Father Fenwick for a moment. "You'll be leaving to start your new post in a week or so, I suppose?"

"Yes, I haven't heard anything definite yet," replied Father Fenwick. "It's not going to be easy though, starting a new parish from scratch, there isn't even a church built yet."

"So where will you say mass?" enquired Father Frederick.

"I'm not sure at the moment," Father Fenwick replied. "I'll be making a visit to the area in the next few days. There is a school building on the estate, but I don't think that it's catholic."

"Mm," uttered Father Frederick. "Mass in a protestant church, well, it's better than nothing."

"Yes," replied Father Fenwick. "I could make a temporary altar in my lounge at first, because I don't expect that I'll have many parishioners to start with."

"I'd certainly like to see that," replied Father Frederick "It would certainly be different, you wouldn't need a sound system anyway."

"Yes, that's true, but I'd certainly need one to play my Bob Marley records," said Father Fenwick with a loud laugh."

"Or my Verdi operas," added Father Frederick.

*

Father Fenwick poured himself a second cup of tea. "And this tea looks like it's been dredged up from the River Mersey," he said laughingly.

The next day he had planned a trip to *New Pastures*, to get a feel of his new parish. He opened the door of the ageing Vauxhall car, which was parked on the drive outside the presbytery, and eased himself into the driver's seat. He breathed a huge sigh of relief when it started first time. He had spent many hours tinkering with the car. It was just as well that he had plenty of practice with repairing motors. His father had owned an old jalopy, and this is why he had once had the desire to become a motor mechanic. He was glad that he would not have oil all over his hands today.

He glanced at his map, to remind himself of the route that he would take. It was about twelve miles. Across the Runcorn bridge and out towards Chester on the M56. He put the car into first gear, with a loud crunching noise, and drove out of the presbytery drive, with a slight jerky movement. The traffic was reasonably light today, which was a relief, because he had no desire to be stuck in a traffic jam, particularly on the Runcorn bridge, which was notorious for congestion.

After forty minutes of driving, a road sign came into view, announcing that he had reached *New Pastures*. Father Fenwick took a left turn which led up a narrow stretch of road, and then gradually led to a much wider road. He took in his first view of what was going to be his new placement and home. *New Pastures* had been built on what had previously been a large meadow, with large, wooded areas. Some trees had been felled, but many were retained, which gave way to little copses and provided a charming backdrop to the houses. The general impression on Father Fenwick was a scene of tranquillity.

The estate comprised twelve separate areas, comprising twenty houses each. Each Close was named after a tree, which would remind the residents that they were living in what had once been a large wooded area. This was so different from his present parish, which comprised rows and rows of terraced houses, with a yard at the rear, instead of a garden.

Father Fenwick continued driving around the perimeter road, noting the various little cul-de-sacs, with their names. In the centre of the estate, he noted a large school. A large noticeboard outside announced that it was called St Edward's. Hopefully, this school could be utilised for the purpose of Sunday mass, in the short term, he thought. It would not be possible to hold mass during the week, due to it being a Non-Catholic school, and the morning assembly would be held there. The plan was, that a new church would be built eventually, for the purpose of ministering to the local Catholic community.

Father Fenwick had been allocated a house at number ten Willow Close. He drove around until he located it and stopped to have a look. It was a nice house, he thought, although similar in design to the other houses on the estate. It was a bit on the small side, but would be large enough for his needs. How different this was from the inner-city presbytery that he was used to.

He got out of the car and walked over to the house, and peered through the window.

"Hmm," he said to himself. "It's a little on the small side, but the lounge will be big enough to install a makeshift altar in the short term." He would certainly be amongst his flock, he thought to himself, smiling.

As he was looking through the window, a rather short, stout gentleman was walking past. He stopped and walked over to where Father Fenwick was standing.

"Hello," he said. "Can I help you?"

"Good afternoon," replied Father Fenwick. "I'm going to become the parish priest for this new area, and I've been allocated this house, I'll be moving in shortly."

"Oh," replied the man. "My name's Bob, and I live at number five Oak Close, but, we haven't' got a parish here."

"Glad to meet you, Bob," replied Father Fenwick. "I'm called Father Fenwick, but you can call me James, or Jim if you prefer, my job will be to establish a parish here eventually, are you Catholic by any chance?"

"Yes, I am," replied Bob. "We moved here six months ago from Walton, it's far better here than our old area, lovely countryside, and we now have a garden."

"Yes," I agree said Father Fenwick. "It is a lovely area, I think that I will be very happy here, where do you go for mass at the present time?"

"We have to go to Saint Mark's, which is a couple of miles outside this estate," replied Bob. "But, it's very awkward if you haven't got a car. It would be much better if we had our own church here on the estate."

"Well, that is the general plan," replied Father Fenwick. "But it may take some time to build a church, my bishop expects great things from me."

"I'm sure that you will do well," said Bob. "It will be good to have our own parish here, a Catholic community on our doorstep."

"Yes," replied Father Fenwick. "When communities are broken up and moved elsewhere, their pastoral needs are very often overlooked. The main priority is to provide more modern accommodation, which is of course important. To get people out of their inner-city environment, and give them a better life, but it may move them further from their jobs, if they have one of course."

"That's true, Father," replied Bob. A lot of people that I know were unemployed before moving here, and they still have little chance of getting a job now, they're just moving to a different job centre. Oh well, I need to be somewhere, you'll have to excuse me Father," he said, changing the subject quite suddenly. "I'll see you again when you move in."

"Yes," replied Father Fenwick. "See you again, Bob, I'll look forward to talking to you again." He watched Bob walk away at a brisk pace, Bob certainly looked like a man in a hurry. "Yes, we'll certainly talk again," he said to himself. He walked back to his car, to continue his look around the estate. Bob will be a useful contact when I move here he thought to himself.

CHAPTER FOUR

Father Fenwick stepped out of the presbytery. He walked down the drive, onto the lawn and turned around. He gazed back at the presbytery, which had been his temporary home for the last fifteen months.

It was the first week of October, and the trees in the garden had already started turning different shades of brown and commenced their annual copper carpeting of the pathway.

Tomorrow, he would move to his new parish in rural Cheshire, and he would be deceiving himself if he didn't feel apprehensive. He had arranged to receive assistance from his friend and fellow priest, Father David O'Donovan, who owned a small van. He assured Father Fenwick that he would be able to transport all of his belongings in one trip, not that it was a great deal.

The house had been fitted out with a kitchen, including a small cooker. Father Fenwick had his own microwave and this would be the most useful piece of equipment, he thought. He didn't regard himself as a chef, but he could knock up the odd meal or so and he could always survive on ready meals. There would be no housekeeper, like Mrs Davies, so he would have to manage on his own.

A folding camper bed would also go with him, it was quite comfortable, as he had used it on several camping trips. Clothing would be no problem, as he didn't own much of a wardrobe. A couple of pairs of jeans, black trousers, for formal clerical duties and dog collars etc. His beloved tracksuit, running shorts and vests, together with his running trainers would be most important in his eyes. His vestments, a chalice, communion hosts and communion wine should of course be the most important, to enable him to complete his priestly duties.

Father Fenwick would need some wood to build an altar initially, if he could locate a joiner to construct one. Although, he had a pasting table, which would suffice in the immediate future.

When a more suitable altar had been made, the pasting table would come in handy for any wallpapering jobs, he thought, smiling broadly to himself.

Father David appeared at just after nine o'clock the following morning.

"Morning, David," said Father Fenwick. "I appreciate your help, it saves all the fuss of booking a removal firm and waiting around for ages."

"That's no problem, James," replied Father David. "I didn't have much on today anyway, and it's nice to have a run out in the country."

Father David was an assistant priest in a similar inner-city parish as was Father Fenwick, although he liked the country, he didn't share Father Fenwick's love of running, and it was obvious when you viewed him from a sideways perspective. They were just about to complete packing the van when a voice behind them made them turn around. "Hello, Father," said the voice.

Father Fenwick was surprised to see Julie Bingham standing there. "Oh hello, Julie," he replied. "What are you doing here?"

"I found out that you were leaving today and I wanted to say goodbye and wish you all the best, I've bought you a parting gift."

"That's very kind of you," replied Father Fenwick, taken aback by her generosity. "But you shouldn't have spent your hard-earned cash on me, but it's a nice gesture all the same."

"It's no big deal, Father," replied Julie, "I thought that you would like this book, it's all about running."

"Thanks very much, Julie." He opened the bag and was surprised and delighted to see that the book was about Josh Naylor, the famous Cumbrian fell runner.

"Gosh," retorted Father Fenwick, "I've heard about this book, but never thought that anyone would go to the trouble of buying me a copy." He coloured slightly. This didn't go unnoticed by Father O' Donovan.

"You've got an admirer for life there, James," he said.

"Yes, so it seems," replied Father Fenwick. He wished that he had more parishioners like Julie.

"I'll certainly miss you Julie," he said fondly. "Maybe I'll see you at mass in my new parish, when it is up and running."

"I hope so, Father," replied Julie. "It will be great if I can come to mass in a brand-new parish, that you have started, so I hope to see you then."

"Yes, I certainly hope that I will see you there Julie, in the meantime, good luck and take care of yourself."

He watched as Julie walked off. In some ways he would miss this parish, if only for a few of his flock and particularly Julie. He certainly hoped that Julie would visit his new parish.

CHAPTER FIVE

It took the two priests fifty-five minutes to get to *New Pastures*. The traffic had been quite heavy and Father O'Donovan was not the fastest of drivers. However, they arrived safely in one piece and Father Fenwick directed his friend to number ten Willow Close.

"Hey," murmured Father O'Donovan. "This place is quite the picture, no heavy traffic and no terraced houses, but fields and trees."

"Yes, that's right," replied Father Fenwick, "I think that I'm going to enjoy being here."

"A nice little house as well," Father O'Donovan pointed out, as they pulled up outside number ten Willow Close.

"Yes," replied Father Fenwick. "Well actually, it's the presbytery, rather than a house. Ha Ha."

They both got out of the van and Father Fenwick got his keys from his pocket and opened the front door. They both stepped inside the house and got their first view of the inside of the property, because Father Fenwick had not been inside himself.

"Not bad at all," said Father O'Donovan, "It's bigger than it looks on the outside."

"Yes," agreed Father Fenwick. "This will suit me very well, and it's much brighter than the presbytery at St Mathew's."

The two priests set about unloading the van. This task would not take long, due to the amount of furniture that was involved. When they had finished unloading, Father Fenwick put the kettle on to make some tea.

"Thanks, David, for your help," he said. "Would you like something to eat before you go back?"

"Just a cup of tea will do," replied Father David. "I have some home visits to do when I get back."

When they had finished their tea, Father David bid Father Fenwick farewell and with a loud honking of the car horn, he was gone.

Father Fenwick suddenly felt quite alone. Well, he thought, this is it, the opening of a new chapter. The beginning of a new parish. He would get himself settled in his new home and would say mass the next morning, even if he was on his own. Then the work would begin.

He then began to think about what he was going to have for his evening meal. This would not be a difficult decision. He looked into the kitchen cupboards, which had been arranged earlier.

"Hmm," he said to himself. He had a loaf of bread and a tin of beans. That would do fine he thought, beans on toast would sustain him until the next day.

He was just thinking about this when there was a knock on the front door. He was quite surprised, because nobody knew he was there yet, although they could have seen the van earlier. When he opened the door, Father Fenwick was surprised to see Bob standing on the doorstep.

"Hello again, Father," said Bob. "I noticed the van outside earlier and saw you and another gentleman moving your furniture in."

Father Fenwick smiled at Bob. "Hi Bob, nice to see you again, I wouldn't go as far as to say it was furniture, more bits and pieces, but I'm sure that it'll be adequate for my requirements for the time being."

"Is there anything that I can help you with Father?" enquired Bob.

"No, I don't think so, at the moment," replied Father Fenwick. "I was just about to have something to eat."

"Yes, I noticed the tin of beans on the kitchen unit," said Bob with a smile. "You are welcome to eat at ours if you like, my wife is cooking a roast, and there'll be plenty for the three of us."

"Hey, that's very kind of you," replied Father Fenwick. "Are you sure that's OK?"

"Yes, of course," Bob replied. "The wife will be glad to meet you."

*

Mrs Jenkins opened the oven door and grimaced. "Tut-tut," she said to herself. "Those roast potatoes look a bit overdone, but Bob won't mind, he's not fussy." She was proud of her standard of cooking, and she didn't like to feel that she was failing in any way, or producing any meal that she was not completely satisfied with.

While she was muttering to herself, she heard the key in the front door and a voice boomed out.

"Hi love, I've brought a guest for dinner."

Mrs Jenkins went into the hall and was surprised to see Father Fenwick standing there with her husband.

"Oh," she announced. "Is this Father Fenwick?, I've been looking forward to meeting you Father, come on in and make yourself comfortable."

"Thank you, Mrs Jenkins," replied Father Fenwick. He immediately felt that he had known this lady for years, she was so welcoming, with a friendly face and a warming smile. He sat down in a rather comfortable looking chair and immediately felt quite relaxed. "Would you like a cup of tea Father?" she asked. "Tea will be ready in about half an hour."

"That's very kind of you, Mrs Jenkins," Father Fenwick replied.

"Milk and no sugar if you please."

"OK, you can call me Vera, although my friends call me Ve for short."

"Vera is the best," said Bob. "She welcomes anyone who visits us, she has been especially interested in meeting you Father. She's been going on since we moved here about having no church of our own. When she heard that we were going to have our own priest and a new parish, she was over the moon."

"Thank you, Bob," replied Father Fenwick, "that is very encouraging to hear, and it makes me feel that moving here will be more positive."

"I'm sure that it will," replied Bob. "We know quite a few Catholics around the estate and I'm sure that they would appreciate a visit from you."

"I do hope so," replied Father Fenwick. "A parish wouldn't be of much use if there were no parishioners."

"That's right," said Bob. "But there has got to be a church for this estate, parishes outside this area will not be too accommodating for us I think."

"Dinner's ready," Mrs Jenkins shouted from the kitchen. There was much clattering of plates and pans as she made herself busy for serving the meal. She came out of the kitchen carrying three plates of roast beef. She then placed a tureen containing mixed vegetables on the table, followed by a jug of gravy.

"My word," announced Father Fenwick. "That does smell good."

"Help yourself to veg and gravy, Father," said Mrs Jenkins. "Oh, and I almost forgot the roast potatoes, I'll get them now. Would you like a glass of wine with your meal, Father?"

"That would be very nice," replied Father Fenwick. "Thank you."

"I'll get that," said Bob. He went into the kitchen and returned with three glasses and a bottle of red wine. "Not exactly your altar wine, it's a lot stronger," Bob said with a loud laugh.

Father Fenwick laughed loudly as well, he was certainly feeling at home here.

After the meal was gratefully consumed, which had included a generous helping of apple pie and custard, to follow the roast beef. Father Fenwick and Bob did the washing up, while Mrs Jenkins had a well-deserved rest.

Father Fenwick said goodbye to Bob and Vera a short time later, he felt that he would fall asleep if he didn't move. "I'll be in touch with you again, Bob," he said. "Things to sort out over the next couple of days."

They waved each other goodbye, and Father Fenwick walked back to his own house, or what was now the presbytery to be exact.

He had really appreciated the meal that he had just eaten. It was much better than beans on toast. He decided that he would invite Vera and Bob to the presbytery one day, and show off his culinary skills. He would have to get himself organised with shopping though, he thought to himself.

CHAPTER SIX

The next morning as Father Fenwick consumed his rather sparse breakfast, consisting of a bowl of muesli and two cups of tea. His position finally dawned on him. When he was in St Matthew's presbytery, everything was laid on for him. There was Mrs Davies, the housekeeper, who provided all the provisions; did the cooking, cleaned, and completed the general housework. Now, he was on his own. He would have to do his own shopping, cook his own meals and clean the house. A housekeeper was not provided; unless he could arrange for his own. However, finances at the present time would not suffice, although some housekeepers provided services on a voluntary basis. But, Father Fenwick would not want this situation and would not expect anyone to work for free, purely for the love of the church, if there was one of course. He felt like he was simply living the life of a bachelor, rather than that of a parish priest.

He had arranged to meet the headmaster of St Edward's Church of England school later in the day. The reason being to request his permission to use the school hall each Sunday, for the purpose of celebrating Sunday mass. Father Fenwick felt that once this had been arranged, and his congregation had begun to come together, the first step had been reached.

As he continued to crunch on his muesli, he contemplated the dawning situation. A parish had to be built from scratch. There was the major problem of building a new church, and this project would require a considerable amount of funding. Also, a congregation had to be formed, and Father Fenwick was not entirely sure if the new residents were churchgoers, and indeed, whether they shared his enthusiasm for getting the whole shooting match off the ground. Let alone, for setting everything up for mass each Sunday. At first, mass could be celebrated in his temporary church living room. As a Roman Catholic priest, he had a duty to celebrate mass each day. Life would have been much more straightforward, had he been a motor mechanic, he thought wistfully. It would have been far easier to sort out problems with a motor car, rather than those that are connected with the Catholic Church and clergy. Father Fenwick turned this over in his mind as he walked to St Edward's school to meet the headmaster, Mr Brian Simmons.

*

Brian Simmons strode into the staff room at St Edward's Church of England school. He was a rather tall man, about five foot eight, thought Father Fenwick. His hair was brushed straight back, a little long over the ears, and he wore a small moustache. He was dressed quite casually, for a headmaster, wearing an open collared shirt and bright blue trousers, but this was how things were in the modern climate.

He greeted Father Fenwick with a hearty handshake.

"Hello, Father, I'm very glad to meet you, I have heard over the grapevine that you had been appointed as parish priest for the Catholic fraternity in this new town."

"Yes," replied Father Fenwick. "For my sins, so to speak, but I'm quite looking forward to being involved in this new parish right from the start, to serve the Catholic community. Obviously, there is no Catholic Church at the present time, but plans are in place for one to be built."

"That may take some time and money," replied Mr Simmons.

Father Fenwick looked a little sheepish. "I think that it will," he said. "My old parish will still be involved in getting this new parish off the ground. In the meantime, I'll need somewhere to say Sunday mass. During the week I could celebrate mass in my front lounge, I have set up a temporary altar in there."

"By, Jove," said Mr Simmons. "What will you do on Sunday?"

"Well that is why I am here," replied Father Fenwick. "It would be very convenient if mass could be celebrated in your school hall."

Mr Simmons was thoughtful for a moment.

"I see," he said. "Mass in a Protestant church, what would the Pope have to say about that?"

"I don't think that we need to ask him," replied Father Fenwick, with a smile. "It's purely a parish matter."

"I see," said Mr Simmons. "I don't see any reason why not, the school is closed at the weekend and it wouldn't pose any problems that I can think of."

"That would be very helpful," replied Father Fenwick. "It would only be until a new church could be built; during the week, I'll say mass at home."

"Well, that will certainly be different," replied Mr Simmons. "I'll arrange with the caretaker to open and close the school for you; when shall you start?"

"I would imagine in a few weeks' time," replied Father Fenwick. "I'll have to arrange a meeting to ascertain how many parishioners that I am likely to be ministering to. "However, I have a few contacts already, who will hopefully spread the word around."

"That's fine," said Mr Simmons. "Just let me know when you want to start and I'll make the necessary arrangements."

"Thanks for your help, Mr Simmons, I really appreciate it," said Father Fenwick.

"Call me Brian," replied Mr Simmons, "I hope that we can achieve a good working relationship."

"OK, Brian, mine is James, or some people just call me Jim."

They bade each other farewell and Father Fenwick walked out of the school. He breathed a sigh of relief. He felt as if the ball had started rolling. Next on the list, was shopping for some provisions, he could not expect to dine with Bob and Vera again.

Later that day, he had returned from the shops, with enough food to keep him going for several days. The provisions comprising tinned food and some ready meals. Not that healthy, but he was going to be quite busy over the next week or so, and he didn't want to get bogged down with too much cooking. Although, he was quite a proficient cook, his culinary skills could be put on hold for the time being. Maybe he would invite Bob and Vera around for a meal one evening when he was more settled.

*

Later that day, there was a knock on the door and on opening it, Father Fenwick was pleased to see Bob standing there.

"Hi, Father James," announced Bob, that was his new way of addressing Father Fenwick, which was quite pleasing to him. It made the friendship more personal and less formal.

"Hello, Bob," he replied, "It's nice to see you again, I wanted to thank you and Vera for an excellent meal last night."

"You're welcome," said Bob. "I wondered if you would like to meet one of my close friends this evening, his name is Steve Farrell?"

"I'd like that, Bob, shall we say about seven?"

"That will be OK," replied Bob, "see you later."

As arranged, Bob called for Father Fenwick at seven. It had

started to rain. So they walked rather briskly, to avoid the possibility of getting soaked.

"How long have you known, Steve?" asked Father Fenwick.

"Since we moved here," replied Bob. "He is also a Catholic, we met in the local pub and got chatting over a pint. We hit it off right away, and the conversation was very fluid, he opened up to me about his life, he needed someone to talk to and offload his troubles."

"How do you mean?" asked Father Fenwick.

"His wife has got Dementia, she was diagnosed three months ago," replied Bob.

"That's very sad," replied Father Fenwick. "I have met a lot of people who are suffering with this condition, it tears people apart, particularly the person who cares for them."

"It does," said Bob. "Steve is doing a grand job looking after Jen, he finds it a real struggle sometimes."

Father Fenwick thought about the situation as they arrived at number eight Oak Close. He admired a husband or wife who cared for their spouse. It would be so easy to put them in a home and let someone else do the caring. Of course, he was aware that there were financial issues with this option that could persuade a person to take the self-caring way forward. But, to want to care for your partner, out of love and put your own life on hold, was the most important Christian act that anyone could do. As a priest, Father Fenwick had the greatest respect for such a person. He knew that he would like Steve before he even met him.

CHAPTER SEVEN

Steve Farrell answered the door after Bob had knocked loudly several times.

"Steve hasn't got around to fitting a bell as yet," said Bob. "They only moved in about four weeks ago."

Father Fenwick nodded, he was well aware how easy it was to put DIY jobs off, leave it till tomorrow was the normal way, and of course tomorrow never comes.

Steve opened the door and greeted them both with a cheery smile.

"Hello, Bob and Father Fenwick," he announced. "I've heard a lot about you, Father."

"Hello, Steve," replied Father Fenwick. "Very glad to meet you, how are you keeping?"

"Oh, not too bad, Father, I vary from day to day, depending on how my wife is."

"Yes, Bob has explained your predicament," replied Father Fenwick. "It must be a difficult time for you."

Steve nodded in agreement, and invited them both in. They were shown into the lounge. Father Fenwick was impressed how clean and tidy the room was, there was hardly anything out of place. In the corner, Steve's wife, Jen, was sitting in a rather large armchair. In her arms she nestled a doll, which she was stroking and singing to as if it were real.

"She loves that doll," said Steve. "She thinks that it's real, and I don't mind because it keeps her quiet and makes her more content. We have never had children you see Father, Jen couldn't have them."

"I'm sorry to hear that," replied Father Fenwick. He could really feel for this couple, not to have children and for his wife to suffer with Dementia.

"How do you manage?" he asked.

"We have support from Social Services," replied Steve. "Help with basic things, such as washing and dressing. She also has help to have a shower five mornings a week."

Bob is a really good mate too, he and Vera help. Vera goes shopping for us quite regularly and sometimes sits with Jen while I go shopping, man shopping that is," he added with a cheeky grin. "Vera will sit with Jen once a week while Steve and I go to the local for a couple of pints," added Bob.

"It sounds like you have got a good support system Steve," said Father Fenwick. "You certainly need it, you have a difficult task on your hands."

"I have, Father," replied Steve. "If it was left to our families, we would be struggling. They never visit. I had what I regarded as good friends in Liverpool, but I rarely see or hear from them nowadays."

"I'm afraid this is a common factor," Father Fenwick said. "People seem to keep their distance when someone has Dementia, they are afraid of the condition almost, and don't know how to handle it."

"Now be a good little girl and go to sleep now," mumbled Jen from her chair in the corner. "That's the way she is," said Steve. "She thinks that the doll is real."

"It is in her world," replied Father Fenwick. "She is happy in her own private world, unfortunately it is the carers who are very often unhappy, because they carry the burden of care."

Father Fenwick and Bob sat down in the dining area, which comprised a small kitchen at one end and the dining area at the other. There was a small dining table and four chairs.

Steve made a pot of tea and placed it on the table, together with a large Victoria sandwich cake. They all busied themselves, pouring tea and cutting the cake.

"How are you settling in, Father?" enquired Steve.

"Very well thank you, Steve," replied Father Fenwick, "I feel that I have been presented with a daunting job, creating a new Catholic parish from scratch."

"There is a need for it here," remarked Steve. "*New Pastures* is not only a new estate, but a complete community. There is a definite need for a church, I mean, we already have a pub."

"Yes," replied Father Fenwick, with a smile. "There certainly is a need for a church as well, although, the attendances at mass, and church generally, have declined considerably, so one can't presume that all Catholics in this area will be churchgoers."

"Well, I think that we will all look forward to the day when the church is built," said Bob.

"Amen to that," Father Fenwick added. "If I can be of any help in any way, you can always contact me at the presbytery."

*

Father Fenwick stood up and looked in the lounge to see how Steve's wife was doing, she appeared quite forlorn and lost in her own world. He bid his goodbyes to Bob and Steve and walked back to the presbytery. He felt quite sad when he thought about Steve and his wife. It felt so unfair that such a nice couple should suffer like this. The more that he thought about the situation, the more angry, and helpless he felt.

The rain had stopped now, so he felt the need for a run to burn up his feelings of frustration and sadness at what he had just witnessed.

CHAPTER EIGHT

Father Fenwick quickly changed into his running gear and went out of his front door. He hadn't had a run since moving to *New Pastures*, and he was concerned that his standard of fitness may have deteriorated somewhat. He eased into a steady pace at first and after a short while, he felt the need to quicken his pace, so he need not have worried.

He ran around the perimeter road of the estate. At the far end, there were the remains of a large, wooded area. As he entered this, he felt a feeling of euphoria. There was such joy in running through woods, the smell of the grass and foliage was a tonic in itself. Father Fenwick was well aware of the benefits of any exercise for the relief of anxiety, and he was feeling quite anxious at the present time.

One of the main causes of his anxiety was the trust that had been placed on him in his ability to build this new parish. In St Matthew's, there was great concern about the diminishing numbers of parishioners who attended mass. Now, in this area, he had to inspire people to not only consider the sacraments, but to attend mass in a Non-Catholic school hall.

As he began to enjoy his run, Father Fenwick began to relax more, why was he so concerned? He would try his best, that's all that he could do. For a start, he had already met and made friends with Bob and Steve, and he was sure that he could inspire people. He would have the support of St Matthew's parish and Bishop Larkin. He wondered how Father Frederick was getting on, eating rubber toast with his wobbly teeth. This thought made him smile, and then he started to laugh quite loudly.

Father Fenwick had always struggled to come to terms with being a Catholic priest. It wasn't like any other job, with regular hours, you were on duty twenty-four seven. You were not only a priest, but you were also a social worker, and a counsellor. Furthermore, the question of celibacy was a major pitfall. Catholic priests were prohibited from any sexual activity with the female of the species. It wasn't as if Father Fenwick didn't admire the female form, he certainly had an eye. The whole ethos of celibacy was a major issue for him. However, there were priests who did dabble on the side, but for Father Fenwick, this was not an issue. He felt that if he were to indulge in any form of sexual activity, what would be the point of being a priest, after taking his vow of celibacy.

He eventually put all of these thoughts to the back of his mind and concentrated on his running. This wooded area was excellent, a natural cross-country course. The area was so quiet and appeared so isolated, and yet, it was only yards from the hustle and bustle of the estate.

Father Fenwick loved cross-country running, it was much more preferable than running on roads and pavements. He also liked fell running, as he had been a keen hill walker since he was twelve years of age. His father used to take him hiking in the Mourne mountains, in Northern Ireland. He used to say to the young James Fenwick. "This is the best exercise to clear and purify your mind, ideal to prepare you for entering the seminary and your priestly training."

Yes, Father Fenwick remembered well his father's obsession with him becoming a priest. This was the end result, and had led to him moving to *New Pastures*, to continue with his ministry, and running here today. Well, maybe it was not so bad, there were people here who may need his help and support, and he was willing, and able to provide it. Maybe, he should have been a social worker instead of a priest he thought wistfully.

As he rounded a corner, he noticed that there was a large pond in front of him, and so he stopped briefly to take a look. I bet there is plenty of wildlife here, he thought. Such a pleasant spot. He stood near the edge and looked into the water, at his reflection for a moment.

"You are Father James Fenwick," he said out loud to himself. "You can do this, God has brought you here, to this beautiful place, to make a difference, so get on with it."

He felt more positive about the whole situation now, and he continued with his run. He felt more energised now, he can do this, he can do anything.

CHAPTER NINE

Over the next couple of weeks, Father Fenwick became more recognised throughout the estate. He was regularly seen running around the area, and he became known as 'The Running Priest.' The Roman Catholic fraternity became aware that he was the new priest in town. Bob and Steve were responsible for this, in no short measure.

There was much interest and excitement that there was going to be a new parish on their estate. Father Fenwick discovered a new energy. He found it exhilarating that he could enjoy running, whilst calling on would be parishioners at the same time.

The locals were very much interested in the opportunity of having a young priest, who ran around the estate in shorts and vest. This discounted the more traditional image of elderly priests, dressed in black clothing and wearing a dog collar. They were more interested and eager to find out what it was all about. "He runs around in a vest and shorts and snazzy trainers, Mum," one little lad said to his mum.

Father Fenwick called Brian Simmons and asked if the school hall could be made available for mass the following Sunday. He thought that the time was right and it would be a test to assess how many people would form the congregation.

Bob was very happy to hear this news, and he offered his services, if assistance was needed. "I'd be very happy to help," he said.

Father Fenwick was glad of the offer, and he felt that it would provide him with the confidence that he needed.

"Should he need assurance?" he asked himself. He was, after all, only human and priests could be lacking in confidence also. It was agreed that Bob would assist Father Fenwick with all that he would need for the mass, which would be at eleven o'clock.

So, the following Sunday, Bob called at the presbytery at ten o'clock. He helped Father Fenwick to pack a suitcase with all that he would need. This included vestments, a chalice, communion hosts, altar wine and the order of mass.

Father Fenwick had not thought about the question of altar servers to assist him though. However, it wouldn't matter at first, but it would be necessary to arrange this for the future. He could arrange to ask parents about this and train any youngsters who would be interested in becoming altar servers.

When Father Fenwick and Bob arrived at St Edward's school, they were duly met by the caretaker, a Mr George Chandler.

"Good morning, Father," he said. "The hall is ready for you, I've arranged a table for the altar and fifty chairs for the congregation."

"Thank you," said Father Fenwick. "I hope we will fill all the chairs, but I'm not that optimistic."

"I'm sure that it'll be fine," said Bob.

They set about with preparation of the altar and Father Fenwick put on his vestments. Bob looked at him and felt that he was seeing the priest for the first time, rather than being dressed in ordinary clothes, he looked more official now.

At quarter to eleven, the congregation started to come in, and very soon nearly all the fifty chairs were filled with expectant people.

Father Fenwick felt relieved and surprised, considering that this was the first mass. Word had certainly spread and this boded well for the future, he thought.

At exactly eleven o'clock, Father Fenwick welcomed all of the congregation and began to celebrate mass.

"In the name of the Father, and of the son, and of the Holy Spirit," he said.

*

When the moment came for the sermon, he had decided to keep it as low-key as possible. He introduced himself, and immediately endeared himself to the people by his manner, they clung to every word that he said.

"Dear friends," he began. "Welcome to this first mass of our new parish. Many of you have probably seen me around the estate, very often wearing only the briefest of attire."

There was a ripple of laughter, as the congregation visualised the spectacle of Father Fenwick in his running gear.

"I feel," he continued, "that priests should not be regarded as individuals who live in ivory towers, and constantly preach to the masses, about how they should conduct their lives. They should also be regarded as a friend, a communicator, someone who they can turn to when in need, a member of the community, just like anyone else."

Father Fenwick was thinking, particularly, about Steve and his wife Jen as he made this statement.

"My father encouraged me to become a priest, although I had other aspirations. But, I can see now that it was the right choice; now that I have been entrusted to come here to *New Pastures* and continue with my vocation."

After his sermon, which he thought went down very well, Father Fenwick continued with the mass, which ended as he said: "The mass is ended, go in peace."

The congregation replied. "Thanks be to God."

*

As he stood outside the school hall, he was heartened at the praise that he got from the various members of the congregation. Everyone appeared to have enjoyed the mass. Not only because they didn't have to travel a fair distance, to the nearest church, but, the fact that they could attend mass on their doorstep, and also, the prospect of a new Catholic church being built on their estate, increased their anticipation, and of course, Father Fenwick's personality certainly went a long way to heightening their enthusiasm.

While Father Fenwick was attending to his flock, Bob was busy inside the school hall, packing away the essentials of the mass in the suitcase. When Father Fenwick had disrobed, and Bob had packed this away in the suitcase also. He looked up thoughtfully and said, "You are the priest in a suitcase."

They both laughed at this statement and walked out of the school.

Father Fenwick was in a euphoric mood for several days following the mass. When, Bob knocked on his front door on the Wednesday morning.

"Morning, Father," Bob said. "I wonder if you can call on Steve, he's not very good at all."

"I'm sorry to hear that," replied Father Fenwick. "Of course, I'll come with you. What's the problem?"

"He's in a funny mood," replied Bob. "I think that it's something to do with Jen."

Father Fenwick put his coat on and accompanied Bob to Steve's house.

Steve opened the door, and it was easy to see that all was not right.

"Come on in," he said with a grunt.

They went inside and sat at the kitchen table.

"Where's Jen?" asked Bob.

"She's still in bed," answered Steve. "The carer couldn't get her up this morning, she absolutely refused, she's just lying there talking rubbish. I'm fed up," he shouted. "Her family know how bad things are, but do they want to know? They don't call, or even ring to ask about her, or how I'm getting on looking after her."

Steve stood up suddenly and kicked the chair to one side, in a flash of anger, which sent it clattering across the kitchen floor. Bob stood up quickly, to console his friend. He picked the chair up and settled Steve back into it.

"I'll make us all a cup of tea," he said, wishing to defuse the situation, and he busied himself with the task.

Father Fenwick was quite moved by what he had just witnessed.

"That's a good idea," he said. "Steve, it must be very hard for you. But, you have friends who you can rely on when the going gets tough. You have Bob, and I like to think that you consider me as a friend, not just a dog collar toting priest."

This remark brought a faint smile to Steve's lips.

"Thank you, Father," he said. "It is a comfort to know that."

Bob placed a tray containing three cups of tea and a plate of biscuits on the table. They both continued to console Steve, and to devise a future plan, to help and support him, in times of need.

"The best thing is to leave Jen for the time being," advised Bob. "I'll ask Vera to come around later and give you a hand to get her out of bed, and to help her to get washed and dressed. At least, she's safe where she is for the moment."

Father Fenwick agreed with this suggestion and Bob promised to call back with Vera an hour or so later. He was quite moved by Bob's empathy and willingness to help Steve. He had a good friend there, if only everyone was the same he thought to himself.

CHAPTER TEN

John Byrne was sprawled in his usual chair in his sparsely furnished lounge. He held a can of lager in his hand, his third so far. The room looked very untidy and there was a heavy smell in the air. On the small coffee table, were the remains of a takeaway from the previous evening. The sink in the kitchen was piled high with unwashed dishes.

John always finished an evening off with a takeaway meal after a night in the pub, usually about three or four nights a week, depending on how his money lasted. He had not worked for four years, following redundancy from a factory where he was employed as a packer.

John had been a good worker, very conscientious. He had a wife and three children and he always made sure that he provided for them. He enjoyed a night out with his mates once a week, and he felt that this was enough for him. His other evenings were spent with his wife and children, they thought that their dad was the best.

John was always well-dressed, and was very particular about his appearance. What a difference now. He was wearing a soiled shirt, tatty old jeans and grubby trainers. Where he had once been clean-shaven, he now had several days of stubble on his face, due to the fact that he couldn't be bothered shaving every day. Who was bothered about how he looked anyway?

Following his redundancy, John changed considerably. He wasn't as keen on his general appearance. He began drinking more often, and he regularly became very angry and aggressive towards his wife. He had tried to get another job, but in Liverpool, employment was scarce, particularly for people like John, who lacked qualifications, which were needed for many of the jobs that were available.

John became involved with the wrong sort of people, similar to himself, unemployed and engaged in heavy drinking. He would often bring his mates home, after nights in the pub. They would become rowdy and John's wife soon got tired of this behaviour. She was afraid that they would wake her children up and the negative effect that it would have on them, seeing their father in this state.

After one particular night, his wife felt that she had suffered enough and she asked him to leave their marital home. John resisted at first, and voices were raised, but John soon realised that the situation had got too bad to carry on. He would not have used any form of physical violence against his wife, John was not a violent man. The abuse was limited to shouting and angry outbursts, during which John would often call his wife names, which he deeply regretted afterwards.

He finally agreed to leave, and moved in with one of his drinking pals, leaving his wife, Lisa to look after their three children and wondering what the future would hold for them. Lisa felt as if her world was crumbling around her. She still loved John, and was concerned as to what would become of him, particularly with him living with one of his mates, and she was worried that he may get into trouble.

John felt exactly the same as his wife. He still loved her and his children, he was concerned himself as to how they would cope without him. But, he was of no use to them in his present state. As to how he could improve his situation, he didn't have a clue.

John and his family had lived in a council house in Liverpool, so there was no problem with mortgage payments, at least his wife wouldn't have to worry about that. He had applied to the council, outlining his present circumstances and had been very fortunate in acquiring the tenancy of thirteen Sycamore Close, on *New Pastures*. He was rather doubtful at first, moving over to Cheshire, but he had little chance of being allocated a council property in the Liverpool area and he thought that he may have more chance of securing employment elsewhere. Furthermore, the move would give him the chance to break away from his mates. If he didn't, he felt that his situation would never improve and, he would continue to decline.

John was in receipt of Income Support and Housing benefit, which paid his rent directly to the Housing Association, so his rent was always paid on time. However, his present problem with alcohol and the neglect of the property could put his tenancy at risk.

When he first moved to *New Pastures*, he was determined to break away from his present mould of slovenly behaviour and maybe win his wife and family back. But, months and months of signing on at the Job Centre, with little prospect of finding a job had worn him down, and seen him revert to his old ways, and here he was again. John mused on this problem for a while, grunted and took another gulp of lager.

CHAPTER ELEVEN

Following his visit with Bob to Steve Farrell and his wife Jen, a few days earlier. Father Fenwick had been quite concerned about the current situation. He had witnessed Steve exhibiting an extreme outburst of anger, which involved him kicking a chair like a football. He was obviously exhibiting a sign of extreme stress. It must be quite a strain on him, caring for his wife, and witnessing her cognitive decline. He made up his mind to visit Steve again, this time without Bob.

When Steve answered the door, he looked quite calm, so different from the previous day.

"Oh hello, Father," he said. "Come on in."

Father Fenwick was led into the lounge, where once again his wife, Jen was sitting in her chair in the corner of the room.

"I thought that I would call again to see how you are doing," said Father Fenwick. "I have been worried about you since my last visit."

"Thanks, Father, that was a bad day, last time you called with Bob. Jen was very difficult, but it's not always like that."

"I'm glad to hear it Steve," Father Fenwick replied. "You certainly look a lot brighter."

Steve put the kettle on, and while he was making the tea, Father Fenwick went over to where Jen was sitting.

"Hello, Mrs Farrell," he said. "How are you today?"

Jen looked up from stroking her doll and peered at Father

Fenwick. At first, he thought that she recognised him from his previous visit.

"He put it in the pog," she mumbled.

"Oh, I'm sorry to hear that," answered Father Fenwick. Whatever a pog was, made no sense to him, but obviously it was stored in Mrs Farrell's brain, if it meant anything at all.

Steve and Father Fenwick sat down to drink their tea at the kitchen table. During this moment together, Father Fenwick assured Steve that he and hopefully, the Catholic, and general community, would offer support when it was needed. There were probably many individuals who were in a similar position as Steve and Jen, and Father Fenwick regarded that his offer of support, was a duty of a priest, and the whole Christian community. Most of the time, the support may consist simply of a shoulder to cry on and a sympathetic ear.

"She talks like that all the time," explained Steve. "I can't make head or tail of it most of the time, it does get me down occasionally, we can't have a sensible conversation like we used to do."

"Yes, that must be very difficult," replied Father Fenwick.

"It's not the caring that gets me down," continued Steve. "I consider it a privilege to look after Jen, I still love her and want to be with her. But, seeing her every day getting worse, almost like a different person, is heart-breaking."

Father Fenwick was silent for a moment, he was turning this situation over in his mind. He felt helpless, what could he do? He was only a priest, who wore a dog collar and praised and preached about a god that nobody can see, but had to believe in, nevertheless. How could he expect people to believe in this god, when suffering like this was going on? All that he could do was offer support, and hopefully be a friend to Steve and people like him, whether they were Catholics, or not. He would step aside from his priestly role and become simply James Fenwick, the one time would be motor mechanic and would be athlete.

He sometimes yearned for an ordinary life. A life where he could meet a girl, get married and have children. How could he understand such matters, when things went wrong in the family? Instead, he was married to the church, where he was expected to conform to the very strict standards which were set by the hierarchy, which was led by the pope.

On the other hand, he was on his own in this new parish, his own boss so to speak. He felt that he was making friends in his new role, as a founding father almost. He hoped that he could help people who were in difficulties, or were going through a rough patch. He especially hoped that he could make a difference. He was, after all, an ordinary man of thirty years of age, who liked running and socialising. He could take off his dog collar and wear ordinary clothes, or his running gear. He would then fit in as any other man in the street, and not just as a priest.

He was wrenched abruptly out of his thoughts, as Steve began to talk again.

"It's like having Jen here with me, or not with me, if you can understand that Father," he said.

"I can understand," Father Fenwick replied. "Jen is still with you in body, but not in spirit."

"That's just it, Father," said Steve. "Jen has gone to her family in Liverpool for short breaks in the past. But, I missed her, even though our life is not the same as it used to be, and conversation is non-existent."

"Hmm," Father Fenwick mumbled. He appreciated what Steve was saying, but as to giving him advice, that was difficult. He was lost in thought again for a moment and then he said.

"I totally understand what you mean Steve. But, it's not easy for me, or anyone else to offer you advice, unless they are having, or have experienced it themselves. One thing is sure though Steve, I am always here to offer any help and support that I can, at any time of day or night."

"Thanks, Father, that's very encouraging to hear," Steve said.

"You can call me James, or Jim, you know," advised Father Fenwick. He felt that it sounded less formal, and more down to earth, it made him appear as an ordinary person, just as he had always wanted. "I'll call around again, but, don't forget, you can call me any time that you need to talk."

With that, Father Fenwick left Steve alone with Jen, wishing that he could do more to help them both.

When he had left, Steve sat quietly for a few moments, contemplating his conversation with Father Fenwick. He felt lonely for most of the time. Both Jen's and his family rarely visited if they visited at all. It was as if Jen had contracted some disease that was contagious. His friends were the same, he hardly saw, or heard from them, except Bob of course. He couldn't have a sensible conversation with Jen any longer. She seemed to be shrinking within herself. She sat in the corner mumbling to herself all of the time. She had a doll which she constantly talked to as if it were real.

Steve was sixty-six years of age. He had retired from working in an office just twelve months previously, and he missed his work intensely, particularly his interaction with his workmates. Jen had not been too bad when he had retired. Sure, she did suffer from some memory problems, but everyone presumed that it was an integral part of ageing.

Following an application to the council for a move from their present accommodation, they were offered the tenancy of eight Oak

Close. Steve thought that it would give them both a more relaxing environment to allow them to enjoy their retirement. But, over the twelve months since their move, Jen's condition started to deteriorate, and she was now completely dependent on Steve for her care. They did have support from Social Services, but the periods in between their visits left Steve feeling lonely, anxious, and depressed.

True, he did have Bob as a friend, but he felt that he could not rely on him and Vera too much, after all, they had a life too. He had taken a liking to Father Fenwick. He wasn't like any other priest that he had known. He gave the impression that he was just an ordinary bloke, who was more concerned about people's welfare, rather than more Godly concerns. Steve felt comforted about Father Fenwick' placement here, he made him feel that he was not alone.

CHAPTER TWELVE

Lisa Byrne breathed a sigh of relief, her three children had been put into bed after a struggle for most of the day.

"Why have we got to go to bed this early?" asked George, the eldest, at eight years of age. "Dad used to take us up and read us a story, when is he coming back, we miss him?"

"He's had to go away to look for a job George, you know how hard up we've been lately," she told him.

"Why can't he get a job here?" asked George.

"There aren't any jobs here, George," replied Lisa. "Hopefully, he'll get a job in Cheshire, and then we can get back to being a normal family again. We can possibly all move over there in the nice countryside, instead of this gloomy place. You can have those new trainers that you have been going on about for ages if dad gets a job."

"Oh goody," said George gleefully, settling down into bed. The prospect of new trainers was enough to settle him down happily.

Lisa didn't like promising her kids too much, but she was hopeful herself that it would turn out all right in the end, although she had her doubts and fears about the future. She was very concerned about John. He had let himself go such a lot, and his friends had dragged him down further.

Finding employment would mean such a lot to him and his family. Lisa had lost contact with him since he moved. He did have a phone when he first moved, but it was cut off. He preferred to spend what little money that he had on drink and take-a-ways, not on phone bills.

Lisa decided to try to find out how John was doing, so she rang her brother Malcolm, to ask if he could pay him a visit.

Malcolm answered the phone promptly. "Hello," he boomed in his loud voice.

"Hi, Malcolm, it's Lisa here, how are you keeping?"

"Oh, not too bad, what can I do for you, Sis?"

"I'm quite worried about John, Malcolm, and I wondered if you could arrange to visit him and see how he is," replied Lisa. "I think that he may have been cut off, because I can't get any answer on his phone."

"I'm not surprised," replied Malcolm. "He's probably not paid his bill. Why are you worried about that useless drunk?"

"That useless drunk just happens to be my husband Malcolm," said Lisa indignantly.

"Oh, yes, sorry about that, Lisa," Malcolm said apologetically. "That came out wrong, I didn't mean to sound so critical."

Malcolm had never liked John, even when he was working and supporting his family. He always thought that John wasn't good enough for his sister, and she could have done better. When John went off the rails, after losing his job, it confirmed what he had thought of him all along. Malcolm had a good job, which he considered very secure. He worked for Liverpool Council, as a clerk in the accounting office. He had always considered himself better than anybody else, the fact that he could be in the same position as John one day, never entered his mind, he never considered it a possibility.

Malcolm wasn't married, so he didn't have a clue what it was like to have a family of his own. Particularly, how difficult and stressful it would be if the main breadwinner was unemployed. He lived on his own in his flat, which was tastefully furnished. He was proud of his expensive hi-fi and his collection of CD's and records. He was particularly proud of his new BMW, which was lovingly cared for, always washed and polished, it was his showpiece.

*

He was doing all right for himself, he thought little of anyone else. He frequented the best nightclubs and pubs in town, and he flirted with many women, he considered that he could take his pick. Who wouldn't want him, with his good looks, fine clothes and a gleaming BMW? If arrogance was in the Olympics, Malcolm would win the gold medal.

"Ok, Sis," he said. "I'll visit him on Saturday morning, I'm not doing anything else."

This statement proved what he was like. Would he have agreed so readily, if he was doing anything special, such as dating a girlfriend? Lisa doubted that he would.

"Thanks," she said gratefully, she was unaware of the pertinence of Malcolm's remark.

*

As promised, Malcolm made his way to thirteen Sycamore Close on Saturday morning. As he stepped out of his car, he glanced in his wing mirror to check that his hair was not out of place. He had no reason to do it, after all he was only going to see John. But, you never know who you will meet, he thought.

As he walked up the path that led to John's front door, he noticed how unkempt the garden was, it was overgrown with weeds, not a flower to be seen. The general appearance of the exterior of the property fared no better. The windows looked like they needed a good clean, as well as the front door. Malcolm breathed a long sigh, he wasn't at all interested in John, he was a no mark in his estimation.

He was here purely because John was married to his sister and had produced three children, and he had promised her that he would call. Why Lisa married him was a mystery to Malcolm, she could have done so much better. She was a very bright girl, attractive too, she could have had any man, someone like him.

He looked around the door frame for a doorbell, but he couldn't see one, so he knocked on the glass loudly. There was no answer, so he peered through the window, although the dirt on the glass didn't provide him with a clear view, he knocked again, still he got no answer.

Malcolm was beginning to get irritated now, the thought of coming all this way for nothing grated on his nerves.

He was just about to walk back to his car, when out of the corner of his eye, he noticed a shambling figure walking towards him. With a shock, he realised that it was John. He was carrying a shopping bag, and was swaying from side to side. He looked completely unkempt, wearing clothes that were in a very poor state of repair. He appeared not to notice Malcolm as he passed him and stumbled up to his front door.

Malcolm guessed that he had been drinking, and he had no desire to confront John at the present time. He stood by his car and watched him disappear shakily through his front door. Malcolm realised that he would not get much sense out of John at the present time, he was much more likely to be on the end of verbal abuse, and he had better things to do anyway. He couldn't tell Lisa what he had just witnessed. He didn't want to worry her unduly, she had enough to be concerned with at the present time. Malcolm got back into his car, put a CD into the player and drove away. When he arrived home, he phoned Lisa and told her that John was all right, he was doing OK, and she shouldn't worry about him. He had no guilty feelings at all about his lies. He had put Lisa's mind at rest, so he was satisfied, job done. He put a record onto the turntable in his hi-fi unit, and settled back into his chair with a glass of whisky, happy that he had done his bit.

CHAPTER THIRTEEN

Father Fenwick had been busy the few days following his visit to Steve and Jen. The question of appointing altar servers to assist at mass was a priority and was high on his mind. He had made many visits to his local parishioners, particularly those with children, with the aim of asking for volunteers. He was pleased that the reaction had been positive. The parents who he had spoken to were very keen on the idea that their child would be on the altar, assisting Father Fenwick to serve mass.

He had arranged a meeting in the presbytery and was in anticipation of a useful outcome. Four children had advised Father Fenwick that they would be happy to volunteer their services. Although, whether they were following their own minds, or were being influenced and pressured by their parents was not clear.

Father Fenwick advised the children that he would arrange the necessary training over the next couple of evenings. One hour on each evening would be sufficient for the children to become accustomed to the role of altar servers. At the present time, those children of parishioners on the *New Pastures* estate attended St Winifred's school, which was outside the catchment area, or so called 'New Town', because as yet there was no catholic school on the estate.

Father Fenwick arranged for two of the new altar servers to commence their duties on the following Sunday. He was aware that it would be a tense time for Paul and Amy, nerves would be frayed, non the less for Father Fenwick, who wanted everything to run smoothly. He need not have been unduly concerned, because there were no hiccups and everything went smoothly at the mass, on the following Sunday, much to the satisfaction of all concerned.

After the mass, Father Fenwick was once again surrounded by appreciative parishioners outside the school, and he was more than happy to give them as much of his time as possible.

Bob and Vera were present of course, but the absence of Steve was to be expected, as he could not leave Jen on her own and Father Fenwick appreciated that Steve would not feel comfortable bringing Jen to the mass, but she would be most welcome if he wished to do so. Those individuals who were suffering with any form of mental infirmity should not be hidden away from social gatherings, particularly those connected with the church. Father Fenwick decided that he would pay them a further visit the following afternoon.

Monday morning dawned bright and clear, it looked as if it was going to be a nice day. Father Fenwick once again celebrated mass in his lounge, there were three parishioners present today. He wondered what it would be like if he had thirty-three, it would be rather crowded he thought with a smile.

Following the mass, he went for his usual run around the estate. He felt exhilarated, and he was moving well. He went through the wooded area, the favourite part of his training route, past the pond and out the other side, he thought of this area as his personal cross-country course. This part of his course always gave him a feeling of peace. He had never seen anybody else in the woods, so there was always the feeling of isolation.

He always slowed down to a jog in this area, whereas, on the roads, he tended to run much faster. A slow jog in the woods gave him the opportunity to notice any wildlife that was about, and allowed him to appreciate the scene fully.

On this particular day, he noticed a squirrel running up a tree, and a robin was singing away loudly in the background. This brought joy to his heart, and it reminded him that he should be happy to be a priest. God had provided all this for us to enjoy, and he was doing his work, wasn't he?

His thoughts then turned to Jen, on the other hand, why did God allow such suffering in the world, when there was so much to enjoy. Jen who had been robbed of her dignity, and was at the mercy of carers, some who were young enough to be her grandchildren. There were many others like her, people who had been engaged in all sorts of employment, mothers, fathers and grandparents. Those who possessed different levels of intellect and skills, but nonetheless, were still of great value to society, despite their infirmity. Running allowed him to consider all these facts as he pounded along.

After his run, Father Fenwick showered and had a bite to eat. He then made his way to Steve and Jens' house. Steve answered the door after the first ring of the bell.

"Hello, Father," he said. He still insisted on calling him by his priestly title and not his first name, a habit hard to break, Father Fenwick thought.

"How are you today, Steve?" he asked.

"Not too bad, Father, I've had worse days, come on in."

Father Fenwick was ushered into the kitchen, as usual and sat down at the kitchen table.

Steve looked rather forlorn for a moment and Father Fenwick thought that he presented an image of a troubled man.

"I don't know how long I can go on with this," he stuttered.

"How do you mean?" asked Father Fenwick.

"Well, Jen is getting much worse now. Even with the carers coming, I feel that I can't cope much longer. The isolation and lack of stimulation is getting to me. She doesn't know who I am any more, it's heart-breaking."

"I'm sure that it is, Steve," replied Father Fenwick. "What is the solution, do you think?"

"Well, I have been talking to Bob about the situation, and we came to the question of whether it's time to put Jen into a care home."

"That's a big decision, Steve," advised Father Fenwick.

"It is, Father, it's not what I want for Jen, the thought of putting her into a home makes me shudder."

"You could give it a trial period Steve, and see how it goes, but you'll need to get advice from a social worker."

"Yes, I know," said Steve. "We already have a social worker, who arranged the care for Jen, her name's Brenda Caddick."

Steve said that he would contact the Social Services office and arrange a visit to discuss the possibility of Jen receiving a period of respite care. It would certainly give him some time on his own, and he could then make a decision for the future, based on how he felt at the time.

However, it was not going to be an easy decision for him. He quite naturally wanted his wife to remain in her own home. After all, she wasn't that difficult to look after, particularly with the help of the carers, but there were times when he got very frustrated.

He was constantly aware of his own shortcomings and his so-called demons. Steve had suffered with Obsessive Compulsive Disorder for years, and this made him feel vulnerable and anxious at times, as the constant checking, and rechecking wore him down. He naturally wanted the best for Jen, but he was not sure that he was always providing it. When his anxiety level rose to extreme heights, he felt that he was disabled and this led to impatience with his wife, which he deeply regretted. On some mornings, Jen was very tearful and her mind appeared to return to when she was a child. Steve felt that something bad had happened during her childhood, but as to what, he could not say.

"Yes," he said to himself when Father Fenwick had left. "I'll speak to the social worker and see what she says."

If Jen could go into a care home for a short time, it would give him a break, and time to think about the future. It would be good for Jen as well. He sat back in his chair, feeling more relaxed now that he had come to a decision.

CHAPTER FOURTEEN

Brenda Caddick sat at her desk in the social work department of Chester Social Services. She grimaced when she considered how large her case load had become. She had been qualified for two years now, and at times she felt as if she was just starting. She had left Manchester University with a first in Sociology.

Following her graduation, she had been unsure which way her career should go. One day one of her lectures suggested that a career in social work would be a good choice, as she possessed the right temperament, a caring personality, coupled with an empathetic approach.

She had continued at university for a further two years, to study for the diploma in social work, and sometimes she wondered if it had been worth the effort. On this particular morning, she had arrived early at the office, and immediately opened her computer. She gritted her teeth when she noticed that her team manager had allocated her four new cases. These new cases would take her caseload to seventy-five. One of the new cases was for a carer's assessment for Steve Farrell.

Jennifer Farrell was already on her caseload, for the provision of social care, which comprised assistance with her personal hygiene and dressing. Steve on the other hand had never received a carer's assessment because he had not requested one. Some social workers would automatically make provision for the carer and assess their needs, but others left it until a request was made by the carer themselves. Steve Farrell had now asked for an assessment, and it was a legal requirement to provide it. Brenda contacted Steve on the phone and made arrangements to visit him the next day when an assessment could be made.

On arrival, Brenda found Steve in a positive mood. He was hoping that a short period of respite from his caring role would enable him to continue in a more positive way, and allow him some time to recuperate, and enjoy some time on his own. As he explained to Brenda, he was willing, and indeed wanted to continue to care for Jen, he considered it as a privilege and a duty, as her husband, he couldn't imagine life without her, despite her condition, and he certainly couldn't imagine her placed in a care home.

"OK, Mr Farrell," said Brenda. "Let's think about how long you will want Jen's respite to last."

"Not too long, maybe a week at first, to see how it goes," replied Steve.

Brenda advised Steve that she would have to put the case to the panel, so that they could agree to the funding, but she didn't think that there would be a problem. Once it was agreed, she could discuss where would be best to place Jen. They would have to take into account her age, she was only sixty-two years of age. Suitable care homes for this young age group were almost non-existent in the area. Finding a placement further afield would not be an option either, because Steve didn't drive, or own a car, so would be unable to visit, if things didn't work out.

Brenda assured Steve that she would make the necessary arrangements and would formulate a list of suitable care homes that had vacancies. Steve thanked her, and escorted her out, after she had completed her carer assessment. Brenda would type up the assessment when she was back in her office, she preferred to do this herself, rather than it sit in an in tray awaiting admin to type it up. She assured Steve that he would receive a copy within a couple of days.

When Brenda had left, Steve wondered if he was doing the right thing, but decided not to concern himself too much. After all, he had to consider what was right for Jen, and Brenda had told him that he must look after himself, so that he could continue with the support. Jen only had Steve for company for most of the time, and in a care home she would enjoy some interaction with other people who were in a similar position as herself. Likewise, Steve would be able to enjoy some freedom and socialise with others for a change.

When Brenda returned to the office later that day, she consulted the notes that she had made regarding Jen and Steve. She would now need to write up her report for the panel, and then hold her breath, awaiting their decision. She felt that this whole process was like writing an essay at school and awaiting the teachers report. Very often the application was refused by the panel, who asked for more information. This delayed the whole process, and Brenda thought that this was the panel's strategy. The panel was a thorn in the side to all the social workers. It consisted mostly of managers, who were unaware of the client and their needs, but were more concerned about the financial constraints placed on them by the council.

As Brenda was reading through her notes and thinking about the most appropriate format for her report, her manager stormed into the office.

Linda Burnham was a well-built woman, who looked more manly than feminine. She dressed in extremely plain clothes, such as tweeds and brogue shoes. Her voice was quite deep, and when she was conversing with others, she adopted a manly stance. The staff in the office thought that she may be a lesbian, she wasn't married and so there were whispers behind her back. She ruled with a rod of iron. When she asked you to jump, you asked how high.

Brenda was fearful of her, and she wasn't the only one. When Linda came into the room, she had the knack of making you stiffen up.

She was all for the management, and had aspirations of becoming Service Manager. As a result, she watched the team finances carefully, and she would question severely any decision that a member of her team would make, if she thought that she could save a few bob. The relevant social worker would then feel deskilled by this approach, after all they were trained for the job, and surely they were the right people to make any decisions regarding intervention.

Brenda's heart sank when she saw Linda come into the office, this was all she needed, a lecture, from her.

"This is not good enough," Linda shouted. "We are falling behind with our reviews, and it's just not on. You need to get a move on with yours, Brenda. We'll go through your caseload at supervision tomorrow."

This was not music to Brenda's ears, supervision sessions were generally ear bashing sessions. It was just like being in the headmaster's office. Memories of schooldays flooded back into Brenda's mind. She was always falling behind in her schoolwork, and being scolded about the standard of the work, as a result of this, she had lacked confidence ever since those days.

"Right then," boomed Linda, "fifteen hundred in my office tomorrow."

"That's fine," replied Brenda. "I'll put it in my diary now."

"Um," grunted Linda, as she strode out of the office. The door shut with a loud bang, followed by a further bang of her own office door.

Brenda felt completely demoralised after the confrontation with Linda. She wobbled over to the kettle to make a cup of tea, wishing that it was something stronger. She would then have to make a start on her report for the panel, and she dreaded the discussion at supervision the next day.

CHAPTER FIFTEEN

Father Fenwick collected his thoughts after celebrating mass in his lounge, or as he affectionately called it, 'Gods' Living Room.' There had been ten parishioners at the mass, seven more than the previous day. It was a bit of a crush, but things were definitely coming together.

As he was wallowing in his success, the telephone rang. The unmistakeable sound of Bishop Larkin's voice sounded in his ear.

"Good morning, Father Fenwick," said the bishop. "I have been hearing positive things about you, it appears that you have made a considerable impression so far. You seem to have got things moving quite quickly."

"Thank you, Bishop Larkin," answered Father Fenwick. "I'm quite satisfied that the Catholic community are rearing to go, so to speak."

"Yes, yes," said the bishop impatiently. "The reason for my call is to inform you that a meeting of the community must be held as soon as possible. *New Pastures* has been declared as a New Town by the Development Council. As such, the planning and development department, together with the department of education have said that a school should be built on the estate as soon as possible, to cater for the local Catholic children.

Father Fenwick's spirits rose when he heard this, the first step in building a church. "Unfortunately, the school must take priority over a church," continued Bishop Larkin. "So, the meeting will be held to advise the local community of the proposed plans. I'll leave you to arrange this Father, maybe you could use the school hall, where you celebrate mass."

"Yes, I'll get onto that," advised Father Fenwick. "I'm sure that there won't be a problem with using the school hall."

"If you'll be good enough to advise me when the meeting has been arranged, I'll make a point of attending. Good day to you, Fenwick." With that Bishop Larkin rang off, leaving Father Fenwick to make the necessary arrangements.

He rang Brian Simmons right away, to ask him if he could arrange a community meeting in the school hall.

"Of course," came the reply. "When do you want to hold it?"

"As soon as possible," replied Father Fenwick. "I think that Bishop Larkin is keen to organise it as soon as possible. The council are going to build a school for the catholic children on the estate."

"That's very good news," said Brian. "The children need a more local school, and one that is specific to the new town. How about a church?" he enquired.

"I'm not sure when that will be built," replied Father Fenwick. "Bishop Larkin didn't mention it. I'm sure that all will be explained at the meeting though."

The meeting was provisionally arranged for the following week, on a Wednesday evening, at 7pm. This would allow plenty of time for flyers to be produced and delivered to the community. It was decided that the meeting would not be restricted to Catholic residents only, but should be open to the community generally, because the new town was for all residents, not barring any other religious groups.

Mr Simmons offered the services of his school pupils, and advised Father Fenwick that the younger pupils would be able to produce posters to advertise the meeting.

"This would be a useful project for them, allowing them to increase their IT skills, while at the same time introducing them to community related projects. The children could also be utilised to deliver the posters, which would ensure that everyone in the community was included in the loop."

Father Fenwick was pleased with this idea, because he felt that the whole community was behind him. The next thing for him to do was to contact the council, to arrange the meeting, and also to contact Bishop Larkin. If all relevant persons could attend the meeting, the date could be definitely confirmed.

Father Fenwick contacted the relevant department in the council, by telephone. It was at times such as this that he missed the use of a car. He felt that it was preferable to speak face to face with the appropriate authorities, to allow them to put a face to a voice. He was directed to a Mr George Thompson, who was Director of County Council Planning.

Mr Thompson was aware of who Father Fenwick was. His fame had even travelled as far as the council.

"Good afternoon, Father," he said in a jovial voice. "Your fame proceeds you."

"Thank you," replied Father Fenwick. "Good afternoon, Mr Thompson. As you are obviously aware, I have been allocated to establish a new parish at *New Pastures*. I have been told by Bishop Larkin that a community meeting should be held to discuss the building of a new school, and possibly a church."

"Yes, that's correct," replied Mr Thompson. "Bishop Larkin has already notified me about this. Because *New Pastures* has been declared as a new town, the council are responsible, and indeed have a duty to provide a school for the Roman Catholic children in the area. This will of course only be up to secondary level."

"I understand," replied Father Fenwick. "The school hall at St Edward's is booked for Wednesday next, at 7 pm. Bishop Larkin will attend."

"That's fine," replied Mr Thompson. "I will be there, together with the Borough Treasurer and a representative from the Works Department. I believe that several local councillors will also be present, so I look forward to meeting you then."

Father Fenwick breathed a sigh of relief as he replaced the receiver, another positive step towards the establishment of the parish, which as yet, had no name.

A few days later, he received a telephone call from Mr Simmons, who advised him that the pupils had produced a poster. When he was asked if he would like to see the finished article, Father Fenwick told him that he would leave it up to Mr Simmons' own judgement. If he was happy with it, then he would be also.

The children were eager to distribute the flyers, to as many houses on the estate as possible. Bob also offered to help out by calling on friends and neighbours, to make them aware of the meeting. The estate became a hub of activity. There was an expectation amongst the residents and they didn't want to miss out on any part of it.

Father Fenwick decided to call on Steve, to see how he was and if he had any news regarding the respite for Jen. Steve should have the opportunity to attend the meeting, if he wanted to, and indeed bring Jen as well. Just because she was a victim of Dementia, she shouldn't live in a bubble.

Steve informed Father Fenwick that he hadn't heard any news regarding the respite, but it was early days yet, and he was still hopeful. He said that he would like to attend the community meeting, but when he questioned who would look after Jen, he was surprised and relieved when Father Fenwick told him that she could come as well, she would be more than welcome, so there should be no problem. Bob and Vera would be there, so they could offer support if it was needed.

CHAPTER SIXTEEN

Brenda sat at her desk frantically arranging her list for her supervision session, this had to be in order, to enable her to run through it as smoothly as possible, it was not unlike preparing a case for court. She had completed her panel application, which she would submit just before her supervision session, which she was dreading, as most of the staff usually did. She knew that she would get plenty of criticism and not much praise. She had several difficult and trying cases on the go at the present time, but arranging respite for Steve should be straightforward, if she kept her fingers crossed.

She glanced quickly at her watch, a quarter to three, just enough time to make a cup of tea, or so she though. As she was getting up to put the kettle on, the office door was flung open. Linda leaned through the door frame, exhibiting her usual strict looking mask.

"You can come in now," she boomed. "I've got a lot on this afternoon, and I need to get it over with."

Brenda felt a bit more relaxed when she heard this, it looked as if her supervision might be over fairly quickly. If Linda was busy, she would be out of everybody's hair.

Brenda gathered her papers and followed Linda into her office, who was already seated behind her large desk, looking every bit like a headmistress.

"Well," she shouted, "what's been happening this week?"

Brenda timidly looked at her list and began explaining what she had worked on over the last week. She felt that she was doing a good job, despite having to get the 'begging' bowl out, when more costly services were required.

Linda listened intently as Brenda went through her list of clients. Every now and again she would butt in and challenge her methods of working. Eventually, she reached the issue of respite for Steve.

"Is there no other way of providing support?" she questioned.

Brenda felt her hackles rise slightly and pointed out that it was a duty of a local authority to provide support for carers. She added that there was little family involvement in this case, and if support wasn't available, then Jen may end up in permanent care. But, short breaks of respite would enable Steve to continue in his caring role and avoid the possibility of 'carer burnout.'

"Mm," grunted Linda. She reluctantly had to agree that Brenda was carrying out her duties appropriately and she couldn't argue with that. Brenda was proud of being a part of the council, it made her feel that she was worth something.

Linda ended the session abruptly, with a few more negative comments, she always liked to have the last word. Brenda was finally free. With a sigh of relief, she walked out of Linda's office, and jumped as her office door shut with her usual loud bang.

Brenda finished off her panel application and was just about to submit it, when her office door was flung open, and Linda peered through the doorway.

"About your panel application," she boomed. "I'll authorise it this time, but just make it for one week. I'll advise panel. I'm sick and tired of all this pussyfooting to the managers. If they object, they'll have me to answer to. We can use *Happy Days Care Home*, as it's a council home, it will be a lot cheaper than these expensive fancy private homes."

Brenda felt relieved, and surprised by Linda's approach. She waited for the usual door bangs, but they never came.

Brenda decided that she would contact Steve on the following day and arrange a visit, to discuss the plan. She was sure that Steve would be happy with it, although Chester was some distance away, Steve would not need to visit. He could then have a complete rest, to recharge his batteries. Brenda could provide the transport to the home, so Steve would not have to concern himself with anything.

The next day, as arranged, Brenda visited Steve and Jen. When Steve answered the door, he smiled broadly and ushered Brenda inside.

"It's good to see you again, Mr Farrell," she announced. "My manager has agreed that Jen can have a week in *Happy Days Care Home*. It's run by the council, so the care is good."

"Oh, thank you for making the arrangements," replied Steve. "I didn't expect it to be so soon, would you like a cup of tea?"

"Thank you, that would be nice," replied Brenda. While Steve was making the tea, Brenda went over to where Jen was sitting.

"Hello, Mrs Farrell," she said. Jen looked up at Brenda, smiled, and placed her hand gently on hers.

"You are going on a little holiday, for a week," Brenda told her. "What do you think of that?" Jen smiled at Brenda again, and continued to touch her hand.

"It's on the other side you know," Jen mumbled.

"Is it?" replied Brenda. "Well we'd better leave it there then."

Brenda had no idea what Jen was talking about, but she knew that it was better to answer as simply as possible, to avoid distressing her.

When Steve had made the tea, they sat down at the kitchen table. Steve played mother and poured the tea.

"Where is *Happy Days* exactly?" he asked.

"It's in Chester, but it is a very good home, I know that it's a distance away, but it's only for a week."

"That's all right," replied Steve. "It will give me some time on my own, to think about the future, and what is the best option for Jen."

"That's the best way of looking at it," advised Brenda. "Leave me to make the necessary arrangements, and I'll get back to you when a date is arranged. Don't worry about transport, I can take you and Jen in my car."

When Brenda had gone, Steve felt a wave of calm come over him. He was sure that everything would be all right.

CHAPTER SEVENTEEN

Father Fenwick was on his rounds once again. He had called at several homes to introduce himself and to advise the occupants about the forthcoming community meeting. On the whole, he had been warmly welcomed by everyone, whatever denomination they were. The word had spread about the 'New Priest' in town and the community were keen to learn more about the forthcoming developments.

Father Fenwick had decided to complete one more call on this day. He approached thirteen Sycamore Close and looked for the doorbell. As there wasn't one, he knocked loudly on the door. There was no answer, so he knocked again.

John Byrne rubbed the grime off his window and peered out, to see who was there.

"It better not be someone selling something," he muttered under his breath. John didn't like anyone calling. He was hounded by people asking him to support this charity or that charity, or to join a lottery scheme. In fact, he didn't have the time of day for anyone at this particular time. He needed to be left alone to wallow in his self-pity.

He reluctantly opened the door, and was confronted by a smiling Father Fenwick.

"Who are you?" he growled. "I don't want anything, and I don't want to give money to no charities." John looked a bit taken aback when he noticed Father Fenwick's dog collar. "I don't want anyone church, saying that they want to help me find God."

er Fenwick smiled broadly.

"I'm not here to help you to find God, or anyone else for that matter," he replied. "Although, if you do manage to find him, I'd be glad if you will tell me where he is, because I'd like a word with him."

John peered at Father Fenwick through squinted eyes, and he smiled weakly. This humorous remark wasn't wasted on John. He perceived that this man of God wasn't the usual high and mighty person that he was used to, he actually had a sense of humour. John didn't have much to do with the community, most people tended to ignore him and walk past fairly quickly. They regarded him as a down-and-out character, a sponger, living on benefits.

Despite this, John had heard about Father Fenwick through the grapevine, and the fact that he was posted here to create a new parish. There weren't many people who hadn't heard of him. This was the way that Father Fenwick wished to be regarded, simply as a member of the community, but the occasional wearer of a dog collar. He didn't feel comfortable wearing it, but it was part of the uniform. Father Fenwick wanted, and in fact craved to fit in. He was aware of the problems within the Catholic Church, and in other religions too, there had been too many cases of abuse within the clergy, mostly surrounding children.

After a moments silence, Father Fenwick explained to John that there was a meeting to be held the following Wednesday, to discuss plans for the new town, and in particular, a new school and church.

"I don't think that I would be welcome there," said John. "I don't get on with people around here, 'ave nothing to do with 'em, and they 'ave nothing to do with me."

Father Fenwick felt sorry for the man in front of him. He recognised a man who was down on his luck, and he felt that he could help him to fit back into society.

"Oh, I'm sure that isn't the case," he said. "The meeting is at seven next Wednesday evening, in St Edward's school hall, I hope to see you there. The presbytery is number Ten Willow Close, if you need any help, or a chat, you can call round any time."

"I'll think about it," John said. "But don't hold your breath."

Father Fenwick wished him all the best and told John that he hoped that he would be there, and bid him goodbye.

John closed the front door and went back into his lounge. He thought about the visit by Father Fenwick. He had rather liked him, because he wasn't preaching to him, but treating him as an individual. It was the first time that he had been treated with some respect for ages, and he appreciated that. He decided that he would make the effort and turn up to the meeting.

He didn't care what people thought about him, let them stew in their own little worlds. For the first time in a long while, John was beginning to feel better about himself. He had met someone who thought that he had some worth, as a member of the local community.

He thought about what he would wear for the meeting, his wardrobe was a bit thin on the wedge at the moment. He would have a bath, wash his hair and have a good shave, it would be a treat to get that stubble off his face. He wouldn't have a drink on the Wednesday, or the evening before. If his breath smelt of alcohol, it would fuel the image that people thought about him. He looked in his wardrobe, or what attempted to be a wardrobe. It consisted of a clothes line, that was attached to screws which John had fixed into each end of the wall. He smiled, to himself as he thought that he still had some DIY skills. He also possessed a chest of drawers, which he had bought from a charity shop. In the drawers were some odds and ends, mostly T-shirts, underwear and socks.

A white shirt was hanging on the clothes line, there was also a smart jacket and trousers, which he last wore when he went on a night out with Lisa. He had a pair of leather shoes, which would polish up nicely, and he was sure that he could find a pair of socks without a hole in them, not that anyone would notice anyway. He would complete this outfit with a tie, which he also had not worn for years. Yes, he would show them, down and out he was not, he was going to be on the up. A dark thought suddenly clouded his euphoria. He was still unemployed, and he was aware that people tended to look down on people who were reliant on benefits, even though it may not be their own fault. Smart clothes alone would not make him totally acceptable within the community. This would be his new beginning, he would try harder to find employment. After all, he was not a shirker, when he had a job, he had worked hard at it.

Yes, John felt that he had something to work for now. He was going to find employment and move up the social ladder. Then maybe, he could win Lisa and his children back, and they could become a proper family once again.

CHAPTER EIGHTEEN

Steve was just on the verge of nodding off in his chair. He hadn't had much sleep on the previous night. Jen had kept him busy, and he felt exhausted. She had been muttering to herself all night, sometimes in a loud voice. He checked on her several times to make sure that she was not getting out of bed, as she had done on previous occasions, to avoid the possibility of her falling. When he clambered back into his own bed, he tossed and turned, and couldn't fall back to sleep. Steve didn't sleep with Jen any more for this reason. He felt that she was much safer in a single bed, and it was better for himself also.

The phone rang and suddenly jerked him out of his repose. Steve rose shakily to his feet, and grumbled to himself about being disturbed. He was quite pleased, however, to hear Brenda's voice on the other end of the phone.

"Hello, Mr Farrell," she said. "I'm pleased to inform you that I have arranged for Jen's placement at *Happy Days*. She can go in tomorrow afternoon, at about 2 pm."

Steve was taken aback, he hadn't expected it to be so soon, but he was relieved to hear the news. Tomorrow was Tuesday, so that meant that he could attend the meeting on the Wednesday evening, without having to worry about Jen.

"That'll be great," he said. "I'll get a suitcase packed tonight, and she'll be ready for when you call tomorrow."

"That's fine, don't worry yourself, Mr Farrell, Jen will be all right," reassured Brenda. "I'll call for you at lunchtime, and we can get her prepared, and then go."

"I'll have a bit of lunch ready for you, if you like," said Steve. "Can't have you driving on an empty stomach."

"That will be very nice, thank you, Mr Farrell," replied Brenda. "I'll see you tomorrow then."

The next day Brenda called at Steve's to help him to get Jen ready for her trip to *Happy Days Care Home*. Steve had already packed a suitcase containing everything that Jen would need for the week.

"I think that I've packed everything," he said.

"Don't worry," replied Brenda. "I'll check it for you, because it would make things difficult if you had forgotten something."

Brenda quickly checked the suitcase and confirmed that Steve had packed all the necessary items.

When this was completed Steve laid the table, with a light lunch. He had made sandwiches and there were some apple tarts. A pot of tea completed the repast.

Jen seemed unaware of what was going on. Brenda spoke to her in her usual soft toned voice. "Hello Jen," she said. "You're going on your holiday today, for a week. You'll have a nice little break, and Steve will as well."

Jen smiled at Brenda and touched her hand lightly, as she had done previously. She mumbled something, which Brenda couldn't understand. Steve seemed rather upset. Although he was going to have a break, he obviously felt a bit guilty about placing her in the home.

"She'll be all right Mr Farrell," Brenda said, in her usual reassuring voice. "Don't upset yourself too much, you're doing the right thing."

"I know," replied Steve. "I just feel that I'm shutting Jen away, even though it's only for a short time. You know, I feel that she won't come out."

"That's quite natural," advised Brenda. "Most people feel the same as you."

Steve was reassured with this advice, which was delivered in Brenda's usual soothing tone. Brenda had such a caring approach, and was full of good advice. He was very grateful for the support that he was receiving.

On the car journey to the care home, Jen was very quiet, and occupied herself with looking out of the car window. Every now and again, she would say something, in her mumbling tone. Steve was very quiet also. He wasn't looking forward to leaving Jen in the care home, although he kept reminding himself that it was only for a week. He wondered what he would do while she was away. He was that used to having a strict timetable, and daily routine, and he thought that he would find it difficult to break away from it.

They reached their destination in just over half an hour. Steve's first impression of *Happy Days* was that it looked very modern, almost welcoming, not run down and gloomy looking, as he imagined most care homes would appear.

"Here we are," said Brenda, looking at Jen. "This will be your home for the next week. It's a very nice hotel." She chose this word carefully, rather than tell Jen that she was going into a care home. Whether Jen understood, Brenda wasn't too sure, but she felt sure in her own mind that she had used the appropriate language.

Steve and Brenda got out of the car, and helped Jen out. Steve got her suitcase out of the boot and sighed. He was about to be separated from Jen for the longest period since they had been married.

"Here we go, Jen," he said. "We'll soon have you in your room."

This remark failed to register on Jen of course, she peered at Steve as if she was meeting him for the first time.

Steve took hold of Jen's arm, and together with Brenda they assisted her to walk up the steps and into the foyer of *Happy Days Care Home*. Once again, Steve was surprised at how modern the inside looked, just like the outside in fact. Indeed, it did look more like a hotel, rather than a care home.

A smartly dressed lady came out of an office, which was off to one side of the foyer. She greeted them with a warm smile.

"Good afternoon," she said brightly. "You must be Mr and Mrs Farrell. I'm Margaret Jones, the manager of *Happy Days*."

"Hello," replied Steve. "This is Jen, my wife. She's here for a week."

"Yes, everything is ready for her," replied Mrs Jones. "You don't have to worry about a thing, she'll be well looked after here."

Steve agreed, and felt that Jen would be very comfortable, and he reassured himself that he needn't have worried. While Brenda went into the office with Mrs Jones to sort out the paperwork and general arrangements, Steve took Jen into a large lounge and sat with her, to reassure her, if this was needed.

There were several residents sitting in the lounge, which was tastefully furnished.

There was a large screen television in one corner, which was showing a film. The residents were glued to it, so they appeared to be happy. There were also several lounge chairs and sofas. In another corner, there was a large display cabinet, containing all sorts of ornaments. The general feel of the lounge was one of opulence and it had a very relaxing atmosphere. Steve settled into a chair, and thought that he could do with a week in here himself.

He was almost nodding off when Mrs Jones and Brenda walked into the room.

"Well that's the formalities done," advised Mrs Jones. "We'll take you up to Jen's room now." She led them back into the foyer, which contained a grand staircase, and a lift. They all got into the lift, and went up to the second floor. When they got out of the lift, they walked along a wide corridor, which would accommodate the largest wheelchair and mobility scooter. They stopped at room thirty-five. Mrs Jones opened the door with a key card.

"As you can see," she said with a smile. "We're not behind the times here."

She led them into Jen's room. Once again, Steve was very impressed. The room was spotlessly clean and tidy. It contained a single divan bed, complete with a bedside table and reading lamp. The bathroom was off to one side. It was also spotless and the whole area was flat, with a shower, toilet and washbasin. Mrs Jones advised Steve that it was a 'Wet Room.' There was no bath, so the occupant wouldn't have to clamber over it. They could simply walk in, it was designed for individuals with any sort of disability.

"This is all very nice," Steve said. He was very impressed. He turned to Jen and told her that this would be her bedroom for the next week.

She smiled and said, "It's gone out."

"Nothing's gone out," replied Steve. "You'll be very comfortable here." He was sure of that.

Mrs Jones advised Steve that it would be best to leave Jen now. They would sort everything out. Unpack her suitcase, and settle her in. To go now, without a fuss, would be less distressing for both parties. Steve agreed, and he reluctantly left the room with Brenda.

When Steve and Brenda were back in the car, Steve felt quite sad. He was aware that Jen would only be in the home for one week, but the whole process of leaving her was upsetting for him. Brenda reassured him in her soft tone of voice.

"It's quite natural for you to feel like this," she said. "Jen will have a relaxing time over the next week, she'll be well looked after, and you will be able to relax a bit yourself, and have the time to recharge your batteries. You could even take up fishing," she said with a smile.

Steve was once again reassured by Brenda's advice, although he wasn't sure about the fishing. He had Bob and Father Fenwick to support him, so everything would be all right.

CHAPTER NINETEEN

Father Fenwick left the presbytery at six pm, on Wednesday evening, for the community meeting. He was full of expectation, expecting positive news, regarding the plans for the development of the new town.

George Chandler, meanwhile, the school caretaker was grumbling to himself, about the extra work that had been placed on him. Normally he was away by six, but now he was expected to work until the meeting had finished, and he had to clear all the tables and chairs away.

"The football's on tonight and I'll miss it," he moaned to himself. "Bloody meetings."

The fact that he had a job, and a steady one at that, never crossed his mind. There was a great deal of unemployment in the locality, and he was lucky to have a job, but he didn't care about that. He had reluctantly placed a large trestle table and four chairs at the front of the hall. There were four large jugs of water and glasses for the 'thirsty buggers', he thought. There were also twenty rows of chairs. It was unclear though, how many residents would actually turn up.

Some of the teachers had volunteered their services in the kitchen, to make tea and coffee. They weren't complaining, and they wouldn't be paid any extra for their services. They felt that it was good community spirit on their part.

Father Fenwick was the first to arrive. "Good evening, Mr Chandler," he said with a smile. "Let's hope that we have a positive meeting tonight."

"Hum," grunted George, "let's hope that it doesn't go on too long."

"Exactly," replied Father Fenwick, walking away briskly, he didn't wish to become embroiled in George's grumbling.

"Good evening, Father Fenwick," came a loud voice suddenly from behind him. He turned around to face Bishop Larkin.

"Oh, good evening, Bishop Larkin, good to see you, thank you for coming," he replied politely.

"Let's hope that we have a good turnout tonight, this is an important meeting," replied Bishop Larkin.

"Yes, I think that we will," replied Father Fenwick.

"You've done a good job so far Father Fenwick. Getting this meeting arranged so quickly is no mean feat. I always knew that you were up to the job."

Father Fenwick was almost knocked sideways. The bishop paying him a compliment, it certainly lifted his spirits and raised his confidence somewhat.

"Thank you, Bishop," he replied, with almost a cocky tone in his voice.

While Father Fenwick was wallowing, following Bishop Larkin's praise. Bob came in with Vera and Steve. Father Fenwick acknowledged them and introduced them to Bishop Larkin.

"How are you feeling, Steve, now that Jen is in the care home?" asked Father Fenwick.

"I still feel a little bit guilty," Steve replied. "The house feels different now that Jen's not there, sort of empty. It's funny, I missed her as soon as we left the care home."

Bishop Larkin shook hands warmly with Bob, Steve and Vera.

"I'm very pleased to meet you all," he said with a smile. He looked in Steve's direction.

"I believe that your wife is suffering with Dementia," he said sympathetically. "Take it from me, you are doing a fine job caring for her. It's not an easy task, by any means. I'll remember you both in our prayers."

"Thank you, Bishop Larkin," Steve answered. He was heartened and comforted by the bishop's words.

Bishop Larkin then spoke to all three of them. "Thank you all for your warm reception for Father Fenwick. I believe that you have been a great help to him in his new venture. It's a substantial task that he has been given, and I know that he appreciates your friendship and support."

They were all taken aback by the bishop's words. They appreciated this and the fact that he acknowledged them was a great boost to them and raised their self-esteem.

There was suddenly quite a bustle, as residents came pouring into the meeting, and the seating arrangements started to fill up. Father Fenwick was amazed at how many people had started to arrive. Bob suggested to Steve and Vera that they should grab a seat while they could. Steve agreed, and they took their seats four rows from the front.

Father Fenwick noticed out of the corner of his eye, three gentlemen walking in together. They asked for him personally, and were directed in his direction.

"Ah," a rather tall man announced. "Father Fenwick, I presume, we spoke on the phone a couple of days ago. I'm George Thompson, Director of Planning."

"Oh, yes," replied Father Fenwick. "I'm very glad to meet you, Mr Thompson. It's good to put a face to a voice, so to speak."

They shook hands warmly, and Mr Thompson introduced the

other two gentlemen.

"This is Mr Charles Burridge, Borough Treasurer, and this is Mr Henry Miller, who is from the Works Department."

Father Fenwick acknowledged both gentlemen, and thanked them for giving up their time to attend the meeting.

They were then introduced to Bishop Larkin, who greeted them with enthusiasm. As the hall continued to fill up quite swiftly, Bishop Larkin suggested that they all take their places at the top table, which they hastily did.

At seven pm on the dot, all the seats were filled, and there was standing room only at the rear of the hall. Mr Thompson stood up and faced the crowd. The chatter ceased suddenly, as he began to speak.

"Good evening everyone," he announced cheerily. "Thank you all for coming to this community meeting. The purpose of which is to inform you all about the plans for building a school for the children in *New Pastures*. As it is designated as a new town, the council has a duty to ensure that there is a school for the local children. Obviously, we are in a school at the present time, but it is a Church of England school. There must be a new school built to cater for the Catholic children in this immediate area."

Father Fenwick stirred anxiously in his seat, as yet there was no mention of a church at this stage of the proceedings.

Mr Thompson continued. "As you will understand, the priority for the council is the building of the school, before a church, although a church is just as important, so we have an ultimatum. The church could be constructed as an adjoining part of the school. A screen would be utilised to close off the school when services are to be held. On the days when there is no service, the screen could be opened, thus allowing the space to be used as a school hall again."

Father Fenwick had been listening to this intently. He was glad to hear that some provision had been made for the church, but as part of the school, he was not entirely convinced that this would work, he would prefer that the church was separate from the school.

Mr Thompson looked in Father Fenwick's direction, expecting a comment from him. He cleared his throat.

"Good evening, Father Fenwick," he said. "I believe that you have made quite an impact since you came here, and it's your drive that will make this venture a success, would you like to say a few words?"

"Thank you for your faith in me, Mr Thompson," replied Father Fenwick. "However I would prefer to be addressed as Father James, it sounds less formal. I have one question. Where would the altar be placed in the building?" he asked sheepishly.

"We anticipate that the sacristy would be at the front of the building, together with the altar," advised Mr Thompson. "Obviously, we wouldn't expect you to use a pasting table."

A ripple of laughter ran around the room. Father Fenwick smiled broadly as well, it was plain to see that his homemade altar in the presbytery was no secret. He nodded and thanked Mr Thompson for his explanation. At least there would be what could be described as a church, with a proper altar, which would be better than what they had at the present time.

Mr Thompson smiled, glad that there had not been any objections so far. "I'll pass you on now to Mr Miller, for his input," he said.

"Good evening everyone," Mr Miller announced. "As Mr Thompson has already mentioned, a school will be built, which will incorporate a chapel. This is the most cost-effective way of doing this. It would be a drain on the council's funds to build a church and a school, so this will provide the best of both worlds in the short term. Furthermore, as a result of the school and the church being in one building, the children will be encouraged to practice their faith and attend church services."

Father Fenwick listened intently to this. He had to agree that it would be convenient for both the church and the school to share one building. However, this maybe only a temporary arrangement, and a separate church could be built in the future, as the parish grew.

Mr Burridge cleared his throat and began to speak next.

"Good evening everyone," he began. "As Mr Miller has mentioned, it will be more cost effective to house both the school and the church in one building. The council have put funding aside for this project, and it's anticipated that work will commence in the near future."

There was a loud voice suddenly from the back of the room, and everyone turned around. "When can we expect the building to be complete?" asked a rather tall, slender gentleman.

Mr Miller and Mr Burridge exchanged glances.

"We anticipate that the work will be completed in about twelve months, give or take a month or two," advised Mr Burridge. "Of course, the progress will depend on conditions, such as the weather and working conditions."

The tall gentleman smirked "Hopefully there won't be any strikes to hold the work up," he said with sarcasm in his voice.

"Well, let's hope that we keep the workers happy then," replied Mr Miller, with a smile. The tall gentleman sat down, obviously satisfied with the reply that he had received.

Everyone would be aware that strikes were possible, it was always a possibility at any time.

Mr Thompson spoke again. "Well, I'd like to thank everyone for coming. If anyone has any other questions, or concerns, we will be mingling for the next half hour, or so."

Everyone present appeared to be happy with what had been discussed at the meeting. The council had laid their cards on the table. The project had been agreed, and the building of the school and church would begin very soon, so that was something to be happy about. There was a community spirit emerging. Residents were starting to converse with one another, whereas, previously they may have just nodded to each other when they passed in the street. A few people introduced themselves to Steve, and asked how Jen was doing. Steve felt quite taken aback, because he had felt isolated for so long, neighbours and family didn't call, and he felt that he was left on his own to struggle. Now, he felt that he was coming out of the darkness, and could hope to have more support from his fellow neighbours in the future.

This was not wasted on Father Fenwick either. He felt that the community was starting to come together. Not just the Catholic fraternity, but people of all denominations. This was so different from St Matthew's parish, probably because the new town covered a much more contained area.

He stood up and looked around the hall. He noticed with some concern that John Byrne was absent. When he had visited John a few days earlier, he had told him that he would attend, although, he did tell him not to hold his breath. He decided that he would visit him in the next day or so and see what had happened to make him change his mind. He was quite concerned about John's welfare, and considered that he had a duty to help him.

When everyone had been refreshed with cups of tea and biscuits, and many questions and concerns had been put to rest, the meeting concluded.

Everyone left, with anticipation, looking ahead to the new school and a new church, a new beginning had been set in motion.

CHAPTER TWENTY

John Byrne opened his second can of lager. He was in a glum mood, because he had previously set his mind on tidying himself up and attending the meeting. This was the way he was, he wallowed in self-pity for most of the time. He felt completely isolated. Nobody called, although what could he expect? He was hardly the sort of person who most people wanted to associate with. He couldn't blame them, he wasn't very sociable at all. Maybe, just maybe, people might like him if he made more effort.

He had told Father Fenwick that he would attend the meeting, and he had every intention of doing so. But, then the dark gloom descended again. The moment of euphoria had passed him by. He had lost touch with his family, his friends, and everybody. Why would he be interested in welcoming the building of a new school, when his own children were in Liverpool, with his wife, and god knows who else. For all he knew, Lisa may have got a new man in her life. He could hardly blame her, after all, he wasn't the catch of the year. So, it went on, this wallowing in self-pity. He cradled his can of lager lovingly, this was his life now. But, what a life, he knew it only led down the road to further decline and misery.

On the other hand though, he felt that he may have missed out on not going to the meeting. It's just possible, he thought, that he may have been welcomed, and not judged by anyone.

The priest, he thought, had seen some worth in him, so maybe others would think the same. He thought about Malcolm. He was such a smart arse. He thought that he was the bees knees, so smug, with his good job and fancy lifestyle. John knew what Malcolm thought of him, a waster, not good enough for his sister.

So, John continued to wallow in his own misery. It was Saturday evening, and here he was on his own. No friends to call on him, or go to the pub with, he felt like a hermit. He downed a further three cans of lager, which were followed by several glasses of whisky. He attempted to stand up, but the room spun around in front of him. He stumbled, and fell heavily onto the floor in a drunken stupor.

It was nine minutes past ten, the next morning, when he woke up from his binge of the night before. His head felt like it had been hit with a sledgehammer, and his mouth felt like something that had been dredged out of the River Mersey. He rolled over onto his side and attempted to get to his feet. Slowly, he got onto his knees.

"Why in God's name did I do this to myself?" he groaned.

After about a further ten minutes, he dragged himself into a chair and slumped into it. He had drunk himself into a stupor in an attempt to mask his misery. But, this didn't help, but merely provided a reverse effect, and he now felt worse for it.

He suddenly thought about Father Fenwick, and remembered that he had not judged him, and had made time for him. Maybe he could call on him in the presbytery, he thought. But, at the moment he wasn't fit for anything. He felt that he couldn't stand, and he needed to eat, but for now he could only sit in the chair, he was afraid that he might fall again.

He decided that he would wait for a while, and then attempt to stand up. If he could get himself something to eat, he would maybe feel a bit better. Although, there wasn't much food in the house.

Maybe a few rounds of stale bread, and a tub of margarine, and a cup of tea would be nice.

The situation suddenly dawned on him. If he continued to go on like this, nothing would improve, and he may even end up in hospital, or on a mortuary slab, he shivered at the thought of it. Yes, he would get over this, and finally make the effort to improve his life.

CHAPTER TWENTY-ONE

It was the Sunday following the community meeting, Father Fenwick, celebrated mass in the school hall once again. Bob had transported all that he needed in the trusty suitcase When the time came for the sermon, Father Fenwick smiled and greeted the congregation warmly.

"My dear friends," he began. "I feel very happy today. Last Wednesday evening we held our meeting in this very hall. We were told that our school, complete with church will commence being built very shortly. We can then look forward to the day when it will be consecrated, and the first mass celebrated therein." The congregation listened intently to what Father Fenwick was saying to them. There was hardly a sound, it was as if they were in a classical concert hall.

He continued. "While I was at the meeting, I noticed with much satisfaction that a community spirit was developing. Let us think about this for a moment. What do we mean by community? The word originates from the Latin word, Communitas, meaning public spirit.

Or Communis, which means shared in common. That is what we must do, as a Christian community. We must continue to build a community spirit, and share our desires, and actions with our neighbours, to help each other to reach a common goal.

In our community, we have the aged, who may struggle to cope with day to day tasks. Those who are suffering with mental trauma of different kinds, and their carers, who may have to put their own lives on hold. Those who are lonely, without friends, and may feel isolated and in despair, and those who have fallen on hard times. We can help all of these people, this is my mission dear friends, and hopefully it will be yours also."

When the mass concluded, Father Fenwick once again stood outside, while Bob packed his essentials away in the suitcase. He welcomed everybody who stopped to talk to him, and there were many. A small boy stopped and spoke to him enthusiastically.

"Hello, Father," he said. "I liked what you said about helping people."

"Thank you," Father Fenwick replied. "What's your name?"

"Robin," the small boy replied. "You're the running priest, aren't you?" he asked.

Father Fenwick smiled broadly and said. "If that's what you want to call me, it's OK by me. But, you can call me Father James as well."

"I'd like to run, my dad says that I'd be good at it," the boy replied.

"Why do you think that you'd be good at it?" asked Father Fenwick.

"Cause the police can't catch me," the small boy replied.

A rather short man walked over smiling.

"Good morning, Father," he said. You'll have to excuse Robin, he got into a little bit of trouble with some other lads from the estate recently. They were trespassing on a building site, and one of the lads started breaking some things. Someone must have called the police, and when they appeared suddenly, the boys ran off. Robin jumped over a metal gate, which was about five feet high, he left the seat of his pants on one of the spikes. The other boys were caught, but Robin was too fast for them, they couldn't catch him. When a police sergeant called at our house later, they said that Robin couldn't half run."

"Ah, I see," said Father Fenwick, laughing. "Only half a run though. I think that's quite a funny story, but you need a whole run if you want to be good. I'm glad that you weren't doing the breaking though. But, if you'd like to start running, I'd be pleased to help you if I can.

I'm not a coach, but I know how to run, so let's see how you go shall we?"

Father Fenwick turned to Robin's father and told him that if he wanted to bring Robin to the presbytery one evening, they could discuss some possibilities.

"That would be very helpful, Father," he said gratefully. "If Robin could get into running and burn up some energy, it may stop him getting into trouble, my name is David Bryant by the way."

"Happy to meet you, Mr Bryant," said Father Fenwick cheerfully.

*

He turned to Robin and said, "I'm glad that you weren't damaging anything, I don't hold with vandalism of any kind. But, if you're keen on taking up running, I hope that I'll be able to steer you in the right direction." A meeting was arranged for the following Tuesday evening, and Father Fenwick looked forward to the opportunity of helping out. He rather fancied himself as a coach. He thought wistfully, that Robin may one day be an Olympic champion.

Bob appeared at the door with Father Fenwick's suitcase. "Ready for the off Father, all packed up," he said cheerfully.

"Thanks, Bob," replied Father Fenwick. They both said their goodbyes to Robin and his father and began walking back to the presbytery. Bob invited Father Fenwick to Sunday dinner later, which he accepted gratefully. Vera's dinners were a joy to behold.

"Steve will be there as well," said Bob. Father Fenwick was pleased to hear this, because he was keen to see how he was getting on without Jen. Later in the afternoon, he would pay a visit to John Byrne, which he felt was overdue.

CHAPTER TWENTY-TWO

After everyone had enjoyed a hearty meal, which had been carefully prepared by Vera, the conversation revolved around Steve and the current situation.

"How have you been coping, Steve?" asked Father Fenwick. Steve replied, appearing a little pensive.

"Not very well, Father. The general idea behind the respite, is to give me a break from looking after Jen. But, although I'm having a rest, I'm missing Jen quite a lot. It's funny really, although the real Jen has gone, and there is no meaningful conversation any longer, I still feel that she is there with me in body. Most people don't understand really. They think that once the person who you care for is not there, you can just switch off. But, it's not as easy as that. The person is still on your mind constantly, even if I went on holiday, I would not be free from the situation, I would still be anxious."

"I am trying to understand," replied Father Fenwick, sympathetically. "Obviously, you've got to be in that situation to realise the extent of the trauma and anxiety that it can cause. All your friends can do, is offer support when it is needed, and I hope that is what we are doing."

Bob had been quiet, but he suddenly chipped in.

"You're like a breath of fresh air, Father James. You can't know how much you have brought to this community in the short time that you've been here. You are like a rock in times of need."

Father Fenwick was taken aback by Bob's comments and it was like music to his ears.

"Thank you, Bob," he said. "I really appreciate what you've said. It makes me feel that my move here has been worthwhile."

Vera added her comments. "I second that Father," she said, smiling warmly, waving a dishcloth in Bob's direction. She was dropping a gentle hint that she would appreciate some help with the dishes, and so they all got up to help with this chore.

Father Fenwick said that it was the least that they could do, after Vera had spent the morning preparing the meal.

The three men got stuck into washing the dishes and clearing them away.

"We make a good team," Bob said smiling warmly, and they all chatted together, until all the utensils and dishes were washed, cleared and put away in their respective places.

When this was done, Father Fenwick explained that he wished to visit John Byrne. Both Bob and Steve where inquisitive and asked who John was. Father Fenwick explained that John had hit on hard times. He explained the position that he was in and said that he was a person who needed help and support. So he thanked Bob and Vera for their much-appreciated hospitality, and bid them all farewell. He wondered what sort of condition that he would find John in, he didn't feel too optimistic, after his previous visit though.

CHAPTER TWENTY-THREE

During the course of the morning, John had managed to get to his feet and totter into the kitchen. He looked at himself in the mirror, and what a sight he saw, surely that couldn't be him. He had a dark bruise down the right side of his face, he looked like he had gone three rounds with Cassius Clay. He was lucky that he had not broken any bones. Maybe the next time he wouldn't be so lucky, if there was a next time, maybe this was the wakeup call that he needed. He had managed to make a few rounds of toast, which was made with stale bread.

This was followed with the last digestive biscuit in the packet, and a cup of tea, with no milk. He really needed to do some shopping, but he was waiting for his money from the social security, which was not due until Tuesday.

He had just finished this meagre repast when he heard a loud knock on the door. He muttered to himself, and crawled to the window to see who it was. He peered through the dirty glass, and when he recognised Father Fenwick, his spirits rose a little. He had been very impressed with Father Fenwick when he had called on him recently. He felt that he was somebody who could give him some hope for the future. John was not a religious person, in fact he had not been to mass for many years, let alone confession. But, he realised that Father Fenwick would not judge him about this and would wish to help him, nevertheless. He appeared as a friend first, and a priest second. He put a person's interests first, rather than just wanting to preach to them.

He started to move his aching body towards the front door and groaned in pain, cursing that he had brought this pain on himself. He opened the front door gingerly.

Father Fenwick looked aghast at the sight that stood before him.

"Good heavens, Mr Bryne," he blurted out. "What has happened to you? Have you been in a fight?"

John explained that he had felt depressed the evening before, and had got drunk, and this had resulted in him falling over.

"That must have been some binge," Father Fenwick said. "Are you in pain?"

"The biggest pain is psychological," explained John. "I can't believe how stupid I've been."

John invited Father Fenwick inside. He looked around and was immediately concerned about the conditions that John was living in. The lounge and kitchen areas were very sparsely furnished, and not in a tidy and hygienic condition. He was aware, particularly about the amount of empty beer cans that were strewn everywhere.

John smiled weakly, and said. "Sorry about the mess Father, I'm afraid that I had to let the maid go."

Father Fenwick also smiled at John's humorous remark. However, it was not really a laughing matter, John shouldn't really continue to live like this. But, he was aware what depression could do, and John was certainly depressed. He had no job, his family were estranged to him, and he had very little income to improve his lifestyle.

"Have you got anyone who can help you out, and give you some support?" enquired Father Fenwick.

"I'm afraid not," John replied. "My mates are the reason that I'm like this. Lisa didn't like them, when I was with them I was encouraged to drink all the time, and they were always talking about breaking into places."

"Hmm, it can't have been easy for you. Losing your job was the start of the problems."

"That's right," agreed John. "Until then we had been a happy family. I had a job, not the greatest in the world, but it provided some income. The kids were doing all right, their school work was up to standard, and I used to help them with their homework, particularly arithmetic."

"There you are," said Father Fenwick. "You were a useful family member then, and you can be again in the future. All you need is some help to get yourself up to speed again."

John thought about this for a few moments.

"Yes, I was," he mumbled. "After losing my job, the arguments between me and Lisa got worse. I got in with the wrong crowd, and that's when the heavy drinking started. I moved out here to be free of them. I had visions that I would make a better life here, and move Lisa and the kids over eventually."

"You still can," Father Fenwick said. "We can help you. I've got two good friends here, Bob and Steve. I'm sure that they'll be only to keen to help you, if you wish, they've been a great support to me since I moved here. Steve's wife isn't very well, and he knows what it's like to struggle."

John seemed more cheerful when he heard this, and he agreed to meet Bob and Steve.

"Leave it to me," Father Fenwick said. "I'll speak to them about it, and we can pop around when it's convenient."

"You won't be able to contact me Father, my phone was cut off some time ago, and I can't afford to have it reconnected."

"Don't worry about it, John, we'll just call around and catch you if you're in."

*

On the way back to the presbytery, Father Fenwick thought about the possibilities that lay ahead. The first task was to get John to believe in himself again. They could all help him to clean up his house, then maybe they could help him to find a job, and ultimately, get his life back on track. The possibilities looked promising.

Father Fenwick regarded Bob and Steve as 'very good chaps', and he was confident that they could work with John and befriend him. John appeared as a very amenable fellow, who would respond well to friendly intervention. After all, the current situation that he was in was no fault of his own. His family life had been progressing very well, he had been a hard-working man, and regarded himself as the breadwinner of the family. Bad luck, and the sign of the times had struck him a cruel blow. With his job gone, and his slow decline into depression, he had let the reins slip. He turned to drink as a means of softening the blow. But this had led him into fraternising with those who were in a similar position as himself.

Although, these so called 'mates' were not like him. They didn't care for family life, or holding down a job, and they were involved in criminal activity as a way of life. John was being sucked in, although he would not involve himself in a criminal lifestyle such as theirs. He had, unknown to himself, made the first move to change his life. Making a move away from his mates had presented him with the opportunity of escaping from his decline.

Unfortunately, not much had improved. Continuing unemployment, shortage of finances, and social exclusion had taken its toll. The worm must turn, and with their help, it could be achieved.

Father Fenwick felt heartened by this, and he made John's

situation his main goal. He was also aware that Robin and his Father were coming to the presbytery on Tuesday evening, to discuss plans for running coaching. Life was becoming busy now, he would get back to the presbytery, change, and go for a run. He had a great deal to think about.

CHAPTER TWENTY-FOUR

It was a dreary, wet Monday morning, Brenda had just got into the office. She took off her coat, made herself a cup of tea, settled into her chair and turned on her computer. She wondered how Jen was doing at *Happy Days*. The seven days period of residential care would be up the next day. She hadn't heard any news, so she thought that all must be going well. She decided that she would contact the home later that morning. She hadn't heard from Steve, so she presumed that he must be coping, otherwise, he would have got in touch with her.

As she was gearing herself up for the day's toil, the door opened and Dot Morrison walked in. Dot was a Senior Practitioner, and was responsible for assisting Linda with the smooth running of the department.

"Hi, Brenda," she said cheerfully. "How's it going?"

"Not too bad, thanks, Dot," replied Brenda.

"That's good, Brenda," Dot replied. "There certainly is a lot going on recently, I've never known so much work for our department. I note that you arranged respite for Steve Farrell."

"Yes, just for one week, it will end tomorrow," Brenda replied.

"Linda has asked me to have a word with you about it," Dot said. "Evidently there has been a problem, and the home have contacted her. She's not very pleased that you haven't contacted them, to review the situation."

Brenda's heart sank. Linda on the warpath, and her in the firing line, was no way to start the week.

"I've been so busy lately," Brenda said meekly. "As I didn't hear anything, I thought that the placement was going well."

"Don't get too stressed about it," Dot said in a soothing voice. "Evidently, Jen has been quite a problem. Shouting for most of the night, and she has been resistant when the care staff have been washing and dressing her, she's also grabbed a few of the carers on their arms. So Linda has asked if we can get together this afternoon and discuss the situation."

They arranged to meet in Linda's office at 2pm. At 2pm exactly, Brenda knocked on Linda's door.

"Come in," boomed the usual loud voice.

On entering Linda's office, Brenda was faced with a steel faced Linda, and sitting opposite her was Dot, who was also not looking too happy.

"Sit down," Linda shouted again. "Dot has informed you why I wish to speak to you today, hasn't she? Although your supervision isn't due till next week."

"Yes, she has spoken to me about it," Brenda said softly.

Linda glared at Brenda and said, "I would have expected you to have completed a review during the week, to see how the placement was going, this would have given us time to make any necessary changes."

Brenda sighed and explained to Linda that she had been so busy, and because she hadn't been advised otherwise, she thought that the placement was proceeding without cause for concern.

"One shouldn't presume in this job, Miss Caddick, one should always review and then take the appropriate action. Right, that's all I want to say about it. I want you and Miss Morrison to go to the home tomorrow morning and complete a review, to assess what we are to do about the situation, if anything. If you can have the assessment notes typed up and put on my desk on Wednesday morning, at nine am, without fail, thank you, good afternoon."

Brenda and Dot stood up and left the office. They closed the office door quietly, before Linda could close it with her usual bang.

They both breathed a sigh of relief and agreed that they would go to *Happy Days Care Home* at 11 am the next morning.

"We'll have to decide whether Mrs Farrell can return to her own home, or remain at the care home a little while longer," said Dot.

"Yes," agreed Brenda. "Mr Farrell is really quite stressed with the current situation, and if his wife returns home in a worse condition than before she went in, he could break down completely."

Dot agreed with Brenda and told her that she would contact Steve right away and inform him about the review on the following day.

When Steve heard the news, he was quite upset. Firstly, he was very anxious that Jen might not be able to return home, and also that he may not be able to look after her if she did.

Dot reassured him and told him not to worry, they were simply going to see how Jen was doing, and also how the staff were coping. As Steve hadn't heard any news, he was expecting a call from Brenda to arrange for them to collect Jen the next day.

Dot arranged to pick Steve up at 10.15 am the next morning, and told him not to be too concerned at the present time. But, of course, Steve was bound to be concerned about the position. He had suffered with acute anxiety for the last two years, and the latest news of Jen's deterioration was very worrying for him. When Dot had rung off, Steve slumped into a chair and decided to give Bob a ring, who always managed to smooth over troubled waters.

Bob was very sympathetic, as expected. "Look, Steve," he said. "I understand how difficult the situation is, but you may have to make a difficult decision. I've seen the strain on your face that looking after Jen has caused. Maybe a care home would be the best option for you, you would be less stressed, and you could visit Jen whenever you wanted, and know that she was being well looked after."

Steve felt tears welling up in his eyes at the thought of this.

"Well," he stuttered. "I'll see how it goes tomorrow. I'm being taken to the home tomorrow morning by the social worker."

"OK, look Steve, I'll pop around shortly, and we'll have a good chat about it. Put the kettle on old man."

Bob told Vera that he was going to see Steve and try to calm him down. He put his coat on and went out of the front door. He wasn't sure that he would be able to console Steve, he knew what the outcome would be in the end.

When Steve opened the door, he looked distraught, and appeared to have lost weight. Bob was quite alarmed at the sight of him. It was plain to see that he had been missing Jen over the last six days. Steve ushered him inside, and they both sat down at the kitchen table. It was a glum meeting, and Bob tried to be as positive as he could.

"Look Steve," he said sympathetically. "Let's not be too despondent at the moment, things may turn out all right in the end. Come around to ours later and have dinner with us. Have you been eating properly?"

"That'll be nice, I haven't really felt like eating lately," Steve replied, feeling slightly better at the offer.

Later that day, Steve walked around to Bob and Vera's house and enjoyed a hearty meal, and their usual hospitality. After dinner, they all sat and watched the news on television.

"Dear oh dear," exclaimed Vera. "It looks like another strike is looming, just what we don't need."

There had been too many strikes lately. These were caused by general unrest, caused mainly by poor wages and long working hours.

"Some people are never happy," said Steve. "When I was working I was glad that I had a job. I used to come home in the evening, and Jen would have my tea ready. I really miss my job since I've retired. Jen was well then, now everything has gone sour. No proper life, no conversation and nothing to look forward to."

Bob and Vera glanced at each other, they didn't know what to say to Steve, to make him feel better. All they could do was try to be his friend and offer him as much support as they were able.

After a few moments silence, Bob spoke up. "Father Fenwick told me about a chap who is living locally, he's having a rough time. Evidentially, he moved out here after losing his job in Liverpool. His wife threw him out, and he's got three children, which his wife has got to look after, with no proper income coming in."

Steve looked pensive for a moment. "That's hard luck, his wife must really be struggling."

"That's right, and John is struggling as well," answered Bob. "Father Fenwick wants us to pay him a visit and see if we can offer him some help."

"Yes, that's a good idea," replied Steve. "We'll arrange to visit him when I know what's happening to Jen. I might feel better if I can help somebody else who's struggling as well."

*

The next morning, Dot and Brenda called for Steve to take him to *Happy Days Care Home*. Mrs Jones came out of her office to greet them.

"I know that we planned to send Mrs Farrell home tomorrow," she said. "But under the circumstances it may not be the right decision. The decision will depend on whether you will be able to look after her Mr Farrell. Your wife appears to have deteriorated quiet significantly over the last week."

Dot spoke up and advised Mrs Jones that they would assess the situation and decide on the most appropriate outcome.

"We would need to decide if an adequate care package could be put into place Mrs Jones. Obviously, it would need to be a significant package, in order to cater for all Mrs Farrell's needs."

"Of course," Mrs Jones replied.

"If we decide that Mrs Farrell can go home, we will need a decision from panel, as they would have to decide if it was viable, and weigh up the cost alternatives. This would necessitate Mrs Farrell remaining here for some more time."

"Yes, that's no problem, the room is free for several weeks yet," advised Mrs Jones.

Brenda listened to this, hanging on to every word. She thought about what Linda would make of it, no doubt she would put her case forward very strongly. The alternative decision would also need to be agreed by the panel, because an extension would require extra funding. She turned to Steve and asked him for his thoughts.

"I'm devastated," he said. "The thought of Jen staying here permanently is certainly not what I was expecting. I hate to think of not having her with me ever again, dear oh dear."

Dot and Brenda felt very sad for Steve, it was a lot for him to take in. It would be very difficult for him to adjust to living on his own. It would be as if his wife had died, and he would suffer the same bereavement process as if she had.

Brenda touched Steve's arm and said. "We'll go up to Jen's room now and see how she is."

"Are we not better to discuss it in the office?" queried Steve.

"No, it's not normal policy," Advised Dot. "Even though your wife cannot follow every word of what we are talking about, we must include her as part of a Person Centred Approach, she is the Relevant Person. It's just possible that she may take in some part of the discussion, we cannot know that she doesn't, and after all, the discussion is about her future as well."

"Oh," I see, said Steve. "I understand."

"Good," said Dot. "We'll go up to the room now."

They all went up to Jen's room, on the second floor. She was sitting in a chair by the window. Steve was shocked when he saw her, her face was grey, and she looked like she had lost a lot of weight.

"Hi love," he said meekly. "How are you today?" All he managed to get from Jen was a low groaning noise.

"She looks terrible," announced a shocked Steve. "What's happened to her?"

"I'm afraid that this deterioration is part of the illness Mr Farrell" advised Dot. "Unfortunately, there is no cure for it; and Jen will continue to get worse over time. All we can do is to look after her, and cater for her immediate needs. This is what we have got to decide today, whether to let her come back home, with an increased package of care, or advise a permanent residential placement."

Steve churned the predicament over in his mind. He wanted Jen to come home, because he missed her a lot while she had been away. On the other hand, to have her back home, and see her getting worse over time would be distressing for him.

Dot and Brenda could see that Jen would need a lot of care. She would need two care workers to attend to her personal care, and this would be required several times a day.

"Can she stand on her own, and walk about?" Dot asked Mrs Jones.

"I'm afraid not," she replied. "We have to use a hoist to get her out of her chair, and wheel her into the bathroom. She screams and grabs the carers when they try to wash her. I doubt that she could be managed very well at home, without considerable adaption, and even then it would be a struggle."

Steve's face dropped, he could see where this was leading. He felt very depressed at the present time.

Dot and Brenda completed their assessment and thanked Mrs Jones for her assistance. They advised her that they would report back to her when a decision had been made. A further couple of weeks would be arranged to sort out the future arrangements.

All three then drove back to *New Pastures*, to drop Steve off. They all felt quite glum, and had little to say to each other. Steve had his own thoughts and demons to worry about. Dot and Brenda geared themselves up for their meeting with Linda the following day. But, before then, they had a significant amount of typing to do. At the present time, they weren't entirely sure which way it would go.

CHAPTER TWENTY-FIVE

Father Fenwick was reading one of his favourite books, *A Christmas Carol*, by Charles Dickens. He admired Dickens, greatly, one of his favourite authors. He particularly enjoyed reading books which were set in a period setting. He felt that there was something atmospheric about stories which were set in the past, and particularly the nineteenth century, which was when Dickens was writing. Although many would regard *A Christmas Carol* as more of a book for children. Father Fenwick would not agree. He perceived that in those times gone by, there was much more of a community spirit. People didn't have as much money, and access to the technology of today, such as motor cars, radio, and mobile phones. They would have had to make their own amusement, and would have had more time for their neighbours, unlike those individuals of today. He particularly liked *A Christmas Carol*, because it demonstrated to the reader how a person can change.

Scrooge had become a hermit, and didn't mix with his neighbours, or his family. He was particularly mean to his employee, Bob Cratchit, refusing to give him a raise in his salary. He wouldn't allow him a day off for Christmas Day. And yet, he eventually changed his ways, becoming a pillar of society, and respected by all.

John Byrne could change his ways also, Father Fenwick was sure of that. He could return to being a respected family man, and once again, becoming a respected pillar of society.

However, he would not have to be visited by three ghosts, and hear clanking chains in the middle of the night to achieve this change.

John was shunned by most people. Not only because he was unemployed, but because of the cause of his circumstances. People were wary of him; they thought that he might be involved with undesirable characters, which he once was.

There was one particular instance a couple of months ago. John had been friendly with Henry Dobbin, who was a well-known local villain. He was known to the police, and had been involved in minor infringements, burglary and petty violence. John had been drinking with him one afternoon in the Dog and Duck pub, when a fight broke out. Tables were overturned, voices raised, and glasses smashed. Another man ended up with cuts and bruises. Although John was not involved in the fracas, he was tarnished with the same brush. The very fact that he was friendly with Henry, and in the same public house, drinking with him.

He got a bad name, and was labelled as a troublemaker also.

After this incident, John had distanced himself from Dobbin, and he had become reclusive again. After all, this was why he had moved out of Liverpool, and he didn't wish to return to his bad old days.

While Father Fenwick was going over this in his mind, there was a knock at the door, and he glanced at his watch, it was seven fifteen. He was expecting Robin Bryant and his father, following their discussion after the mass on the previous Sunday, when he had said that he may help Robin with his interest in running.

Father Fenwick answered the door, and greeted them both warmly. He ushered them into his kitchen come dining area, and they all sat down at the table.

"Well, Robin," he said. "Have you considered my offer of help with your running?"

His father spoke up for him. "He certainly has, Father," he said. "He's very keen to get started."

"I am Father," Robin answered, enthusiastically. "Me mates, Gaz' and Eddy think that it's a mad idea, but I'll be able to run faster when the 'scuffers' are after us."

Mr Bryant coughed nervously, as Father Fenwick told Robin that the idea wasn't to run away from the police, but to enjoy himself, get fit and hopefully become a good athlete.

"I hope that he does," Mr Bryant said. "It'll certainly do him good, and put a bit of discipline into him."

"Yes, it certainly will. We'll get started as soon as possible Robin. But, tell your mates that it's not to help you to run from the police. It's to make you a good runner, and get you really fit. It won't be easy at first, but you appear to have some natural talent. So I'll let your dad know when we can begin."

With that, Father Fenwick bid Robin and his father goodnight. As they went out through the front door, he considered the future and smiled as he said to himself. "The Running Priest Harriers Club has been born."

He decided that he would pay a further visit to John Byrne the next day; he would invite Bob and Steve if they wished to accompany him. They had previously expressed their wish to visit him. Maybe, John would like to get involved with a bit of coaching himself. It would be good for his morale, and give him the feeling that he was doing his bit for the community; it would also get him started on the path to respectability once again. This was his plan anyway, he hoped that it would work.

CHAPTER TWENTY-SIX

"Well," boomed Linda, as she scanned Dot and Brenda's assessment notes, on Wednesday afternoon. "What do you make of it?"

"Things haven't been going too well," Dot advised meekly. "It appears that Mrs Farrell has deteriorated somewhat over the last week. The care staff have had a struggle with her. Mostly with behavioural issues and her mobility has got worse."

"How do you mean," Linda demanded.

"Well, she wasn't that bad when she went into the home, but now it appears that she has trouble walking, and they have to use a hoist."

"Hmm," grunted Linda. "Private care homes eh? I don't like them at all; we haven't any idea how good the care has been; I believe in good NHS care, on a geriatric ward; Mrs Farrell shouldn't have gone down so swiftly. If a certain social worker had reviewed mid-term, we may have had a better idea how things were going."

Brenda cringed slightly, she was aware that Linda's rather toxic tone was aimed in her direction. Sometimes she felt that Linda hated her; she certainly had little respect for any of the social workers on her team. She appeared to take pleasure in bullying people, and showing them who was boss.

"Taking stock of the situation," Linda continued. "I would like you to try to transfer her to a geriatric ward at Brampton Hospital. I feel that she would receive much better care in an NHS facility, and she could be assessed properly. I believe that these long stay geriatric wards are the right choice; never mind these people with fancy ideas, who believe in the private sector as being a better choice and providing better care; sheer poppycock."

Dot chipped in at this point of the proceedings. "Mrs Farrell is hardly a geriatric, she's only sixty-two, Linda; so I feel that it would be wrong to place her on a ward with much older people. Also, I feel that we may have a struggle to get her into an NHS hospital. We would need to get doctors on board to support our case."

"Hmm," Linda muttered. "You're not paid to feel anything. But you may be correct regarding admittance to a geriatric ward not being in the best interests of Mrs Farrell; but we'll have to see how it goes. We may have no choice even if these private homes can't cope. Well then, let's get to it shall we? I definitely feel that Mrs Farrell would receive a higher standard of care in hospital whatever, so let's aim for it shall we?"

Dot and Brenda were slightly taken aback when Linda had agreed with them, regarding the point about a geriatric ward. But, they knew only too well, that Linda would make a point of it and would push to achieve her own goals.

"It's obvious, we know how she works," said Dot. "We wouldn't have to pay anything if Mrs Farrell was placed on a long stay ward. But, if she went home, or remained in a private home, we would have to foot the bill."

"That's true," replied Brenda. "Although she would be assessed as to her ability to pay. I doubt if the Farrell's have got much capital, if any. So, we'll have to arrange a meeting at Brampton Hospital to see if it's possible to get her admitted; maybe on a section, if her health is at risk."

"Or, possibly get her home, with a care package," added Dot.

"I can't see that working," replied Brenda. "I doubt if Mr Farrell would be able to cope with her. He looked all in last time I saw him."

"Right then," advised Dot. "We'll get working on it. Linda has authorised a further two weeks at *Happy Days*, to allow us time to make the appropriate arrangements."

"How did she manage that, without going to panel?"

"You know how Linda works, Brenda. She strode into the service manager's office, and told them how it was going to be; Dawn crumbled when she saw her face."

"Gosh," said Brenda, smiling. "Linda may be a tough old boot, but she certainly gets the job done."

They both laughed, and went back to their separate offices.

*

When Brenda was back in her own office, she decided to give Steve a ring to ask how he was coping. When he answered her call, he didn't sound too good at all.

"Hello," he said, almost in a whisper.

"Good afternoon Mr Farrell. I thought that I'd give you a ring to see how you were feeling, after our meeting yesterday," she said.

"I'm feeling very down," Steve replied. "I just don't know how things are going to work out. I've done nothing but turn the situation over in my mind. Jen's not coming home again, is she?"

"Well, we don't know that for certain, but we are keeping an open mind," said Brenda. She didn't want to give Steve false hopes, but deep down, she knew what the answer would be; and it wouldn't be what Steve wanted to hear.

"I can't rest," explained Steve again. "It's not like it used to be, we used to do things together; go places together. Now, it's all ended, no hope for the future. I sit here on my own, I see nobody most of the time. What am I going to do Brenda?"

Brenda was at a loss for words. She didn't know what to say. She couldn't tell him the truth, but at the same time, she didn't want to lie.

"Don't get too depressed about the situation," she advised. "We will do everything that we can; it will just take a little time to sort things out."

"OK," replied Steve. "I'll just have to hope for the best."

Brenda put the phone down, and felt quite sad regarding the situation. This was the part of her job that she hated. It was all right when things went well. But when they didn't they had plenty of publicity. Social workers were demonised. Most of the time, there were successful outcomes, but there was a lack of publicity then; bad news is good news, as far as the media is concerned.

Brenda would put her trust in Dot, she was a good social worker, and had been qualified for ten years. She took comfort in this. They would work hard to achieve a positive end result, but for whom?

CHAPTER TWENTY-SEVEN

Father Fenwick had rung Bob and asked him if he and Steve would like to accompany him to visit John Byrne, the following morning.

"Yes, Father," Bob said. "That will be a good idea. Steve rang me yesterday, he had spoken to Brenda, and he told me that he felt very low; Jen may not be able to come home again."

"Dear me, that is bad news," replied Father Fenwick. "Poor Steve, maybe we could cheer him up, and John at the same time."

"That sounds a good idea, Father; how about if we go to John's at about eleven in the morning?"

"That sounds good to me," replied Father Fenwick. "It will give me time to say morning mass and gather myself together; I'll have time for a short run as well; I've got something that I want to discuss with you."

"Right, we'll meet at Steve's house at quarter to eleven then, and walk around to John's, after we've had a good chat and a cup of tea."

Bob said that he would ring Steve and advise him about the arrangements. They hoped that they would find John at home, although it was unlikely that he would be out, due to his present situation.

The next morning, Steve heard a rousing knock on his front door. He had been feeling depressed all morning, but when he saw the two cheery faces of Bob and Father Fenwick, he felt instantly better; he could see some hope and friendship in their happy faces.

"Come on in my friends," Steve said in a welcoming tone. "How are you feeling today Steve?" asked Bob.

"Much better for seeing you two," Steve replied.

Father Fenwick shook Steve's hand and told him that he hoped that he would feel a little better when they had been to see John.

"I hope so, Father," replied Steve. "I need something to take my mind off Jen; I can't sleep, or rest thinking about the future without her."

Father Fenwick was keen to allay Steve's fears, although he felt that he may struggle to achieve it.

"Try not to worry too much, Steve," he told him. "Thing's will turn out all right in the end, I'm sure, we are here to support you, we are your friends."

"I certainly hope and pray that they will, Father."

"I'm sure with God's help, and your prayers, you can rely on the best outcome for Jen and yourself."

"Thank you, Father. Let's all sit down for a few minutes, I've made a pot of tea."

They all sat around the small dining room table, chatted, and sipped their tea, after which they all began to feel a little better, and felt that they were ready to meet John.

Steve was thoughtful for a few moments. "Who is John?" he asked Father Fenwick.

"Well, Steve," he replied. "John used to live in Liverpool, he has a wife, and three children, and he once had a steady job, which provided him with a reasonable income, which enabled him to look after his family.

Unfortunately, fate dealt him a bad hand, and he was made redundant. He became depressed because he felt that he was letting his family down. So, he began drinking heavily, and mixing with undesirable acquaintances. Unfortunately, he was led astray, and got into some minor trouble with the police, through no fault of his own.

His wife became weary of his late-night binges, and so she asked him to leave their marital home. He managed to get a house on this estate, thinking that the move would provide him with a new start. Unfortunately, he got in with the wrong crowd again, and this lead him to falling foul of the law once more. So, he withdrew into a reclusive lifestyle, and alcohol abuse once again."

"I see, it sounds like he has gone through a rough patch; so, do you think that we can help him Father?" asked Steve.

"We can certainly give it a try, Steve, and Bob is keen as well. So, let's go for it, shall we?"

"Yes, let's all try and help him, just like the 'Three Just Men'," replied Steve.

"Well I'm not so sure about that Steve, but I think that they were four, weren't they, if I remember rightly?" Bob pointed out.

"Yes, I think that you're right Bob. Well, we will be three then, we'll be smoothing over the injustices of society."

They all agreed about that, and were in a more determined mood now than earlier. Steve was looking forward to meeting John, and thought that with his help and empathetic approach, it may help him to get over his current problems. Steve was aware that he was not the only one who was suffering with the trials of life, if he could help someone else to feel better about themselves, and take a step up, he would possibly help himself to feel better as well. He needed something to take his mind off his current situation.

So in a more positive mood, the 'Three Just Men' set off for John's house.

CHAPTER TWENTY-EIGHT

They all set off at a brisk pace, and reached John's house in a short time. They chatted to each other as they walked, and they wondered how they would find John.

To their surprise, John answered the door almost immediately, and invited them inside. Father Fenwick was surprised, that John looked quite smart, he had obviously made an effort to make a good impression. The lounge, looked different also. The room appeared very tidy, not like it had been last time Father Fenwick had visited.

This was the first visit for Bob and Steve, so they couldn't compare it with prior visits. But, for Father Fenwick, he was taken aback when he witnessed the scene. It was obvious that John had been swayed by his earlier visits, and had made the effort to improve.

He greeted Bob and Steve warmly, shaking their hands, while smiling broadly.

"I'm glad to meet you two gentlemen," he said. "I've heard a lot about you from Father Fenwick."

"All good, I hope," said Bob smiling.

"Yes," replied John. "Father Fenwick has told me that you've given him a lot of support since he moved here, to take over the parish. I'm afraid that I've not had much time for religion for some time now."

"Well, we haven't done that much," Bob said, smiling.

"Ah, you're too modest," Father Fenwick said. "You've been a great help to me. Getting me contacts, which has saved me a great deal of time. I'm sure the local residents have felt a lot more comfortable with you than they would with me. People tend to be wary of priests, they can feel intimidated, and think that they are going to preach to them on their doorsteps."

"But you are not like most priests," advised Bob. "You're more like one of us, ordinary like."

This was music to Father Fenwick's ears. This was what he had always yearned for, not to be seen as a priestly figure, but as an ordinary 'man in the street.' He was more at home like this; and meeting Bob and Steve, had presented him with the opportunity that he wanted.

Now, he would like to count John as a friend also.

"It's good of you all to come around," John said. "When the father called at first, I thought that he was going to preach to me and get me to go to church. I haven't been for years now, but I have tried to live a good life; that is, until I lost my job, and everything fell apart after that. I met a few blokes and thought that they would be my friends, but they turned out just like my so-called mates in Liverpool."

"Well," said Steve. "Things could get better now if you want to accept us as your friends. We are willing to help you, and I promise you that we are nothing like your previous 'so-called' friends."

"Thanks for that," agreed John. "Things can't get much worse than they are now, I constantly have this dread that nothing is going to get better. I feel that I've lost Lisa and the kids for ever."

John started to well up, and tears rolled down his cheeks, he looked quite forlorn.

There were a few moments silence, during which the three friends felt quite helpless and a feeling of emptiness overcame them.

"Look," Bob blurted out suddenly. "I'll put the kettle on shall I? We'll have a cup of tea and formulate a plan. Your future starts here, John, and it looks bright."

"How can you help me? I feel that I've made such a mess of my life. Letting my family down and running away over here."

"You've not made a mess of your life, John, or run away," said Father Fenwick soothingly. "It's not your fault that you lost your job, it's a sign of the times. You were floating in a sea, with no wind in your sails."

John reluctantly agreed with what Father Fenwick had told him. It wasn't his fault that his job had disappeared. The government was to blame, not him. The factory where he had worked had made small electrical parts for cars, condensers and electrical points to fit inside the distributor. John's job had been to pack the parts in their packaging and box them up. He loved the job, although it could be tedious at times, he got a great deal of satisfaction from it. At the end of his shift, he felt that he had played his part.

The company decided that the costs of production were increasing and constant strikes were crippling their business. As a result of this, production was transferred abroad, where workers would work for next to nothing. The government allowed it, instead of improving the working conditions for everyone. Yes, the government were to blame, and John hated them. He felt that they were responsible for his downfall.

"What I need most is a job," John said. "I can't hope to get myself together unless I'm working again. Maybe if I had a job, Lisa would think that I was worth taking back. She could come to live here with the kids, she'd certainly like that, it would be much better than where she's living at the moment."

"You're certainly worth taking back, John, whether you have a job or not," said Father Fenwick.

"But, I take your point, a job would improve your chances of getting your wife back. Also, you do need to work again, for your own peace of mind."

"I'm sick of living on benefits, I want to feel that I've earned my money. People tend to look down on the unemployed."

"Unfortunately, that's true," said Bob. "It's very unfair though. I know that you get the lazy sods who don't want to work, and are happy to live on state handouts. But, it's very unfair to tar everyone with the same brush."

"I'm retired now, but I still miss my job," said Steve. "I sometimes feel that I'm living on benefits myself. It's funny really, I've earned my pension, through paying into the system for years, but still feel like a scrounger at times."

"I know what you mean, Steve," said Bob. "But you've been looking after Jen, a full-time carer, so you've nothing to feel guilty about. You've paid your dues all of your working life."

"Yes, I believe that your wife isn't well, Steve, and you've been looking after her," said John.

"I have John, she's got Dementia, life will never be the same any more, and she doesn't even know who I am. She's in a home at the moment, and I don't know if she will be coming home."

"I'm sorry to hear that Steve," said John sympathetically. "It must be very difficult for you. And I thought that I had it rough."

Bob chirped up suddenly. "Enough of this doom and gloom," he said. "Things will be better if we all stick together. How would you all like to come around to our house tomorrow night for a meal? I'll ask Jen."

"That sounds great," said John. "Are you sure that she won't mind?"

"I'm sure that will be ok, just leave it to me, I'll fix it. Shall we say at six?"

John was taken aback at the offer from Bob. For the first time in what seemed an age, he had friends who thought that he was worth the effort and didn't judge him for his downfall; friends who he would be able to rely on, and who would not be involved in criminal activity. He felt that his luck was about to change, he really had a reason to believe it.

CHAPTER TWENTY-NINE

The next week passed without any problems. Father Fenwick was satisfied the way the situation was moving along. John had enjoyed his meal at Bob's house. He had received a warm welcome from Vera, and had been made to feel at home. He had a more positive outlook now, and felt that his future was about to improve, he considered that he was moving out of the shadows. Father Fenwick had already noticed a change in him. He had made the effort to make himself more tidy regarding his clothing, and he was clean-shaven. It was obvious that the recent bonding with Bob and Steve had paid off, and he realised that his outlook could improve if he trusted in the help of his newfound friends, something which he hadn't enjoyed previously.

Steve, on the other hand was still feeling very unhappy, and insecure. He didn't know what was going to happen to Jen, and he was missing her very much, and he now needed the support of his friends more than ever.

Father Fenwick had received notification that plans had been put into motion regarding the construction of the new school. Building was due to commence over the following weeks. Surveyors had moved onto the building site, and there was much activity. There were several men on the site, in yellow high visibility jackets, and hard hats, peering through their theodolites.

Mobile office units and toilets had been placed at various

locations, and there was a large placard, displaying the name Todmore Construction Ltd.

This was a welcome sight for sore eyes to Father Fenwick. As he watched with interest, he suddenly had an idea. They would need workers. Obviously, this would be for qualified builders, such as bricklayers, plasterers, electricians, and so on. But, they would also need labourers, there would be much need for these extra workers.

Father Fenwick took it upon himself to enquire without delay. He walked over to one of the men, who was busy holding a measuring pole.

"Excuse me," he said, feeling that he was intruding. "I'm sorry to disturb you. I believe that construction is about to start on the new school?"

"That's right," replied the man. "Once we've got all our calculations worked out, the lads will move in, probably over the next few weeks. We need to make a start, before the bad weather sets in."

"I was just thinking, will there be any vacancies going for labourers?" asked Father Fenwick.

"There will be. But, you'll have to apply at the local job centre. Are you looking for a change of career Father?" The man asked, peering at Father Fenwick's dog collar.

"Not at the moment, it's for a friend of mine, who's looking for work," replied Father Fenwick.

"Well, he'll have to hot foot it to the job centre, they'll be holding interviews shortly."

"Thanks for your time," said Father Fenwick, walking away briskly. "I'll tell him."

He decided to walk around to John's house. He would tell him that the building site would be looking for labourers. He felt sure that John would jump at the chance of applying, but he would need to visit the job centre himself and apply for a job on the site.

John was very keen when he was told that there may be work going.

"Do you think that I'll have a chance of getting a job on the site Father?" he asked.

"I don't see why not John," replied Father Fenwick. "You have a good working record in the past, so there shouldn't be any reason why you wouldn't be taken on, and you're a robust looking chap."

"There'll be a lot of blokes after the jobs, unemployment is widespread in this area," John said, with a frown.

"That's right," replied Father Fenwick. "But if you get there by tomorrow at the latest, you should be in with a chance. If you need a reference, I'll only be too glad to give you one."

"That's very kind of you Father. I'll go to the job centre first thing in the morning."

"Well, all the best John, I'll look forward to hearing your good news then," Father Fenwick said, with a positive tone in his voice.

John hoped that he would have good news. The following morning he went to the local job centre, which was a thirty-minute walk. He was slightly alarmed when he saw how many people were there, not thinking that many were there just to sign on. There were a considerable amount of individuals who were happy to remain on the dole, and receive unemployment benefit, like the friends that John had once mixed with. They wouldn't want to work on a building site, which they would regard as hard work, which they weren't used to.

John waited until one of the desks was free and told the clerk that he had come to enquire about a job on the building site at *New Pastures*.

"Are you signing on here?" Snapped the clerk, a rather wiry looking lady, with grey hair, and a rather pointed nose.

"Yes," replied John. "I sign on Wednesdays."

"Name," she snapped again.

"John Byrne."

The clerk clicked on her computer keys. "Ah yes," she said. "Mr Byrne, you've been signing on here for six months now, and you've shown no sign of finding a job."

"Yes," replied John. "I've had anxiety problems. My wife threw me out and I met up with some people who were unreliable, then I moved out here to try to make a new life."

"Um," grunted the clerk. "Have you worked on a building site before?"

"No, my last job was as a packer in a factory, it was quite hard work. I'm not afraid of hard work. I was good at the job, but the factory closed down, and I was made redundant."

"Well, I don't see any reason why you won't be suitable, you seem keener than the rest. The main thing is for the unemployed to want to work That's a rare commodity around here. I'll give you a form to fill in. The site office will be open from nine on Monday morning. Just present yourself with the completed form and you will be interviewed and considered suitable, or not, good luck."

John took the form gratefully, thanked the clerk, and left the job centre. He felt hopeful that he would be successful. Monday couldn't come quick enough.

As soon as he got home, John read the form. He wasn't particularly good at filling forms in. He groaned as he read some of the questions, particularly those that referred to qualifications. He had left school at sixteen, without taking any GCSE's. Many of his friends had stayed on to further their education, but John needed to earn some money. He had been going out with Lisa for six months, and she was pregnant at the time. He regretted not getting any qualifications, but his job at the factory had earned him enough money to enable him to support Lisa and the baby, so at that time, he had decided to leave school and get a job, which he had managed to keep until his redundancy.

Anyway, that was behind him now, in the past. He had married Lisa, and produced three children with her. So, now he had to move on; he felt that he had messed things up.

Although it wasn't his fault that he was made redundant, but he had allowed himself to mix with the wrong crowd, and that definitely was his fault, so now, he must make amends. With that in mind, John set about filling in the application form.

CHAPTER THIRTY

Father Fenwick's feet pounded on the tarmac, during his daily run. His mind was working on overdrive. That morning he had received disturbing news. Bishop Larkin had called him to tell him that Father Frederick was in hospital; he had suffered a stroke in the early hours of the morning. Since Father Fenwick had moved to *New Pastures*, the diocese had been unable to replace him at St Matthew's, because there was currently a shortage of priests.

Consequently, poor Father Frederick had to manage on his own, which was bound to put a strain on him, due to his eighty plus years.

Bishop Larkin told Father Fenwick that he would need to return to St Matthew's for a short while, during Father Frederick's absence. This had disturbed Father Fenwick greatly. He felt that he couldn't leave his new parish at the present time, things were just starting to happen. The new school was about to undergo construction, not to mention leaving his friends there. He was particularly concerned about Steve. He needed support at the present time, although he still had Bob, and just lately, John also.

Maybe he was working himself up too much, the move would only be a temporary measure, while Father Frederick was recovering. It was essential that *New Pastures* had a resident priest, as it couldn't be left without one during the initial organisation. There were some smaller parishes that didn't have a regular parish priest, and were reliant on priests who served several parishes in turn, on a mobile basis, what Bob had termed 'A Priest in a Suitcase.'

Bishop Larkin had emphasised that his main concern for the time being was for a priest to be made available to say Sunday mass at Saint Matthew's, which was most vital, particularly as it was an established parish. A priest could be available as a 'long arm' member of the parish, however. Anyway, Bishop Larkin had said that it was important for a replacement to be made as a matter of urgency, so Father Fenwick would only fill the gap in the short term, because he was needed during the establishment of the new parish on *New Pastures*. It was unclear how severe Father Frederick's stroke had been at this stage; although, even if it wasn't that severe, he would be unable to return to his duties immediately following his discharge from hospital.

When Father Fenwick returned to his presbytery, there was a message on his answer phone. He clicked on the receive button to hear a further message from Bishop Larkin.

"Good morning once again, Father Fenwick," he announced. "I appreciate that you have had a shock regarding the news about Father Frederick; I have been informed that he has only suffered a minor stroke, thank the lord. He seems quite well, on the contrary. He is eating everything that they put in front of him, as usual. He is creating quite a fuss though because the hospital appeared to have mislaid his teeth. They brought somebody else's teeth to him, and he got quite irritated about it, he told them that they wouldn't fit into his mouth."

"I can imagine that," said a relieved Father Fenwick, laughing.

"Obviously, you are needed at *New Pastures*, so I will arrange for you to spend most of your time there, and visit St Matthew's when necessary. I'll be visiting Father Frederick in the hospital tomorrow, so I will have a clearer picture then of how soon he will be able to return. But, I anticipate that he may need a period of respite for a short while, before he can return to the parish, if at all."

Father Fenwick didn't wish to contemplate Bishop Larkin's last words; but he thought that he was thinking of himself, rather than Father Frederick's health.

"I suggest that you come back to St Matthew's on Thursday, mingle, and make it clear to the parishioners that you are only back as a temporary come and go measure. Then you can return to your parish after Sunday mass. So, don't concern yourself too much Father James, I am aware that you have made an excellent impression so far, and you've got things moving; so I wouldn't want you to be away for longer than necessary."

Father Fenwick breathed a sigh of relief, maybe he shouldn't have worried after all. He would explain to his friends and the parishioners about the situation and allay their fears, as he didn't want to make them feel that he was leaving them already, now that the first steps of the new parish had begun. First though, he would explain to Bob, Steve and John what was about to happen, that he wouldn't always be there all the time for a few weeks. He wouldn't want them to fret about it, and think that they were about to lose him.

Bishop Larkin had told him that he would have use of the car from St Matthew's parish during his comings and goings. But, maybe it was time for him to purchase his own car; his knowledge of motors would be of great help when choosing one, he would be able to go over it with a fine-tooth comb, and get the best car possible, for what he could afford, which was not much. In the meantime, he could ask his old friend, David O'Donovan to help him out with his first visit to St Matthew's.

He dialled his number, at St Joseph's, which was situated in St Helens, not far from Liverpool. Father Richard Andrews answered the phone. "Hello," he announced brightly. "St Joseph's presbytery."

"Oh hello," Father Fenwick answered. "It's Father Fenwick here."

"Oh hi," came the reply, Father Richard was always quite flippant and easy going, similar to Father Fenwick in fact. "I've heard that you're getting along famously at *New Pastures*."

"Yes, I am, thanks for that. I suppose that you've heard about Father Frederick?"

"Yes, it's quite a shock, I hope that the old boy will be all right."

"I sincerely hope so. I've been asked by Bishop Larkin to step into his shoes at St Matthew's while Father Frederick is absent."

"Yes, it's because of the shortage of priests, isn't it? Sometimes I think that we'd get more recruits if the pope dropped the celibacy rule."

Father Fenwick smiled to himself. "Not much chance of that happening."

"No, unfortunately, I'd be one of the first to dive in, if that happened."

Father Fenwick smiled to himself again. He could understand where Father Richard was coming from, but he didn't necessarily think like him.

"Anyway, I wanted to speak to Father David, is he there?"

"Yes, he's got his head buried in a book at the moment, the Karma Sutra, I think."

Father Fenwick was rather shocked when he heard this remark, but then he realised that this was a flippant remark, so typical of Father Richard.

"Only joking, old boy," Father Richard said laughing loudly. "He's reading one of his football mags, about Everton, I think."

"By Jove, that's worse," Father Fenwick joked back.

"I'll just get, David, speak to you again, all the best for the future."

"Thanks, Richard, speak to you again. We must meet up some day."

"Hello James, how are you keeping?" asked Father David.

"Oh, very well thanks, David. I've just explained to Richard, that due to Father Frederick being indisposed for a while, I've been asked to fill in at St Matthew's for a short period, but mostly to say mass on Sundays. So, I'll be going back and forth for a while. I wondered if you are free to give me a lift this Thursday? I'll be able to make my own way back in the parish car."

"No problem," Father David replied. "It's going to be hard work, you'll be tired out, no energy left for your running."

"Oh, no fear about that, nothing will keep me away from my running," Father Fenwick replied, with a determined edge to his voice.

"Whatever you say," replied Father David. "Shall I pick you up at around ten on Thursday?"

"That'll be fine, David, I look forward to that. I should be able to drive back to *New Pastures* after Sunday mass. I'll have to say mass there; it'll probably have to be an evening mass, at six."

After ringing off, Father Fenwick decided to tell Bob about the situation. He would be able to inform Steve and John, and any other parishioners who were concerned. A notice would be put up at the school, in case anyone turned up on Sunday, expecting the morning mass. Father Fenwick would also be able to inform the few parishioners who attended his morning mass at the presbytery.

It was an inconvenient situation, but under the circumstances, it was a necessary one. The parishioners at St Matthew's would be concerned on hearing the news about Father Frederick, and they would feel far happier that Father Fenwick was stepping in temporarily, rather than a priest, whom they did not know.

Bob was alarmed when he heard the news, but became less

concerned when he realised that it would not be a permanent situation.

"I'm relieved to hear that," he said. "I thought that we were going to lose you, just when everything was going smoothly."

"Yes, that's what I thought at first," Father Fenwick replied. "But, it's only right that I fill in while poor Father Frederick is indisposed. The parishioners will be relieved that I will be making an appearance, rather than a priest who they are not familiar with. I'll be going on Thursday, and returning on Sunday after mass."

"I'll let Steve and John know tomorrow," said Bob. "I'm sure that they'll understand."

"Thanks, Bob, one of my fellow priests is collecting me, David, he brought me here when I first moved."

"Ah, yes. I remember noticing the two of you together," said Bob.

"Anyway, I'll be back on Sunday afternoon. I'll call on Steve to see how he's getting on then, and it's John's interview on Monday, so I'll pop in to see him as well."

"Thanks, Father James, I'm sure he'll appreciate it, we'll see you then, I hope that all goes well," said Bob.

"Thanks, Bob, I'm sure that it will, I just hope that Father Frederick will be OK."

CHAPTER THIRTY-ONE

Mrs Davies was busy bustling around the presbytery, dusting here and polishing there. She was looking forward to Father Fenwick returning, if only for a brief period of time. She was concerned about Father Frederick though. He was over eighty, and she felt that he needed to have support from another priest. He had made it clear that he didn't want to retire. He says that priests are like old soldiers, they don't die, they just fade away.

She had prepared Father Fenwick's room, and had prepared a casserole, and baked some scones. It was obvious that she was very fond of Father Fenwick. She thought that he had a positive outlook, and always wanted to detach himself from his priestly roles at times, he didn't give the impression of being high and mighty, he treated everyone that he came into contact with the same jovial and happy stance. He looked beyond his role as a priest, so that he could function as if he had not taken on the role at all.

Mrs Davies suddenly felt worn out, it was hard work keeping the presbytery clean, and she was getting on in years herself. She made herself a cup of tea, and put her feet up, to allow herself to have a short rest. She breathed in the peace and calmness, around her. It wouldn't be so quiet when Father Frederick returned, but she hoped that it wouldn't be too long. She missed his moans about this and that, there was always something that he could find fault with, particularly his teeth.

She was quite thoughtful as she sipped her tea. The size of the congregation had not increased since Father Fenwick had left, but this didn't mean that only one priest was needed to cater for the needs of the sparse parishioners who bothered to attend; she had a genuine concern for the future of the Catholic Church. There was criticism regarding celibacy between priests. Many would ask how they could advise about marriage problems, when it went wrong, if they didn't experience it themselves. There was much pressure on the Pope to change this arrangement, but Mrs Davies wasn't sure whether the church should consider it or not.

She was about to doze off when there was a ring of the doorbell. She eased herself out of the chair and went to the door. She opened it, and was confronted by Mrs Jennings. She was a lady of eighty-six years, who had suffered with loneliness since her husband had passed away twelve months previously. Her main communication with the outside world was St Matthew's. She called at the presbytery on a regular basis, and Mrs Davies always invited her in for a cup of tea, even though she delayed her working routine.

"Oh hello, Mrs Jennings," she announced. "Have you called for your daily cup of tea?"

"Thank you, Mrs Davies, that would be very nice," replied Mrs Jennings. "You know, I haven't spoken to a soul for days."

Mrs Davies smiled, she was only in the presbytery the day before.

Mrs Davies poured her a cup of tea, and placed a few ginger biscuits on a plate. They both drank the tea and there was much crunching of the biscuits, there was certainly nothing wrong with Mrs Jennings teeth.

"Father Fenwick is coming back to see us for a few days, Mrs Jennings," said Mrs Davies.

"Oh, that will be very nice," replied Mrs Jennings warmly. "He's such a wonderful young man, very dashing in his dog collar, and when he goes running in those shorts, I wish that I was forty years younger."

Mrs Davies smiled broadly, Mrs Jennings obviously didn't consider that he had taken a vow of celibacy. But, she understood perfectly what she meant, she felt the same about him herself. She often thought that he was wasted as a priest, such a handsome man, he would make someone a lovely husband. But reproached herself for thinking this way.

The conversation then turned to Father Frederick. Mrs Jennings was no less fond of him, but, of course, unlike her fondness for Father Fenwick.

"I hope that he is recovering," said Mrs Jennings. "He is such a kindly man, and not bad looking either for his age." Mrs Davies couldn't help smiling broadly again at Mrs Jennings remarks.

"When is Father Fenwick coming back?" she asked.

"Well, I'm expecting him later today," Mrs Davies replied. "But, he is only here until Sunday afternoon. He's got to go back to his new parish in Cheshire, which I hear is coming along very well."

"Yes, I believe that he's making a very good impression there, but he's such a loss to our parish," said Mrs Jennings, rather sadly. "Thank you very much for the tea, I'll call in tomorrow to see Father Fenwick, goodbye." Mrs Davies had no doubt that she would. She continued with her cleaning, nothing was too good for Father Fenwick.

CHAPTER THIRTY-TWO

Linda leaned back in her chair, her arms stretched behind her head. She had been summoned. The Head of Service had the audacity to summon her. Mr Harold Spencer had informed her that she had no authority to allow a member of her staff to extend a residential placement, without referral to the panel. Linda had nothing but contempt for the panel. They were simply managers and pen pushers, in her estimation. She, on the other hand was a qualified social worker. Linda Burnham BA, Dip (SW), MA. She had studied for years at university to qualify as a social worker, so she took offence that these managers were telling her what she could, or could not do.

Linda often reflected on her past when she was not busy with the ever-increasing paperwork, which seemed to plague all Social Services departments nowadays. She was aware that all her staff looked upon her as if she was an ogre, and were afraid to challenge her, but simply thought it best to agree with her, and take what she said as gospel. But, if they knew the torment that she was going through, they may think of her differently.

Linda had not had a happy childhood. Her parents were strict Methodists, and made sure that the young Linda went to church every Sunday, attended Sunday School, and studied the Bible every day. Indeed she had studied the Bible under duress, each day at home. She never seemed to have much fun, and particularly when she reached her teens, her parents forbade her to have a boyfriend. It was, therefore, no surprise that she developed a hard as iron exterior herself.

At university, she was a good student and passed all of her exams with ease. Towards the end of her academic life, her father had died of Cancer, leaving her to support her mother, who was not well herself; she suffered with anxiety and depression. Linda hardly ever went out to meet anybody, and so never had a boyfriend. She began to develop a very hard exterior, and began to treat with contempt those whom she came into contact with. She never bought trendy clothes, or those that were deemed as fashionable at the time, like many young women of her age, but dressed in dowdy clothes, that looked as if they came from the last century.

Linda thought long and hard about which career she would take. So, when she read an advert in the local paper, for social workers in Chester Social Services, she decided to apply. Linda thought that if she made the grade, and became a team leader, she could use her power to control people on her team. Of course, she was successful at interview, and was accepted as a level one social worker. She eventually reached level three, and then was appointed as Team Manager, on the Mental Health Team.

As she sat in her office, she contemplated how much had been missing in her life. She was now fifty years of age and had hardly any experience with the male species. She did have a boyfriend once, but he soon discovered what she was really like and ended the relationship.

Linda eventually developed a more masculine frame. She started to wear clothing in a more matronly fashion, mostly tweeds skirts and heavy brogue shoes. She was aware what sort of impression this gave to her staff. She knew that they talked about her behind her back, and they thought that she was a lesbian. Nothing could be further from the truth. Even now, she desired to have a relationship with a man, but she realised that it was too late, she had missed her chances, by being tied to her mother's apron strings all those years ago. This was why she treated her staff so badly now, bullying them, it made her feel more powerful. In her mind, it made up for all the failures in life. However, she disliked herself for it, and this side of her personality made her more miserable. All she had was her job now, and nobody was going to take that away from her.

Linda reluctantly got out of her chair, straightened her back, bent her knuckles with a crack, and went out of her office, slamming the door behind her, as she always was in the habit of doing. She walked down the corridor, and went out, across the courtyard, to the main building block. Mr Spencer's office was straight down the corridor, the last door on the right. She took a deep breath and knocked on the door, ready for the confrontation.

"Come in," came a voice from within.

Linda opened the door and strode in, keen not to appear rattled in any way by Mr Spencer's summons.

"Ah, Miss Burnham, Good Morning. Thank you for your time, I know how busy you are," said Mr Spencer.

Linda thought that this was an odd way to greet her, considering that he had summoned her to his office.

"Yes, I am busy, so let's make it brief shall we?" Linda answered, with a sharp edge to her voice.

Mr Spencer was quite shocked by Linda's tone, he wouldn't usually stand for subordination from staff who were further down the pecking order than he was; but Linda had a reputation for taking no prisoners, and he was wary of her persona.

"I must remind you Miss Burnham to whom you are speaking to, and would ask you to show a little respect, if you please," he said dryly.

Linda felt her whole body stiffen, and her finger nails dug into her tweed skirt; it certainly didn't please her to be in Mr Spencer's office.

"Right, now let's get down to business shall we? The reason that I've asked you here today is to make it quite clear about the protocol regarding panel applications. You are obviously aware of the procedure, are you not?"

"I am," Linda answered, with the same sharp tone to her voice.

"Now, regarding the case of Mrs Farrell, I believe that she's still in *Happy Days Care Home*, is she not?"

Linda felt quite irritated now. She hated the way Mr Spencer turned his statements into a question.

"Yes, she is still there, until we can assess her properly, and provide the most appropriate care setting for her."

"Ah, yes. I appreciate that, but it is the omission of a panel application that I am concerned with here."

Linda realised that she should be quite open and clear at this point, and stick to her guns, and why she made the decision to go ahead.

"In my view," she explained. "An application to panel would have delayed things. Mrs Farrell was already in the care home, so we couldn't just move her out. I simply decided that we couldn't wait for managers to get their act into gear, I had to make a decision. I believe that the outcome would have been the same, so why stand on ceremony?"

It was Mr Spencer's turn to be irritated now. He could feel his hackles rising, his knuckles were white, as he gripped his pen, he struggled to keep his composure.

"Miss Burnham," he said, with irritation in his voice. "I appreciate why you took this course of action. However, you could have made a panel application after your decision to press on ahead. I am not stating that decisions should not be made before a panel application; but, if it is deemed necessary to take action, in order to safeguard a client, an application should be sent to the panel at the earliest possible juncture afterwards, explaining the situation. The role of the panel is to manage the council's finances, and to make sure that any expenditure is utilised correctly, and not spent willy-nilly. I wish to make this quite clear, for future reference."

"Hmm," Linda said gruffly. She stood up and leaning over Mr Spencer's desk, she said. "I'll bear it in mind, now if you don't mind, I'll get back to my paperwork, good afternoon." She marched back to her office, huffing and puffing, her brogues beating time, as if she was on the parade ground.

Mr Spencer had grimaced when Linda had leered at him over his desk and left his office, his door was shut with a loud bang. He leaned back in his chair and sighed loudly. He had never known anything like it during his whole career. Mr Spencer then pressed the button on his intercom system. "Jane, take a memo please."

CHAPTER THIRTY-THREE

Steve felt very miserable. He had been sitting in his chair for over an hour, thinking about Jen, and the more that he turned things over in his mind, the angrier he got. He despised Jen's family now. He regretted feeling like this, but, he felt that they had deserted her. No visits had been made, not even a phone call to ask how she was.

He had not seen Bob for a couple of days, but he wasn't angry with him. He had his own life to get on with, he was a good friend, and he thought that maybe he wished to give him some space.

Father Fenwick was away in Liverpool as well, so he couldn't turn to him for a bit of moral support. However, he would be back in a few days, so that wasn't too bad. He wondered how John was getting on. Maybe he could call on him, so he decided that he would walk around to see him later on. John was not feeling too happy either, so maybe they could cheer each other up.

Steve decided to go out for a walk in the meantime, he would surely feel better if he got out of the house for a while. Feeling like a prisoner inside the house was making him feel remorseful, because there was so much there to remind him of Jen.

As soon as he was out in the fresh air, Steve began to feel a little better, he began to breathe more deeply. He walked along the road, nodding to a few people who he passed on his way. He eventually came to the site of the new school. There were several lorries parked there, with workers busy unloading the various building materials that would be needed. Steve thought about John, and he was reminded that he would be interviewed for a job on the site on the following Monday, he hoped that he would be successful, he certainly needed a lift in his life.

After stopping for a few moments, Steve continued with his walk. He remembered Father Fenwick telling him about the wooded area, that he regularly ran through on his training spins, and how peaceful and calm it was, full of wildlife, and in particular, how it gave him a renewed peace of mind. Father Fenwick had told him that it was the most favourite part of his runs, and in particular, he mentioned the large pond that was there, which seemed to appear out of the blue, when you rounded a corner.

Just thinking about this, provided Steve with a more calming peace of mind, and he couldn't wait to get there, off the hard, unforgiving pavements, and onto the soft soil and undergrowth beneath his feet. He reached the wooded area in twenty minutes, and began relishing in the calming atmosphere almost immediately.

He stopped and listened to the calm, there was the sound of a bird twittering in one of the trees, but apart from that, there was no sound at all. Just like Father Fenwick had told him, it felt like the road and the estate behind him was a million miles away. He heard a rustling noise behind him, and looked around nervously, expecting an assailant about to creep up on him. But no, there was no one in sight, simply a rabbit scampering across the path. He smiled to himself and thought that he was being too jumpy, but it is best to be wary at all times, even in such a quiet place as this. No, nothing would spoil his sense of calm at the moment. He continued deeper into the woods. It was amazing how vast the area was, Steve felt that he could almost get lost in here.

He rounded a corner, and then, almost to his surprise, was the pond. Father Fenwick had certainly not exaggerated. It seemed to appear out of nowhere. Steve stood by the side of it and admired how clear the water was, he imagined that there was a vast variety of living organisms in there. It was much larger than he had imagined it would be; he wondered how deep it was, probably not much more than a couple of feet he thought.

Steve knelt down and peered in, to have a closer look. He studied the reflection of his face in the water, and saw that it mirrored the image of his inner anxiety and distress. But then, quite suddenly, something scuttled across the water. His image was distorted for a while, as the ripples wiped it out, and in his mind, it was replaced with a completely altered image, an image that reflected a changed perspective. Steve was startled by the thoughts that flooded into his mind. Of course, this was a sign of change. Gone was the blackness that had surrounded his mind over the last months, and in its place was a new more positive mind, the blackness blown away, as the sunshine flooded through the clouds.

This was it. He was going to cast aside his weaknesses of the past, the self-pity that he had wallowed in. He was going to be stronger for Jen, more positive. Of course, she would not get better, there was no miracle cure for Dementia. She would continue to decline at an ever-increasing rate. But, he would be there for her until the end. To honour his vow that he made on their wedding day.

Surely, the pond had shown him a sign and given him the inner strength that he would need in the future. Just like the feeling of positivity that Father Fenwick had realised when he visited the pond. Steve decided there and then, he would push to have Jen back home again, not to allow her to deteriorate in some care home, where she would be out of his sight. With the help from the carers, he would be a tower of strength, he was one of the 'Three Just Men.' From now on, this place would have a special place in his heart. He would visit the pond whenever he needed to rejuvenate his strength. He would regard this as his '*Magic Pond*'.

CHAPTER THIRTY-FOUR

Father Fenwick had returned to St Matthew's a few days earlier, carefully chauffeured by his good friend, and partner in clergy, Father David O'Donovan. It had felt quite strange for him to be back in his old parish at first. Since moving to *New Pastures*, he had enjoyed a different, more free way of life.

While he had been at St Matthew's he had been very much a loner, bound more strictly by his priestly role. Apart from Father Frederick, he had no acquaintances. But, at *New Pastures*, he had made friends, Bob, Steve and John, and this friendship, he perceived, diluted his priestly role somewhat. It made him feel more normal, which is what he had always wanted. At *New Pastures*, he had more freedom, more time to go running, and visiting. He also had time to consider his role as a priest, and whether he wanted to continue in this role.

Becoming a Catholic priest was a major step to take in a young man's life. There was so much to consider. You had to give up so much of life that was considered normal by society in general. Of course, the major downfall was the vow of celibacy. The church presumed that young men would have no interest in having a sexual relationship, let alone if they were gay. During his time at the seminary, he had discussed this with his fellow students. The general consensus was that they all accepted it. However, those who regarded themselves as gay, had the idea that it was more acceptable to have a male relationship, rather than a female one.

They had the idea that the church was closing their eyes to this fact. Whether this was true or not, Father Fenwick had his own agenda. If you took a vow of celibacy, you had to stick to it, or leave the priesthood. It was like a tug of war, being pulled one way or the other.

There was little doubt, that he was given a warm welcome when he returned to St Matthew's. Mrs Davies gave him a firm hug, told him to put his feet up, and made him a mug of tea. Mrs Jennings was true to her word and called the day after he arrived.

"It's lovely to have you back, Father," she had told him warmly.

"Well, I'm not back permanently," replied Father Fenwick. "It's only until Father Frederick is well enough to come back, I'm very busy with my new parish at the present time. So I'll be travelling to and fro between the two parishes."

Father Fenwick had decided to visit Father Frederick in hospital. He was very fond of him, and it wouldn't look very good if he failed to visit him.

So, on a bright sunny Friday morning, he drove to Chester General Hospital in the trusty Vauxhall Vectra. There was the usual whirring and spluttering, as it struggled to start, followed by the crunching of gears. He arrived at the hospital and entered the car park. After much driving backwards and forwards, he managed to locate a parking space in the large hospital car park. It's strange, he thought to himself, no matter how large a car park is, they were always full to capacity, extend them, and they were full again in no time. He parked the car, and walked into the main foyer of the hospital. He was faced by a large notice board, that advised him where all the various departments were located.

Ward G was located on the second floor. Father Fenwick walked up the stairs and took a right turn. He entered the ward and walked to the nurses' station. A rather large nurse in a dark blue uniform was sitting at the desk, who Father Fenwick presumed was a sister, she was filling in a form of some kind. Father Fenwick coughed to gain her attention.

"Just a moment please," she asked him politely. "I just need to complete this form and send it to the discharge lounge." Father Fenwick waited patiently until the nurse had finished writing.

"Right," she said, "can I help you, Father?"

"Oh yes," replied Father Fenwick. "I'm here to visit Father Frederick."

"Ah," said the nurse, with a broad grin. "Well, he's quite a character to be sure, he always gives us a laugh, he's a pleasure to look after. He never has a word of complaint, except when we couldn't find his teeth, they got mixed up with some other patient's teeth, we have quite a lot of them here. You'll find the father in the third cubicle on your left."

Father Fenwick thanked the nurse with a smile, and left her chuckling to herself. The six cubicles on Ward G comprised six beds each, males in the first three, and female in the second three. Father Fenwick entered the cubicle that the nurse had indicated. Father Frederick was in the last bed on the left, near the window. Father Fenwick was rather surprised that Father Frederick was not in a single room, but sharing a cubicle with five other patients. He recognised Father Fenwick as soon as he walked in.

"Ah, young Fenwick," he uttered, with a chuckle. "It's nice to see you."

"Hello, Father Frederick," replied Father Fenwick. "You look well, how have you been?"

"Oh, so, so," replied Father Frederick. "I've stayed in better guest houses," he said, jokingly.

"Oh, I'm sure that you have," replied Father Fenwick with a smile. He knew of course, that Father Frederick was joking, although at first, he had a thought that the stroke had affected his memory, but all appeared well. "I'm surprised though, that you are not in a room of your own, with you being a priest."

"They wanted to put me in a separate room, but I didn't want any of it," Father Frederick explained. "To be honest, it's refreshing to step out of the priestly role for a short time, and feel like a normal person. In fact, the other fellows here don't know that I'm a priest, they just know me as Fred. You know, James. I've had plenty of time to think while I've been in here. The time that I've spent being a priest, feels like a life lost. There's so many other things that I could have done. Like getting married, having children, and having a normal job."

Father Fenwick was quite surprised when he heard this. Father Frederick had always appeared to be a sincere and committed priest, and somebody that Father Fenwick had always looked up to.

"In fact," Father Frederick continued, "after my convalescence, I may not come back. I could retire and enjoy the rest of my life."

"Well, yes. You could have retired at seventy, but obviously you wanted to carry on."

"Yes, I did. But, I still wonder if it was worth it. Open all hours, and not to mention the celibacy."

"What would you do?" queried Father Fenwick. He was quite worried now. The thought of Father Frederick retiring may mean that he would have to return to St Matthew's on a more permanent basis.

"I would live a simple life, for how long that I've got left on this earth. I would be allowed to move into the rest home for retired priests, with a pension. At least I'd be able to have a lie in, and not have to get up early for morning mass. And, when I think of all those sessions at confession. Parishioners coming in, telling me all their sins, and maybe not all, and promising that they wouldn't do it again. Three Hail Mary's and one Our Father, and Bob's your Uncle."

Father Fenwick listened to this intently, and with concern. Earlier that day, he had similar thoughts regarding his ministry. Some of what Father Frederick had mentioned, had certainly mirrored his own feelings.

"You should consider your own position James," Father Frederick continued. "Decide whether it's all worth it, the sacrifices that you're expected to make. When you reach retirement age, the church doesn't want to know. You could end up living in poverty. You are young now. The Bishop could move you to where he thinks fit. Severing any ties that you may have built up, not that you'll have many that is."

After turning this over in his mind, Father Fenwick said rather meekly. "I've brought you some grapes Father Frederick. I believe that this is the normal thing to bring."

"I'd rather have a bottle of whisky, but it's rather rare around here."

"Have you any idea when you are likely to be discharged?" queried Father Fenwick.

"I think in about a week's time, and then they're planning to send me to the priests rest home in North Wales for a few weeks."

"That'll be a nice break for you," said Father Fenwick. "A bit of country air."

"Yes, it'll be a change from Liverpool, and it'll give me time to reflect on my future. Ha, Ha, my future at eighty-three years of age, I'll be ready to push up the daisies," he chuckled.

"I'm sure that you're far from that yet," Father Fenwick said in a soothing voice.

"I don't know, James, this stroke could be a reminder from the boss to get ready to meet him."

Father Fenwick laughed, Father Frederick certainly hadn't lost his sense of humour. The bell sounded loudly, to signify that visiting time was over.

"Right, I'd better be off then, Father. I'll visit you in Wales when you're there, shall I?"

"Okay, James, I'll look forward to that, and think on what I've said."

He bade Father Frederick farewell, and walked out of the hospital, to his car. He certainly had a great deal to consider. If he decided to leave the priesthood, it would not be as straightforward as he thought. When a Catholic priest is ordained, it's a lifelong commitment. One simply can't walk out. Well, you could, but the church would frown upon it. It would mean having to forfeit your pension. You couldn't become a lay person, which would mean that you wouldn't be able to give communion, like lay people could. The only priestly duty that would be possible, would be to hear the confession of a dying person. But, did he want to leave the priesthood? It's not as if it was his choice alone to become a priest. He wanted to be a motor mechanic, or a soldier, it was his father's wishes that he become a priest.

When he arrived back at St Matthew's, he went into the church and sat on one of the pews, for a moment's reflection. He had to admit to himself that he loved the peace and serenity that an empty church gave him, particularly the echoing that even the smallest sound made. His eyes alighted on the altar, and the statue of Our Lady. He looked up at the organ, how majestic the pipes looked, so silent now, but brought into life at the touch of the keys, by the organist, George. He would have loved to make it sing, like George.

He had had some piano lessons as a child, but it didn't last long, he was too keen on playing out with his mates.

Why would he want to resign from the priesthood? He was very happy at *New Pastures*. There was so much to look forward to, particularly the new building, which would house the school and the church. He had made good friends, Bob, Steve and John, just as if he had been just another resident, without the background of ordination. But, maybe he had gained their friendship because he was their priest. However, one thought concerned him. When the new parish was finally established, he may be moved to another parish, and he would miss his friends, just like Father Frederick had told him. It wouldn't be the first time that he had been moved. Anyway, he would be back at *New Pastures* on Sunday, and would be able to chill out again.

As he sat and contemplated, George walked in, his heavy boots echoing around the church. "Good morning Father James," he announced cheerfully. "I see that you're having a bit of peace and quiet, I'll soon put an end to that."

"Hi, George," replied Father Fenwick, smiling broadly. George had come for his usual morning organ practice; although Father Fenwick thought that he didn't need it. He was an excellent organist, with a wide programme of music.

"Any requests?" George asked, with a smile.

"Oh, I wouldn't want to re-arrange your practice session," Father Fenwick replied. "Although *'War March of the Priests'* would be good, it's a favourite of mine."

"Okey-dokey," George replied, pulling stops and couplers out, and setting his position on the bench.

The peace was suddenly broken as George commenced the requested piece. The organ belted out the music, and the church reverberated with the sound. The hairs on the back of Father Fenwick's neck stood on end, it was only church organ music that had this effect on him.

He listened intently and allowed the music to wash over him, while George was playing. When he had finished, George turned to face Father Fenwick.

"Play it again, Sam," Father Fenwick said with a wide grin.

CHAPTER THIRTY-FIVE

Heavy lorries rumbled along the road on the estate, as they made their way towards the building site. John was on his way to his interview at the site. He had not had an interview for fifteen years, and he was unsure how he would conduct himself, while at the same time making a good impression. He thought in his own mind that he was up for the job, but of course, it wasn't his decision. He felt desperate to get the job, he had been unemployed for so long, and it would improve his chances of getting back with Lisa and his children.

Furthermore, Christmas was fast approaching, and it would be nice for him to be in a position to buy some presents for his family.

There were several Portacabins on the site, and John walked towards the one with a sign that indicated it was the main office. He was surprised that there were no other applicants there, he had expected a large queue. John approached the desk where a young woman was seated.

"Good morning," he said. "I've called about the vacancies for labourers on the site."

The young lady looked up from her laptop and asked John if he had an application form with him.

"Yes," he replied, passing it over to her.

"Thank you," she replied. "I'll just check it over, and then hand it to Mr Burke. If you can take a seat, there's a coffee machine over there, feel free to help yourself."

John dispensed himself a cup of coffee from the machine and sat down on one of the seats. He suddenly felt very apprehensive about getting a job on the site. For a start, he felt that he hadn't made a very good job at filling in the application form. His writing had never been one of his stronger points, and there was some crossing out on the form.

After ten minutes, the receptionist told him that Mr Burke would see him now. John was ushered into his office. Mr Burke was seated behind his desk. He was a burly gentleman, sporting a large moustache. He was wearing a high-vis' jacket and a hard hat. John wondered why he had a hard hat on in the office, he didn't think that the ceiling was about to collapse, at least, he hoped not.

"Good morning, Mr Byrne," he said to John. "How are you today?"

"I'm very well, thank you," John replied.

"Well now, Mr Byrne. I've read through your application form." John's heart sank, he felt that he knew what was coming next.

"I note that you are twenty-eight years of age, and you have been unemployed for some three years now, am I correct?"

"Yes," replied John. "I was made redundant from my previous job, through no fault of my own. I worked in an electrical manufacturing factory, they made car parts."

"Why were you made redundant?" queried Mr Burke.

"Oh, they found it cheaper, and more profitable to make certain parts abroad, and so they had to reduce the workforce," replied John.

"I presume that it was your particular section that bore the brunt of the cuts, that was hard luck," Mr Burke said sympathetically.

"Yes, it was. It was nothing to do with my work record. I was hardly ever off sick, and I worked hard," advised John.

"I see," replied Mr Burke. "Well, as you can see, we are already moving with the building of the new school. The foundations will be laid over the next couple of weeks, and then we'll be ready for the build itself. We are looking for extra workers, I hate using the term labourers. In my book, all our workers have a particular skill to offer. At Todmore Construction, we value all our employees, and training is available, if the individuals are interested, and of course, suitable. Some of our employees just want to do the job and collect their wages, others, who are more enthusiastic, can move on."

John listened to what Mr Burke was saying with interest, but was he being offered employment? He held his breath.

"Ok, Mr Byrne," Mr Burke continued. "I am prepared to offer you employment with this company. You have demonstrated your enthusiasm, completing the application form, and turning up promptly for interview. You appear to be a robust fellow, who have suffered years of unemployment, through no fault of your own. The work will be quite strenuous, but I'm sure that you'll be up to it. There are plenty of unemployed people who I've interviewed, who want an easy pay-check, and are not prepared for graft. You're not that sort of person, I can see that. So, are you prepared to take the job on?"

"Yes, I certainly am, thank you," replied John. He struggled to restrain himself, he couldn't believe that he was being offered work at last.

"Right then," Mr Burke continued. "We'll get a contract of employment sorted out, and then we'll be able to give you a start date. Your job, as an ancillary worker will be to assist the plasterer's and the 'brickies.' That involves mixing plaster, cement, and carrying bricks etc; how does that sound? Initially, you'll be on a trial for three months, just to see how you go. If all goes well, you'll eventually be given the chance to train, either as a plasterer, or a bricklayer, or even an electrician, if you have the aptitude."

"It's music to my ears," replied John. "Thank you, I'm eager to get started."

"I'm sure that you are," said Mr Burke warmly. "Leave it with me, and we'll be in touch shortly, to arrange a start date, in the meantime, thanks for attending, and the best of luck."

John shook hands with Mr Burke and walked out of the office. He couldn't believe that he had a job at last. He felt like shouting it from the rooftops, but he thought that restraint was needed at this stage, he would wait until he had actually started before telling Lisa. He would tell Father Fenwick, and Bob and Steve though. They had helped him to rediscover himself, and had stood by him when others didn't. And if the church hadn't been planned, then Father Fenwick wouldn't have arrived, and he wouldn't be here now, looking forward to starting work again. John smiled to himself, as he walked to Father Fenwick's house. He really felt sure that his life was beginning to turn around.

CHAPTER THIRTY-SIX

It was Tuesday morning, bright and clear. Brenda felt particularly good on this day, her work had been going smoothly, until now. Her office door was suddenly flung open, and the usual booming voice filtered in. "Miss Caddick, I believe that the extra two weeks for Mrs Farrell, at *Happy Days Care Home* are almost up. I've spoken to the manager and suggested a further assessment is needed. We need to tie this up one way or the other."

"Right," said Brenda.

"So, I've arranged a meeting this afternoon at the home, I will attend this time with you, as well," advised Linda.

So, at 2 pm precisely, Brenda was escorted to Linda's car. Linda plonked her ample frame into the seat and buckled up, Brenda did the same. Linda started the engine, put the car into gear, and accelerated out of the car park, with a loud screeching of tyres, everything about Linda was loud, Brenda thought.

Brenda found herself gripping the sides of the seat, as her head was flung backwards. "Nice bit of gumption in this car," Linda said. Her loud voice seemed to reverberate all around the car, and Brenda was sure that she would start with a migraine. She felt quite uncomfortable, being in close proximity of her boss, and she felt stuck for conversation.

Linda soon put her mind at rest, as she spoke in a much softer tone, that Brenda had never realised that she had.

"Do you like your job?" she asked, completely out of the blue.

"Yes, I do," Brenda replied. "It's what I wanted to do, help people."

"I see," Linda said. "But you could have helped people as a guard on a train, or a bus driver."

Brenda wasn't sure how to answer. She felt so uncomfortable, sitting so close to Linda. And yet, she seemed so different now that she was out of the office.

Linda laughed. "I quite understand where you're coming from Brenda. Make no mistake, you are a good social worker, a little bit haphazard at times, but you get the job done eventually."

Brenda wasn't sure how to take this. Was it a compliment, or a rebuff? She tried to go on the defensive.

"I do try to get the work done in the best possible manner, but there is so much to get through. So many clients, and the paperwork keeps mounting up."

Linda laughed again. "Don't let that worry you... What the... you bloody idiot."

There was a screech of brakes as Linda stamped her right brogue on the brake pedal. The car slewed slightly sideways, and came to a halt about six inches from the car in front. Brenda felt herself jerked to the left, which left her feeling breathless for a moment.

"You bloody fool," Linda boomed out of the window, get a licence!"

The driver in front was an elderly lady, and she poked her head out of the car window.

"Sorry," she almost whispered. "A cat ran in front of me, I almost ran over it."

"Mm," Linda grunted. "Shouldn't still be driving at her age. As I was saying. You are doing all right. I know that I come over as a bit of an ogre in the office, and everyone thinks that it's because I'm an old maid, and they're probably right. But, I like to get the job done properly, and I'll always stand up for my staff. Those bloody pen pushers in the office don't know what it's all about, and they're on my back all the time, so I have to show them that the job's done properly."

Brenda was suddenly beginning to see Linda in a different light. Out of the office, she appeared a decent person, maybe she was a rather sad and lonely person at that. She obviously didn't have any social life, or friends. Brenda began to like her a lot more, and more importantly, to respect her position, after all, she was the team manager. She was feeling a lot more comfortable with her now, apart from her erratic driving.

Brenda was relieved when they reached the care home. They both got out of the car, Brenda rather shakily, following her ride on the dodgems and walked into the vestibule. Mrs Jones came out of her office on cue and greeted them both. Linda spoke up first.

"Good morning. I'm Linda Burnham, Manager of the Mental Health Team, I spoke to you yesterday on the phone."

"Ah, yes," replied Mrs Jones. "You've called regarding Mrs Farrell. You haven't brought Mr Farrell with you this time, I see."

"That's correct, I thought it best to review the situation on our own first, and discuss the implications with Mr Farrell after. That way, we can reduce the distress that it may cause him."

"Exactly," agreed Mrs Jones, looking at Linda rather warily. "We wouldn't want that, would we?" There was slight sarcasm in her tone.

"Mrs Farrell is in the lounge, she doesn't appear very well today though, but we thought it best if she could stay out of her room for a while."

"I don't hold with clients being kept in their rooms for long periods," Linda said, rather sharply. "I've experience of it. Individuals just sat in a chair all day with no interaction with others. Then they're manhandled into a wheelchair to take them to the toilet, very often when they are wet through. This practice makes it easier for the care staff. No attempt made to get them mobilising, it's no wonder these poor individuals lose their mobility completely."

Mrs Jones looked rather shaken by Linda's outburst. "I can assure you Mrs Burnham, that this is not the way that we work here."

"Mm," retorted Linda. "It's Miss by the way."

They walked into the lounge, where they were welcomed by the sound of a blaring television and the slight smell of urine. Both Linda's and Brenda's noses twitched.

They walked over to where Jen was seated, in a corner, as usual she appeared to be segregated from the other residents, and was mumbling to herself, as she always did.

"Why is Mrs Farrell seated on her own?" asked Linda, acidly.

"Well, she tends to shout at times, and this upsets the other residents. The other day, Mrs Frobisher walked over to her and told her to shut up. That set everyone off, and they were unsettled for the rest of the day."

Linda was quiet for a while, taking this in, then her voice boomed out. "You must realise that Mrs Farrell is suffering from Dementia. I can clearly see that this is the wrong environment for her, and my assessment is that she would be better at home with her husband, I'm sure that my colleague here will agree with me."

Brenda felt in her own mind that she had to agree with Linda. She could see that Jen would continue to deteriorate if she was left in *Happy Days* much longer, and Steve deserved some time with her.

"But," stuttered Mrs Jones. "Mrs Farrell could hardly go home, her husband wouldn't be able to cope with her."

"That is in your estimation," shouted Linda. "It's up to us what she can, or cannot do. She deserves the chance to be in her own home with her husband."

"But, she can hardly stand," explained a concerned Mrs Jones.

"I'm sure she can't while she's in here, I know what these homes are like, take the easiest option. Plonk them in a wheelchair, and wheel them to the dining room, and then to the toilet; no wonder they lose the use of their legs."

Mrs Jones was lost for words. She hadn't had to face anyone like Linda before, she felt at a loss for words. After all, she was the social worker in charge, and surely must know best, so she was happy to agree.

"Right," Linda advised. "We'll arrange to get Mrs Farrell home, and have an O/T assessment. Brenda, we'll make the necessary arrangements back at the office."

Brenda had been very quiet. She had been happy to leave all the talking to Linda. But, she was pleased that Steve would have the opportunity to have Jen home again.

"I'll leave it up to you to advise Mr Farrell what's happening Brenda, and we'll take it from there."

Brenda would be happy to tell Steve the good news. After all, he did want Jen home again. With the proper support, he would be able to cope.

They both returned to the car, and Brenda prepared herself for the 'white knuckle' ride back to the office. She wasn't disappointed. Linda buckled up, started the engine, put the car into gear, and thrust the car forward, with a screech of tyres, and a puff of black smoke from the exhaust. They sped out of the car park, narrowly missing a parked motorbike. Brenda gripped the edges of the seat once again and took a deep breath.

CHAPTER THIRTY-SEVEN

Father Fenwick was delighted when he heard John's news. He told him that he would arrange a celebration with Bob and Steve later in the day. Following John's visit, he decided to go for a run, which always cleared his mind.

After his run he decided to make a few home visits. He had been informed by Bob that there were many older people who had been moved onto the estate. These included people who were living on their own. Either they had never married, or were widowers.

So, after his run, he showered and got dressed. He decided not to wear his clerical attire, complete with dog collar, but to go out in jeans and trainers, as he preferred. He hoped that this would present a more normal, relaxed image. He was only too aware that some people felt uncomfortable when a priest or vicar knocked on their front door. They may presume that they were in for a 'bible bashing.'

He was just about to go out of his front door when his telephone rang. He felt like ignoring it, but thought better of it. He was surprised when he heard the voice of Mr Bryant, who didn't sound too cheerful.

"Hello, Father," he said. "I'm sorry to bother you, but I would like to speak to you about Robin."

"Oh," replied Father Fenwick. "How's he doing? His running is coming on very well, he may well have promise."

"Yes, that maybe so, but I'm afraid that he's using his ability to get into trouble again with his mates."

Father Fenwick decided to forego his visiting for later on, and he invited Mr Bryant to come around to the presbytery for a chat.

"Well, what's the problem?" asked a rather bemused Father Fenwick, as he greeted Mr Bryant at the front door.

Mr Bryant settled himself into a chair, sipping a cup of tea, which Father Fenwick had kindly provided.

"Well," he began. Robin was out with his so-called mates last week. He presented Father Fenwick with such a vivid picture of the events, that he felt that he was actually there. "Robin was walking along the road with Graham and Harold, when Harold produced a box of matches. He suggested that they could have a bit of fun."

"What sort of fun?" asked Father Fenwick.

"Harold suggested that they could light a fire. Evidently He's always had a fascination with matches."

"That sounds quite serious," added Father Fenwick.

"Yes, it is. But, I don't think that they mean setting fire to buildings, or people's property. Its small things, like grass."

"Oh, I see," replied Father Fenwick, feeling quite concerned at this point. "So, what happened?"

"Well, they went to the park, it's a small park just outside the estate. All the local kids go there, to play football and the like."

"OK."

"Robin arrived home out of breath. He told me what had happened, and that he ran away from the scene as swiftly as he could go. Evidently, they went to an area at the far end of the park, near the railway line. There's an old wooden fence there, to stop people trespassing on the railway lines. Anyway, Harold took the book of matches and some paper out of his pocket."

Father Fenwick was starting to get the picture at this point, although he wasn't allowing himself to start to panic. He continued to listen to Mr Bryant's description of events.

Mr Bryant continued. "Harold crumpled the paper up and set it down on the grass. He struck one of his matches and lit the paper, which was alight immediately. Unfortunately, with all the dry weather that we've been having lately, the grass was ablaze very quickly, and the fire spread at an alarming rate. The boys were shocked by the speed of it all. It spread to the wooden fence, which started to burn out of control.

"We better get out of here fast," shouted Graham, with panic in his voice, the coppers will be on us if we hang around here."

"Oy," a loud voice shouted.

"Cripes," exclaimed Harold. "That bloke's seen us, and there are coppers running over."

With that, the three boys started running away from the shouter, but Graham and Harold were out of breath in minutes. Robin, though, sprinted away at a brisk pace and put some distance from his friends in minutes. He glanced back as he ran, and was alarmed to see that the flames were spreading, producing thick plumes of black smoke, like a giant dragon reaching out.

Robin continued running until he got home, his training with Father Fenwick had paid dividends, and his pace got quicker and quicker, which made him feel alive. Although he wasn't sure what his father would say, when he got home, and this put a damper on his euphoria. He was sure that his friends would grass on him, although he had done nothing wrong himself, it wasn't his idea to light the fire.

"So, that is what happened, and I must say that it's very worrying. I'm sure that Robin wasn't directly involved, but he was with the two boys at the time, so he is seen as an accomplice. Anyway, to cut a long story short, the police called to see me. The police sergeant told me that he knew that Harold was the main perpetrator, he comes from a notorious family. His father has served a prison sentence for burglary, and handling stolen goods, so unfortunately, it's possible that Robin has been affected by the family dynamics."

Father Fenwick was thoughtful for a moment. "I see," he said quietly. "Maybe I could have a word with Harold. If I could arouse an interest in running like Robin, he could then channel his energy towards more practical things; it's clear that Robin has benefited by my training sessions with him, he shows some promise as a runner. Very often, this is all that is needed, someone to take an interest in these kids; it's obvious that his father isn't interested in Harold. It would be very sad if he was eventually facing a future in borstal, when he could show promise in other applications."

"I agree, if you could approach Harold's father when you have time father, and have a word with him, it may help," Mr Bryant suggested. "He's more likely to listen to you."

So it was agreed that Father Fenwick would attempt to speak to Harold's father. He thought back to the days of his own boyhood, in Ireland. He wasn't always as squeaky clean as he should have been, which often gave his father some headaches, but it didn't involve lighting fires. Mischief was one thing, but arson was another, which could lead to someone getting hurt.

When Mr Bryant had left, Father Fenwick went out on his rounds. Wherever he went, he was always made welcome, whether the tenants were Catholics, or not, they were always glad of the opportunity to chat with him, very often he was the only person whom they spoke to.

Apart from his priestly duties, Father Fenwick was striving to bring the community together. In older, larger communities, such as St Matthew's parish, this wouldn't be so straightforward, due to the fact that the community was larger, and well established, with all the negative factors built in. However, in *New Pastures*, the picture was completely different.

For a start, the estate was smaller, more contained, and newer, and the rot would not have had time to develop.

He had been busy thinking and planning lately. He had been made particularly aware of the problems, following Mr Bryant's visit. Because this was a new estate, young people would have nowhere to go to meet friends, and they may become involved in creating mayhem as a result of this. Older people, and those who were very elderly could be isolated, which could affect their mental health. This was particularly true of those who were suffering from various forms of Dementia. They needed a considerable amount of support from others.

If only there was a community centre that could be made available to all of them. A place where the young and the not so young could mix and socialise. Harold and his friends had crossed onto the wrong side of the law through their mischievous activity, which had got out of control. If this was left to ferment further, they could become criminals of the future.

Father Fenwick yearned for the day when the school was built. The building could be used as a community centre, until a separate building could be constructed. Until then, maybe St Edward's school hall could be made available for this purpose. He would approach Mr Simmons again and ask if it could be possible.

Ideas were flooding into Father Fenwick's mind. If he could get this project off the ground, community meetings could be held on a weekly basis. If Robin could encourage his friends to take up running, a small club could be formed. It could be called '*New Pastures* Harriers.'

*

The question of a name for the parish had also been on Father Fenwick's mind. As yet no name had been identified. However, Father Fenwick had thought that the parish could be called 'The Parish of St Michael.' Michael being the spiritual name for Jesus, and he thought that it would be an ideal name for the parish. He would need to put this to Bishop Larkin, however, for approval. He would approach him in the next day or so. With Christmas approaching fast, it would be ideal to have a name for the parish by the time that the first Christmas mass was celebrated, even though it didn't have its own church at the present time, it was still a parish.

Father Fenwick decided not to approach Harold's father for the time being. He would need to approach him from the right direction. If he rushed in like a mad bull in a china shop, he could get on the wrong side of him, and then he would have no chance of success.

He made a right turn onto 'The Brambles', and approached number ten. He had been informed by Bob that an elderly gentleman, a Mr Samuel James, lived there on his own. He knocked on the door, and after a short while a wiry looking gentleman opened the door. He was well-dressed, wearing tight jeans, a multi-coloured waistcoat, and bright red trainers. He wore his long grey hair in a ponytail, he wasn't what Father Fenwick expected at all. He introduced himself to the gentleman and was greeted with a warm handshake.

"Ah, you must be Father Fenwick," the gentleman announced brightly, in what appeared to be an East London accent. "Bob has told me about you, and he said that you may call. My name's Samuel, but I'm better known as "Cockney Sam" by my friends."

He invited Father Fenwick inside, allowing him to enter first. He was directed into the lounge, which was quite sparsely furnished, although clean and tidy. In one corner was a large armchair, which faced a large 55inch television. Under the window, was a large sofa, which looked very comfortable. Leaning against the sofa was a guitar, a saxophone and a large keyboard.

"Oh," exclaimed Father Fenwick. "You're a musician?"

"I was," Sam replied. "Back in the days, in the old East End. We were a band, me and three other geezers. Quite good we wus as well, we used to play in all the pubs in the area. Then 'er indoors died and I lost heart in it, but, I still keep in touch with it you know."

"I'm sorry to hear that," said Father Fenwick sympathetically. "When did your good wife die?"

"Five years ago now, she had Cancer. After she died I took to the bottle, and did nothing. But, then I realised that it would not solve anythin', gave up the booze, and got back to my music. I got quite a few gigs an' all, until I decided to move away, too many memories, so I ended up here."

"That's quite a story, Sam, you don't mind me calling you Sam do you?"

"Not at all, Father. I'm not Catholic by the way."

"That's not important, Sam. I like to think that I'm here for everyone, whatever they are. Since I moved here to take on this new parish, I've tried to merge in with the community generally, it doesn't matter to me which God you believe in, or if you don't believe in one at all."

"That's good to hear," said Sam. "I've never been one for church-going, but I try to live as good a life as I can."

"That's all that matters, Sam. God must appreciate you, because he's given you the gift of music."

"I hope so, Father. Would you like me to play you something?"

"That would be very nice, Sam," replied Father Fenwick. "Whatever you like."

Sam picked up his guitar and started strumming. "Here's a song that I particularly like," he said with a smile. He commenced to play the Beatles classic 'Can't Buy me Love.'

Father Fenwick was very impressed with what he was hearing. Sam was improvising, making the simple song sound much different to the original version, he made it his own.

When he had finished, Sam slumped down in his chair, with a satisfied look on his face. Father Fenwick had been spellbound when Sam was playing, and he stood up to go, as he didn't wish to tire him out. "Well, I'll be off now Sam, give you time to rest. But I'd love to call again and listen to some more of your music."

"There's plenty more where that came from," replied Sam. Father Fenwick left Sam in peace. As he walked along the road, the tune whirled around in his mind.

CHAPTER THIRTY-EIGHT

It was two weeks before Christmas, and Father Fenwick was keen to get everything organised for the event. He had spoken to Mr Simmons, regarding the availability of the school hall, for the celebration of Christmas mass. The prospects looked very favourable for Father Fenwick. Bishop Larkin had advised him that a priest had been appointed at St Matthew's, as a temporary measure, until a permanent appointment could be made. It was unclear at this point whether Father Frederick would return to the parish, if he was able, or indeed if he wished to return, and decided to choose retirement instead. The latest news, was that he was recovering well, and would be discharged soon.

The appointment of the 'locum' priest was good news to Father Fenwick, which meant that he did not have to travel back and forth to Saint Matthew's, and could devote all of his time to the newly named Parish of Saint Michael. This name had been agreed by Bishop Larkin, and the Archbishop had indeed welcomed the title, because of its importance and relevance to the heavenly name of Jesus.

Jen had returned home from *Happy Days Care Home*, to a rapturous welcome from the community. Steve had noticed that she appeared to recognise her own home, as she was helped out of the ambulance, and she actually smiled.

Her mobility had improved somewhat also. This was due in no

small measure to Linda arranging for a physiotherapist and an occupational therapist to become involved, and they had spent many long hours in getting her mobilised once again. True, she needed a Zimmer frame for support, when moving around, but this was nothing to what she had endured in the care home. Sitting in a chair for hours on end, and then being shuffled into a wheelchair for transportation around the home.

John had started his job on the building site, which he had taken up with relish. He regarded himself lucky that he had hit on Todmore Construction, and he felt that this was due to Father Fenwick's intervention. He had been provided with stout working boots, a hard hat, and overalls, which John would have been stretched to purchase himself; workwear such as this would have been too expensive for him to purchase. He felt good, and sang to himself as he mixed a load of cement, shovelling large amounts of sand and aggregate into the mixer, for Bill, the 'brickie.'

"How's that mix doing?" Bill shouted in a gravelly voice. "We should get a lot done today, you're doing ok John."

"Thanks, Bill," retorted John.

He was feeling the strain a bit, the work was very strenuous, but John was eager not to let himself down, or his employer, he had a good chance now to prove himself, and sweep aside his past few years. He shovelled the last of the aggregate into the mixer and stood back as it whirled round. The foundations of the building were taking place at a quick rate, illustrating how large the completed structure would eventually be. John could look forward to the time when it was complete, and he could think to himself that he had played a small part in its completion. A further week, and he would contact Lisa and give her the good news, just in time for the Christmas celebrations. This thought made him feel very happy.

*

Meanwhile, Mrs Davies had been busy once again doing her usual chores at St Matthew's presbytery. She was pleased in one way that a locum priest had been appointed, but rather sad that she would see less of Father Fenwick. However, it would save him the time travelling to and from St Matthew's. She made herself a cup of tea before she left and, sat down in a comfortable chair by the window.

She was suddenly aware that a woman was walking around the garden, and her curiosity was aroused. "Who can that be?" she said out loud to herself. She couldn't see too clearly because the woman was quite a distance away. She was dressed very smartly, in a red coat, a dark blue skirt and black boots. She had long blonde hair, and this accentuated her slim figure. Mrs Davies thought that she was attractive, and looked quite young. She appeared quite interested in the garden, and stopped every now and again to study the various plants that were still resplendent in the autumn sunlight.

Mrs Davies thought that she shouldn't be there, and was quite nosey, although she wasn't doing any harm, so she didn't concern herself unduly. Maybe it was one of Father Fenwick's admirers, she thought to herself with a smile, or Father Frederick's, which made her smile even more broadly. After a while, the woman walked down the path and was gone. She must have just been passing, and was inquisitive to have a look at the garden, so Mrs Davies thought no more about it, but concentrated on her tea and biscuits.

Father Joseph Jameson, the temporary priest, was due on the next day. Mrs Davies was confident that everything was ready for him. She knew nothing about him, and would much rather have had Father Fenwick back, as she wasn't keen on new faces. Evidently he was on loan from a parish in Warrington, which was large enough to have several priests, and could spare one over the Christmas period. She finished her tea and biscuits, washed the few dishes that she had used, and went home, her cat would be ready for his lunch, so she decided to hurry. As she walked down the drive, she couldn't stop thinking about the lady in the red coat. Why this was on her mind was a mystery to her.

The following day, at exactly eleven in the morning, a small car rumbled up the drive towards the presbytery. After a short while, a slender young man got out of the car, and opening the boot, took out a large suitcase. A few minutes later, there was a loud ringing of the front doorbell. Mrs Davies on opening the door, was faced by an extremely handsome young man. Mrs Davies noticed that he wasn't wearing a dog collar, and was casually dressed in jeans, a polo shirt and trainers.

"Good morning," he said, in a very cultured voice. "I'm Father Jameson, your temporary replacement for Father Frederick."

"Ah yes, good morning, Father, we have been expecting you, I'm Mrs Davies, the housekeeper," she said, thinking that the priests were getting younger nowadays, but she had also thought the same about policemen.

She showed Father Jameson to his room and told him to make himself comfortable, and unpack in his own time.

"I'll make you a cup of tea and some biscuits, or would you rather have a sandwich Father?"

"Oh, just a cup of tea will be fine, Mrs Davies, thank you."

Mrs Davies left Father Jameson to unpack and went downstairs to make him his tea. He seems nice, she thought to herself. But, it's hard to imagine him as a priest, the way that he's dressed at the moment.

Father Jameson unpacked very quickly and came down the stairs, just as Mrs Davies had finished brewing up.

"That's very kind of you, Mrs Davies," he said with a smile. "I believe that Father Fenwick has moved to Cheshire to start a new parish."

"That's right," replied Mrs Davies. "We miss him a great deal here, but he seems very happy in his new post. Of course we are missing Father Frederick as well."

"Yes, it must be difficult for you, nobody likes change, but sometimes things can work out very well in the long run. I believe that Father Frederick is over eighty."

"He is," replied Mrs Davies. "He could have retired at seventy, but he wanted to go on as long as he could, and with a shortage of priests, he thought it best to stay on, he's very popular with the parishioners, as was Father Fenwick."

"That's a good sign, but in Warrington, the priests are coming out of the woodwork, there's no shortage," said Father Jameson laughing.

"So you can be spared for a while then?"

"Yes, maybe the bishop will allow me to stay on here."

"We'll have to see then," replied Mrs Davies. "I'm sure that you'll be popular here."

"I hope so. Thanks for the tea, I'll have a walk around then, have a look at the grounds, and go into the church. Have a good look at my new patch, so to speak." Father Jameson walked out into the grounds, smiling as he went. "See you later."

Mrs Davies watched him go, and she wondered if he would be a suitable replacement for Father Fenwick. He appeared to have the right personality, he was young and outgoing.

Bishop Larkin would hope that he would encourage younger people to return to the church, just like his aspirations had been for Father Fenwick, which didn't bear fruit, unfortunately. Time would tell. With that thought in her mind, Mrs Davies set off for home.

CHAPTER THIRTY-NINE

Father Fenwick had asked Mr Simmons if the school hall could be used to hold a pre-Christmas community function, which he had agreed to willingly. Father Fenwick would produce a flyer which would provide information about the Christmas mass arrangements, which would have to fit in with the opening of the school on Christmas Day.

Since Father Fenwick had arrived at *New Pastures* he had been successful in bringing the community together, and enabled them to look out for each other, and offer support where it was needed. Things were moving along smoothly. The new school was under construction, and John had found a part to play in it, the project had provided an invaluable opportunity for him to find employment, and improve his life, and standing in society, which had been turned upside down for some years. Jen had returned home from the care home, much to Steve's relief, although how long she could remain there was unclear at the present time. Then there was the question of Harold. Father Fenwick had not talked to his father yet, but had thought deeply about whether he should. He didn't wish to appear as a 'busy body', and there was the possibility that he would object to a priest interfering with his life, being too high and mighty. It may produce the wrong 'vibes.' So he had decided that he would speak to a few people who were acquainted with him, which he hoped would produce a more practical response.

Father Fenwick had heard that there was a new priest at St Matthew's, which had relieved the pressure on him, but as he had only just arrived, it was too early for feedback from Mrs Davies.

Steve was very enthusiastic when he heard about the plan for a pre-Christmas bash, and he told Father Fenwick that Vera would be only too pleased to make some cakes and other 'goodies' for the event. Bob was also very enthusiastic about it, as it would help to take him temporarily out of the bubble that he was living in at the present time.

Father Fenwick wondered if Sam would provide the music, it would make it much more successful if they could enjoy his music; he may also inspire the younger members to take it up. He decided that he would call on him again over the next day or so to ask him.

Father Frederick had been discharged from hospital, much to the relief of the nursing staff, they had never had to nurse a priest who was so outward looking, and unlike a priest. He had insisted on speaking to each of the other patients in his cubicle each day, telling them jokes, and not so clean ones at that. He would sometimes ramble up and down the ward singing at the top of his voice. He had explained to the nurses that he had to pretend to himself that he had drunk a few glasses of whisky. He would often look the nursing staff up and down and tell them that they had a lovely figure, and if he was younger! They certainly didn't know which way to handle this priest at all. On his discharge, Sister Roberts, a devout Catholic, was seen to make the sign of the cross, and say three Hail Marys under her breath.

Following his discharge, Father Frederick had been sent to a nursing home in Chester to recuperate.

"What will they make of him there?" A young nurse asked Sister Roberts.

"Heaven knows," she answered with a smile.

The *Five Oaks Residential Home* was a fairly new building, not more than five years old. It had been constructed to look much older, with oak beams along the front fascia, and stained-glass windows, which reminded Father Frederick of a church. The gardens were immaculately maintained, with fine lawned areas, colourful flower beds and a large water feature, complete with two fountains. The interior was just as impressive. There were two large lounges, with thick pile carpeting, fine oak furniture, and a large television. There was also a games room, which contained a snooker table, a dartboard and several card tables. The icing on the cake for Father Frederick, was a bar, which was positioned by the large window.

"My word," he whispered to himself. "The church are certainly looking after me here, it's more like a gentleman's club than a rest home." He was escorted into a large lift, which took him up to the fourth floor. He exited the lift into a wide corridor, which was also thickly carpeted. The door leading into room 55 was open, and he stepped inside. He wasn't disappointed here either. The room was tastefully furnished, and comprised a single bed, built in wardrobes, and a television. There was a large shower room off to one side, which was immaculately clean, containing a bath and an open shower. Father Frederick decided that he would unpack and settle in, go downstairs and have a good look around. His convalescence had begun, he could certainly live here.

*

Mrs Davies was very relieved that Father Frederick had been discharged to the rest home. She was keen to visit him, but unless someone could take her there, this wouldn't be possible. Father Jameson had begun to settle in, and had celebrated his first mass, which surprisingly for a weekday morning, witnessed quite a large congregation. The parishioners were keen to see their new priest, and they weren't disappointed, due to Father Jameson's easy-going style and youthful good looks.

Mrs Jennings had made her usual daily visit to the presbytery, for her cup of tea and a chat, which of course revolved around Father Jameson, she was just being her usual nosey self really.

"He's a nice young man," she had said approvingly. "Not unlike Father Fenwick." That meant of course, that he was accepted, if Mrs Jennings had put her stamp of approval on it.

Over the next couple of days, Father Jameson had made himself known in the parish. He had visited many of the parishioners and had proved a 'hit' with all that he made contact with. His morning masses had continued to be well attended, and this was in no short measure due to his sermons, which were enlightening and dotted with humour. As one parishioner put it: 'He ain't boring.'

Mrs Davies was becoming much more comfortable with the new arrangement, as had not been the case at the outset. On the downside, if there was one, it was his choice of music, which was what she would call music with no decent tune in it. Father Jameson would turn the volume up, which grated on Mrs Davies' hearing aid, which she had to turn down to very near its lowest level. She was glad that she didn't live in the presbytery, otherwise she would have to discard her hearing aid.

CHAPTER FORTY

Steve sat on the edge of his bed, his head in his hands. He was listening to Jen, who was making a weird wailing noise, a mixture of crying and moaning. This was happening on a regular basis now. She spent the day mumbling to herself, as she had done before going into *Happy Days Care Home* and her apparent distress at night.

Steve had been glad to have her back home with him at first, but now he was beginning to wonder if he had done the right thing in bringing her home. It wasn't as if he didn't want her home with him. He still felt that it was the right thing to do, to care for her, after all she was his wife, but not the wife who he had married, and lived with for over forty years.

Most people used to attempt to console him and tell him that they knew what he was going through, but how could they possibly know, unless they were going through it themselves.

Steve would tell them that it was like a bereavement. His wife was still there, but was like a stranger, as if the spirit had been removed from her. Things would never be the same as they used to be. Everything that they used to enjoy had gone. Holidays, walks in the park and family occasions, they had all diminished in a flash. Steve lay back down on his bed, and allowed his mind to drift back to when he had first met Jen, and their early life together.

*

Steve was just nineteen years of age and had gone into his local shop to buy a packet of cigs' for his father. There was a young girl serving behind the counter, who he had fancied for some time. She was very slim, about five-foot tall, with long blonde curly hair. In fact, many times Steve had gone into the shop merely to see if she was working. He had wondered if she was seeing anyone at the time, and he convinced himself that she was, so that he bottled out of asking her out. Each time he left the shop, he reproached himself for his timid outlook, after all, she could only say no.

One day he told himself that he would pluck up the courage and ask her. So, he walked boldly into the shop, with determination written all over his face, which was erased as soon as he saw an older lady serving behind the counter. Steve just stood there dithering, wondering what to do.

"Hello, can I help you?" the lady asked him.

"Er, I knew there was something that I wanted, but I've forgotten what it was," was his bumbling reply.

"Ok," replied the lady. "Maybe you'll remember later, you can come back then."

"Er, yes," Steve replied. "See you again, bye."

This went on for a few days, until one day Steve went into the shop once more, hoping to see her. However, she was not there once again, and Steve must have looked very forlorn, because the same lady behind the counter must have read his mind, smiled and said. "If you're looking for Jennifer, I'm afraid she's left."

"Oh," was Steve's reaction. "Do you know where she's gone?"

"Yes I do," was the reply. "She's working in Dobson's Haberdashery Store on Market Street, I suspect that you want to ask her out?"

"Er..." mumbled Steve, his face going bright red. He didn't know what to say.

"I'll have a word with her tonight," the lady said smiling broadly. "She's my daughter, and she's looking for a nice boy to go out with. She often talked about you, and said what a nice lad you were, always smart and polite."

Steve thanked her, feeling very embarrassed and awkward. He wrote his name and address on a piece of paper and handed it to the lady. He left the shop feeling that he was on cloud nine. The lady behind the counter was true to her word, and a few days later, they went out on their first date. Steve took Jen to the pictures, and they enjoyed watching the film, holding hands. They soon became inseparable, and six months later they got engaged, and married the next year.

Their early married life was amazing, and they were very rarely apart. They went out regularly together, on walks, to parties, and to the cinema. When Steve came home from work, Jen had prepared a good meal for him. She was a very good cook, so Steve always sat down to a good meal.

Jen had undergone fertility tests and was told that she would never be able to have children. This was a shock for Steve, as he had always dreamt of having children, he thought that he would make a good father. However, this wasn't to be. To make matters worse, some of Jen's friends had children, and she offered to babysit for them when they wanted to go out. She loved to be surrounded by children. Steve always had to be on his guard, when talking about children, in case he upset Jen. Bob and Vera hadn't had children either, but at least, they had each other for company. Bob was a good friend, and now he regarded Father Fenwick as a friend also.

As Steve sat on his bed now, he regretted that they had never thought about adopting a child. But, it was never discussed. Steve presumed that adoption wouldn't make up for not having a child of their own, so he never brought the subject up, neither did Jen. As he listened to her now, tears rolled down his cheeks, and he felt totally alone. It was in the evening that this was the worst time for him. At times like this, Steve felt that if they had children, they would have helped to soften the blow of losing Jen, and would have been able to support him. This was how it felt. Although Jen was still present in the flesh, she was gone in spirit, and he could not have a proper conversation with her. People always told him that he was doing a good job. Maybe he was, he was certainly caring for Jen as he should, but was he doing a good job looking after himself? Others only saw the picture through shaded glass. On the outside he always appeared to be strong and in good spirits, but this was less so on the inside. But there was more to it, and people would never consider Steve's inner, more pressing needs, they would never attempt to see the picture through clear glass, which was a shame. Steve lay down and tried to get to sleep, maybe the morning would make him feel better.

*

Mrs Jennings was walking back from her daily shopping trip, carrying a bag of 'goodies.' She didn't do much cooking nowadays, since she had lived on her own. She usually relied on ready meals, or if she wasn't particularly hungry, she would just make some toast. She had a very sweet tooth, and loved her cakes and biscuits.

She decided that she would deviate from her usual route home, and take what she called 'the more scenic route.' This particular route would take her past St Matthew's presbytery. She thought that she may call in on Father Jameson, on the pretence that she had popped into the church; in fact, she was just being her usual nosey self. She was in the process of walking up the path to the presbytery when she came to an abrupt halt.

She noticed a woman who was about to go into the presbytery. Even with her reduced vision, she could tell that the woman was quite young. She was well-dressed in what would be considered modern attire by the younger generation nowadays. She had blonde hair, which was gathered in a ponytail. Mrs Jennings thought that she looked a bit 'tarty.'

"Oh my God," she muttered to herself. "She can't be a parishioner surely."

She had never noticed anyone looking like her in the church. Of course, Mrs Jennings would expect everybody to fit into her model of an ideal churchgoer.

She was quite concerned, and her mind went into overdrive. What if Father Jameson had a fancy woman? Surely not. She couldn't think why she had come to this conclusion, there must be a logical reason. Although Father Jameson was very handsome, and she was aware about the conflict surrounding celibacy with the younger priests of today. She decided that she would have a word with Mrs Davies about it next time she saw her. She turned around, and continued with her walk home, while mulling over in her mind what she had just seen.

Toast, and a large cream cake were calling. The mystery lady turned around and looked over her shoulder, smiled to herself, and went into the presbytery.

CHAPTER FORTY-ONE

"What, he's got a job?" shouted Malcolm down the phone line. "What's he doing, working for the local burglary firm?"

Lisa treated this remark with the contempt that it deserved. "Of course not," she said with a slightly mocking tone in her voice. "He's working on the building site, which is going to be the new school, and church."

"Ha, that's a first, since when did John ever get near a church."

"You can talk," replied Lisa sharply. "When did you ever go near a church? Anyway, since when did you even need to go to church to work on a church building site?"

"Point taken," replied Malcolm, apologetically. "I am glad you know, sis. He'll certainly have more money in his pocket then, and hopefully, he has changed."

Lisa cleared her throat and said. "As it's nearly Christmas, I wondered if you would take me and the kids to see him? It's ages now since we've even spoken."

"If you want, but your kids will have to behave in my motor. No crisps or chocolate, I don't want my seats stained."

"It's a deal," replied Lisa. She was excited at the thought of seeing John again. The last time that she had seen him, he was down and out, she wondered what he was like now.

So an arrangement was made for the following Saturday, one week before Christmas. Lisa was so excited at the thought of seeing John again, particularly so near Christmas, and she couldn't wait to tell the kids. They were over the moon when they heard the news. George, their eldest, jumped up and down, at the prospect of seeing his dad again. The younger girls, Molly and Sarah, were just as excited, and whooped loudly at the mention of their father's name.

Lisa started going through her wardrobe to sort out what she would wear. She would want to look her best for John. She had put a little weight on, so it was a struggle to find something that would fit nicely. She decided on a brightly coloured summer dress, a white cardigan, with a red jacket, no tights, as was the fashion now, and a pair of 'flats.'

"That'll do fine," she said to herself. She wouldn't want John to think that she had let herself go, she thought.

Lisa was full of expectation. Would it be possible to be reunited with John she thought? She would like nothing better, to be a proper family once again. She remembered all the arguments, the heavy drinking and his rough mates coming back with him from the pub at all hours. But, that was when he had lost his job, and he had become depressed. Now he had moved away from the rundown part of Liverpool, where they had lived for years, and moved out into the country, to a new estate. And, now, he had started working again. When he had phoned her, he emphasised how happy and content that he was now. He was enjoying working again. The job was hard work, but just to be working and earning a wage made up for that. The men on the building site were great to work with as well, and apart from the hard work, there was much friendly banter at breaktime, and the odd pint after work. Lisa couldn't wait until Saturday, when the family would be reunited again, if only for a short time.

*

Lisa thought that there was much to look forward to. Of course, she wished more than anything else that she could get back with John. But also, he was now living in a much newer area, a brand-new estate, where the air was fresh and trees were in abundance. Now that he was working, and free of his mates from Liverpool, he had made a vast improvement to his lifestyle. If they were back together, there would be far less tension, which would lead to a happy family, no dodgy mates and heavy nights out on the booze. However, this would depend on whether John wanted her back again. She didn't think that he would prefer to live the life of a bachelor. The children would also need to find a place in a local school, there was certainly a lot of discussion to be done, and Lisa couldn't wait.

*

Sam sat back in his chair. The sweet smell of Cannabis was in the air. He had agreed to play at the community Christmas bash on the following Tuesday. While he puffed on his spliff he thought about what he would play. A mixture, he thought, most relevant for the age groups of the people who would be there. He picked up his saxophone and started to play.

Baker Street was one of his favourites, an excellent tune for the sax he thought. He played the tune with gusto, a bit of the old 'Weed' always helped him to relax. Not strictly lawful, but Sam thought that in his own home, it was not doing anybody any harm.

Since moving to *New Pastures*, Sam had become a very lonely man, a recluse almost. He passed his day playing his instruments, his music kept him going, kept him alive. He went shopping a couple of times a week for his essential provisions. His cannabis was supplied by an old friend in London, as he certainly wouldn't have had access to it in *New Pastures*. Sam would certainly not wish to get involved with any local suppliers, not that he knew any of course. His supply came from an old musician pal in the East End each month. Just a small packet to keep him going.

Sam didn't regard himself as an addict. It helped to ease the anxiety that he felt constantly, regarding his lonely life, his new life, without his wife, and his increasing age. He had a son and daughter, but they didn't keep in touch with him. In some ways Sam thought that they blamed him for their mother's death. Although, nothing could be further from the truth. As a musician he was often away from home for nights on end, playing on gigs, which had involved drinking and cannabis smoking, the habit of those who chose a musical way of life. But, Sam had been a good husband to his wife in all other respects, but his way of life caused his wife to suffer from periods of anxiety, and this is why his children kept their distance from him.

When she was diagnosed with the Cancer, Sam became much more attentive, he gave up playing in the band and provided care for her until the end. Her death had hit him pretty hard, and his son and daughter offered him little sympathy, or support. The funeral was a typical Cockney funeral, with black horses pulling the hearse. There was a large crowd watching as the funeral procession went by, Edna had been very popular in the community. The funeral was followed by a real Cockney knees-up in the local pub, Sam played a refrain on his sax, as the mourners sang in the background.

He placed his sax back in its stand, and let the memories flood back in. His present life was now completely different from his past in the East End. He was alone for most of the time, with only his memories and his music to keep him going.

Sam only left the house to buy what he needed from the shops. He was almost afraid to go out sometimes, because he had been on the receiving end of mockery and 'catcalls' from the younger generation, on several occasions. He had often been called a 'Sixties Hippy', and an old 'Josser.' Although he thought that this could technically be true, Sam felt quite hurt by these taunts. He felt uncomfortable and quite sad about how the younger generation viewed the older generation. They would probably consider his music as 'old hat', but he could play anything that they asked him to, old, or modern. He was an expert musician. He would prove this at the Christmas social on the following Tuesday. He would show 'em.

*

John was getting quite nervous at the thought of Lisa and the children's impending visit. At the same time, he was not happy about meeting Malcolm again, who had always considered him as a waster, and not good enough for his sister. But, he had changed now, he had a job and was getting his life back on track, so surely he would view him in a new light. He had made a special effort on this bright Saturday morning. He had made sure that the house was as clean and tidy as possible. Bob and Father Fenwick had helped him to get it ready. The house had been dusted from top to bottom, and everything was made neat and tidy. Apart from that, there wasn't a great deal to do, due to the extent of the sparsely furnished property. A buffet had been laid out on the kitchen table, and John had made sure that there was some wine for Lisa, a few cans of beer for him, and non-alcoholic refreshment for the kids. He was determined to make a good impression.

*

"Well," said Bob. "I think that everything should go well."

"Thanks, Bob, and Father Fenwick. You've both been a great help to me over the last month," replied John. "Steve has as well, of course, how is he doing?"

"He's not feeling too happy at the moment," replied Father

Fenwick. "He's struggling with looking after Jen. He isn't sure if he's done the right thing bringing her home."

"He's a good man for sure," replied John. "It's not everyone who would make the effort, I'm not sure that I could go through with it."

"I'm sure that you would John. Well, time will tell," advised Bob. "We're all here to support him."

There was little doubt about that. Bob and Father Fenwick left John to await the arrival of his estranged family. John asked them if they would like to call back later on in the afternoon and meet his family.

"I'm sure that Lisa would love to meet you both," he said. "I hope that Steve can come as well, if that's possible."

They all agreed that they would make a special effort to do just that.

*

At just after one o clock, there was a loud knocking on John's front door. He gingerly stood up and slowly walked to answer it. He felt quite nervous, although he didn't know why. He hadn't seen Lisa and his children for over six months now, and a lot had happened since then. Slowly, he opened the door, and was immediately greeted with yells of delight from the children. John felt very awkward as Lisa moved forward to give him a big hug.

"Hi, Lisa," he almost spoke in a whisper. "You've actually come."

"Of course we've come you big clod, why did you think that we wouldn't?"

"It just seemed too good to be true," John replied, awkwardly.

Malcolm stood in the background and told Lisa to ring him when they wanted to return home. Lisa thanked him and told him that she would. She didn't think that Malcolm was being difficult, but merely wanted to give them the time together to sort things out, she was thankful for that. They all went inside joyfully, and so began the happy reunion, that John never thought would happen. Later on in the afternoon, Father Fenwick, Bob and Steve came around to join in the festivities, and a good time was had by all. John couldn't have been happier, better times were around the corner, the best Christmas present he could have wished for ever.

Lisa phoned Malcolm at six o clock, to ask him to drive them home. Allowing for his travel time of about forty-five minutes either way, it would be getting quite late when they eventually got back to Liverpool, and the three children would be tired. The children didn't want to leave their dad, but they couldn't stay with John, due to the lack of sleeping arrangements.

"It would be great if we could all be together at Christmas," Lisa said wistfully.

"It certainly would," John replied. "But that would be difficult at the moment, unless..." They both came to the same conclusion. John could go back to stay with them in his former home in Liverpool, that way, they could all be together for the Christmas festivities.

"I doubt if Mal would want to come for me though, unless I could cadge a lift off somebody else."

John decided to look into the possibility, after all, it would be a shame not to spend Christmas together, as a family, now that they had made the first move to get back together again, at least, he certainly hoped that this would happen.

"Leave it to me," said Father Fenwick. "I'll only be too glad to take you over to Liverpool."

"That's very kind of you, Father," replied John. "But I couldn't expect you to be a taxi service for me."

"It will be my pleasure John. I've still got the use of the car from St Matthew's, I could use the trip to call in on the presbytery, and meet Father Jameson, kill two birds with one stone so to speak."

So it was arranged that Father Fenwick would drive John to Liverpool. He looked forward to meeting Father Jameson and see how things were going at his old presbytery at St Matthew's.

CHAPTER FORTY-TWO

"Mm," Mrs Jennings muttered to herself. She was on her way back from her usual daily trip to the shops. As she had started to do, she arranged her route which took her past St Matthew's presbytery. She did this, not because it was more convenient for her, in fact it was a longer distance. She was just inquisitive. She had got it into her mind that something was going on. She imagined that Father Jameson had a lady friend.

On this particular day, she wasn't disappointed. There was that lady again, dressed very similar as the previous time that she had seen her. She was coming out of the presbytery and walking towards her. Mrs Jennings didn't want to approach her, or allow her to get too close, so she put her shopping bag down on the pavement briefly, for a short time, to make it look like she was having a rest. As the lady got nearer, she waved in her direction and briskly walked on. She would definitely speak to Mrs Davies about it now, although she was imagining all sorts of scenarios, and it would give her the opportunity of something to gossip about, which she loved to do, particularly over a cup of tea and a slice of cake.

The lady had been seen by several people, most of whom really took no notice. However, she hadn't been seen while Mrs Davies was present, which added credence to the possibility of something underhanded going on.

One day Mrs Jennings spoke to Mrs Davies about it. She didn't seem overly concerned about it, like Mrs Jennings was.

"She's probably a parishioner," she said, brushing it off lightly. "Or, she could be the mother of one of the children parishioners, probably to discuss a baptism, or first communion. So you needn't concern yourself too much about it, but to put your mind at rest, I'll speak to Father Jameson about it."

So, one morning when Mrs Davies was going about her usual duties at the presbytery, she chose an appropriate moment to bring the subject of the 'mystery lady' up. Father Jameson was sitting at the kitchen table, working on his sermon for the Sunday mass. She had thought long and hard about how she would approach the subject, after all, it was hardly her business. She decided that a casual approach was the best option, to just drop it into the conversation.

Father Jameson didn't seem at all concerned about her inquisitiveness.

"Oh, you mean Rita?" he replied. "She's an old friend of mine from way back, she calls in occasionally to see me, we go back a long way. She's not my girlfriend, if that's what people are thinking. I can assure you Mrs Davies, I took a vow of celibacy, and I have no intention of breaking it."

"I hope you don't mind me mentioning it?" Mrs Davies said apologetically.

"Not at all," replied Father Jameson. "I hope that it hasn't set too many tongues wagging."

It certainly had, as far as Mrs Jennings was concerned. Perhaps now, that would be an end to it.

It certainly wasn't the end of it. Rita was seen walking around the grounds on several occasions. She was also seen walking outside the presbytery grounds, along the road, and going into shops. She never seemed to stop to talk to anyone, but merely nodded and walked on briskly. This appeared to augment the air of mystery that surrounded her. Why was she not friendly? But was happy to keep to herself, this became obvious to several parishioners, she was having a fling with Father Jameson, and nobody would convince them otherwise.

The lady had been seen to enter various shops on the High Street. She was always polite, but never became involved in any conversation. When questioned on one occasion, she merely said that she was a friend of Father Jameson.

On one particular day, pedestrians heard a shrieking of tyres on the road. Dismayed, they saw a child had run in front of a car. One witness reported that a lady had rushed into the road and pulled the child to safety. Following this brave action, after ensuring that the child was unhurt, she reunited the child with its mother and walked away without any further interaction. Why this woman should arouse anyone's interest was a mystery, particularly to Mrs Davies. She said that Rita was a friend of Father Jameson and that was it.

Father Jameson was completely unaware about all the talk, and suggestions regarding Rita and himself, and neither did it concern him. A little gossip was always good for the soul as far as he was concerned. So he had little time for chit-chat.

*

Brenda was in Linda's office. The discussion concerned Steve, and his increasing anxiety about Jen, and his ability to continue to care for her. "He's been very concerned lately, almost to the point of becoming unstable," Advised Brenda.

"Mm, that's a bad sign," replied Linda.

Brenda had looked upon Linda under a different light since their visit to *Happy Days Care Home*. Their working relationship had been a lot better. Gone was the ogre that Linda used to be, and a much more amenable Linda had materialised, at least when she was discussing anything with Brenda. But, she appeared to be the same old Linda with everyone else.

"It must be very difficult to live with someone who used to be your better half, and now they are a mere shadow of the way that they were in the past," continued Linda.

"That's very true," said Brenda pensively. "But what are we going to do about it?, that is the question."

"Well, I think that we both must pay them a visit, and then we can really get a feel about the situation. We can, hopefully, ease the pressure for both of them, and come to the right conclusion. You know that I am against residential care, unless it is absolutely necessary, and will avoid it if possible, particularly residential care in a private home. Care as a business goes against my principles, as you know."

Linda left it in Brenda's hands, to arrange the visit, and advised her that she would leave her diary open, to accommodate the visit when practical.

*

Steve was feeling very unsettled. He had contacted Father Fenwick and asked him to pay him a visit. He felt like he was cracking up. It wasn't purely the strain of witnessing his wife's deterioration from day to day, it was his own behaviour that was concerning him. He had felt very lonely for some time. Although he had Jen with him, she was a mere shadow of her former self, and it was almost as if she wasn't there at all, this was very difficult for others to comprehend.

"I wish to receive confession Father," Steve told Father Fenwick, when he had settled himself into a chair. It seemed strange for him to make such a request, because he had regarded him as a friend for some time, but now, he was talking to him as a priest.

"That's ok," Father Fenwick replied. "We can do that now. We don't need a confessional box, a confession can be made at any time, in any place."

"It's a long time since my last confession Father. I can't say how long actually."

"Don't worry, you're making it now, so when you're ready," Father Fenwick spoke in a soothing voice, as if he was actually behind a screen in the confessional box.

"A man has many needs Father, and I'm no different from the next man. For some time now I have longed for affection once again. Um," Steve appeared to struggle to go on. "The affection that Jen can no longer give me. So I got talking to a certain lady who lives locally, she's a widow. We got along very well. So, while Jen was in hospital, things took off."

"Go on," urged Father Fenwick. "Well, we started to get closer."

"By that you mean a sexual relationship?"

"Yes, that's right, and we've been meeting up ever since, I feel so guilty about it, cheating on Jen."

"Well I can understand your predicament Steve, and can certainly sympathise with you. But, you know that I can't absolve you from this sin, because sexual relations outside marriage are frowned upon by the Catholic Church."

"I understand, Father, and I promise that I will end it and repent."

Father Fenwick was lost in thought for a moment. "However, Steve. I can't forgive you as a priest. But, on the other hand, I'm your friend as well, and can understand the reason behind your action. So let's forget what you have confessed shall we, I wouldn't wish to taint our friendship."

"You mean that I don't have to end it?"

"That's up to you Steve. I'll leave it to your own judgement. If you decide to end it, I can absolve you, but not if you carry on doing it. I mean, I've taken a vow of celibacy. People simply accept it as a necessary role for a priest to take. Very few parishioners would even let it cross their mind. But, I go through the same thing as you every single day. Don't you think that I look at women, and think to myself, if only? But, I have to put it to the back of my mind and just get on with my priestly duties. However, in every other respect, I can be an ordinary bloke."

Steve looked at Father Fenwick, and they both broke down laughing. "Now let's think about the Christmas social next week, and make some arrangements. I'm relying on you, Steve for your support."

Steve agreed that he would provide as much support as he could, he was looking forward to the social himself. He breathed a huge sigh of relief. He was happy to have made his confession to Father Fenwick, to get it off his chest, although not as the church would have accepted it as a valid confession, if he was planning to continue with the relationship on an intimate basis. But he still had Father Fenwick who he regarded as a friend, and who would turn a non-judgemental blind eye to his affair with this lady, as a friend, but not as a priest.

Steve couldn't help feeling guilty about his relationship with Sheila though. He hadn't disclosed her name to Father Fenwick, and of course, he was sure that he would respect their confidentiality. Steve would have to examine his own conscience, and decide whether to continue to see Sheila, on a friends only basis, or on an intimate one. That would be a difficult decision for him to make.

CHAPTER FORTY-THREE

Sam was busy sifting through his music for the social gathering the following evening. He had decided on a mixed repertoire, which he hoped would cater for all age groups. He had a wide selection of tunes in his head, which he had played many times over countless years, but he also had collected a great deal of sheet music, most of it was much more modern music, up to date 'pop stuff,' he called it.

He had just lit up a spliff and sat down for a break when his phone rang. On answering it he recognised a familiar voice, with a Cockney accent. "Hello, Sam, me old geezer," said the voice. It was Frank Dinmore. Frank was his weed supplier and one-time friend, and that's all that Sam wanted to do with him nowadays. He was happy to have Frank as a supplier, but that was as far as it went.

Frank was a minor criminal in the East End, and mixed with some very dubious characters, who Sam would rather forget. A few years ago Sam was at a low ebb, and money was in short supply. Frank had told him that he could help him out of his current currency shortfall. George Oakes was a night security guard at a warehouse, which stored booze and cigs.

George was a local villain, and was known to the police, but this didn't involve violence, theft was his speciality.

Frank had been drinking with George in the Dog and Gun pub one night, when George suggested that he could organise a robbery from the warehouse the following night. He was the only security guard on the premises, so risk would be low. Booze and cigs could make them quite a profit on the 'black market.' Frank was very interested, the mere thought of a night-time robbery thrilled him, it's what he lived for. The possible risk of being caught didn't concern him one little bit. It was this risk that made it all worthwhile as far as Frank was concerned, it was a pure adrenalin rush for him.

"I've got another couple of mates on board," advised George. "But, we'll need someone to drive the getaway van."

"I think that I've got just the man," replied Frank. "An' he's looking for a bit of cash at the moment." So it was all arranged for the following night. Sam reluctantly agreed to drive the van, although he had reservations about it, and he couldn't see any other way of making a quick buck. He didn't have a criminal record at the time, but he did need some cash urgently.

So, the following night a white Ford Transit van, driven by Sam slid silently to the goods outward entrance of Bates and Son Wholesale Warehouse. George had got everything prepared. He had ensured that the security cameras and alarms were turned off. Several boxes of wines and spirits, and cigarettes were stacked by the door. Sam, as well as the getaway driver, was to keep a lookout. The warehouse was situated in a quite alley on an industrial estate. The four men ensured that they were completely alone in the alley. Sam sat nervously in the van wishing that this nightmare would soon be over, he didn't feel that he should be there at all. Quietly, they opened the rear doors of the van, and the first boxes were loaded into it. Fifteen minutes later, they had loaded five cartons of cigarettes, each containing five hundred packets of twenty. Also loaded were ten boxes of wine and a further ten containing cans of beer and whisky.

All appeared to have gone without a hitch, and Sam was instructed to start the engine ready for their getaway. The last box was loaded, and the van doors were closed quietly. The three men piled in, patting themselves on the back, for their excellent work. George had a last look around, and waved them off to continue with his shift. To add to the realism, George's wrists were bound tightly. Although George didn't relish the thought of spending the rest of the shift with his wrists tied, it would make it appear that the robbery hadn't been staged, and he wasn't a part of it.

Sam was instructed to put his foot down and show a clean pair of heels. They sped down the alley, and turned into the exit road of the industrial estate. To their horror, several loud sirens shook them to the core. Their euphoria was short-lived, as three police cars, with blue lights flashing, blocked their path. Their downfall had been a security camera at the far end of the alley. George had been diligent in checking the security equipment in the warehouse, but had completely overlooked the camera in the alley.

Following their arrest, all the men were bailed to appear before magistrates the following week. They subsequently received jail terms of twelve months each. However, Sam only served nine months, due to it being his first offence. So after all, he failed to improve his finances, suffered nine months in Pentonville Prison, and now he had a criminal record to boot.

As he now listened to Frank wittering on, it all came back to him. It was an event that he had wished had never happened and wanted to forget. He had told people that his regular gigs had caused his wife's anxiety. But in fact, it was his prison sentence that had been the true cause.

"How's life in Cheshire me old mate?" Frank said, in an almost mocking tone. "Not like the old East End eh, living out in the sticks now?"

"Not at all, Frank," replied Sam. "The East End has too many memories for me, an' not all good ones at that. I've got a new life 'ere and met some decent people, an' I'm playing my music again."

"If only your new friends knew about your past eh, Sam?"

"They're not going to find out, are they, Frank?"

"Well, that would be a shame if they did Sam. Now for the reason I rang. I've got news of a job coming off, an' we need a driver, absolutely rock-solid Sam, me old geezer, nothing can go wrong."

"What? No chance, I'm surprised that you asked. I was tempted by your offers once before, an' now look at me, I've got a criminal record. So you can forget it Frank."

"Well, it's your choice, Sam, but it would be a pity if your weed supply stopped."

Sam thought about this for a moment. Frank was actually blackmailing him, like holding a carrot to a donkey. "So, if I don't play your game, you'll cut off my supply?"

"Got it in a nutshell old man."

"I don't care," replied Sam. "I'll be happy to give it up, and go legal like, I don't need it anyway. So you don't have to bother me again Frank. I've got a new life 'ere."

"It's your loss, Sammy boy," and with that Frank rang off.

Sam thought long and hard for a few minutes. He didn't need the weed now anyway. He hoped that he wouldn't hear from Frank again. He had been a good friend in the past, and he was happy to get his 'weed' from him, it was convenient for him at the time, but the friendship changed following the bundled robbery. Frank was part of his past, a past that he didn't wish to revisit. Sam was anxious that his dark secret wouldn't come back to haunt him, and he didn't trust Frank one little bit.

*

Steve was anxiously awaiting Brenda's visit. He was aware that Linda would be with her, and he'd had a taster of what she could be like. He had been feeling a little better now that he had told Father Fenwick about his affair with Sheila. But, as to what he should do about it, he wasn't sure. Should he now confide in Bob? He had considered it. If Bob didn't condemn him, he would feel even more assured.

He was aware of a sudden loud screech outside, and peering out of the window, he saw a car coming into the close quite fast. The car braked sharply outside his front door. After a few moments Linda climbed out of the driver's side, followed by Brenda on the passenger side.

Steve opened the front door, thanked them for coming, and let them in.

"How are things going, Mr Farrell?" Asked Linda, she knew of course that the situation wasn't running as smoothly as he had hoped.

"It's been quite difficult," advised Steve. "It's not that I don't want Jen home, but to see her every day like she is, is very distressing."

Both Brenda and Linda were well aware how difficult the situation could be. This was the challenge with caring for someone with Dementia, there was no cure, no way out, and only a downhill slope. But, of course, it was much worse when the individual was your wife or husband.

Brenda and Linda sat down and Brenda opened her file. Steve offered them a cup of tea, which was accepted thankfully.

Brenda asked Steve if the carers were doing a good job with the care.

"Well," replied Steve, "they come three times a day, but they are out of the door as quick as they can. It's as if they haven't got enough time to do the job, no time for social chit-chat."

"How does Jen accept this?" asked Linda.

"Well, she screams a lot. The carers don't give her any time to adapt to them. They come in, drag her into the bathroom, and then they're out in about ten minutes."

"How do you feel about this?" asked Linda.

"I have to go outside sometimes, so I can't hear her crying."

Linda gritted her teeth. She felt the same about private home care as she did about residential care.

"This doesn't sound good at all," she said sharply. "Leave it to us, we'll get a better arrangement sorted for you. In my estimation, and I'm sure that Brenda will agree, what you need, is a good package of daily support. To enhance that, you need regular periods of respite. Meaning that your wife can go into a reputable care home for short periods. That way, you won't have to feel guilty about it. Mrs Farrell will have short breaks, and you will as well. We'll check regularly that the residential part of the care is carried out to as high a standard as possible, and ensure that she doesn't sit in a chair all day, to make life easier for the carers."

"I've had an idea, Steve, you could have a wheelchair, then you could take Jen out for fresh air, to get her out of the house," suggested Brenda.

"Hey, that's a good idea. It would give me some exercise as well, pushing it," said Steve enthusiastically, patting his ample waistline.

Linda chirped up in her usual loud voice. "I agree, it would benefit both of you. Right, that's sorted then. We'll arrange that for you Mr Farrell. We want to provide the best possible support for you, it's what you both deserve. Right Brenda, I think it's time for lunch, on the council, of course." So the two of them left Steve to ponder, and to dine at the expense of the council.

When they had left, Steve sat down and evaluated his situation. He liked the idea of the wheelchair. Jen didn't get out of the house at any time, and this was reflected in her mood, he was sure of that. Furthermore, Steve felt tied to the house himself, only getting out for short periods, to do the shopping. If they had the wheelchair, they, both could leave the house more frequently. Steve could push Jen, and this would help him to increase his fitness level as well. He had reached a decision about Sheila, after pondering long and hard, he felt that he had to do the right thing. He would end the relationship. He would not wish to let her down, but he felt too guilty for continuing a sexual relationship with her. To continue as a friend was possible, if that is what she would be willing to do, but he realised that she had needs as well. His level of guilt was high, and he regretted his actions so far, for getting in so deep in the first place. He felt that he was betraying Jen, even though a full relationship with her was no longer possible. Now that he had reached a decision, his level of anxiety had diminished somewhat. Although, the prospect of a future of celibacy, didn't appeal to him one little bit.

CHAPTER FORTY-FOUR

George Chandler was busy preparing the school hall for the social that evening. As was usual for George, he was cursing under his breath, he just didn't like any extra work that was placed on him. "Blooming late finishing again," he muttered to himself. "Father Fenwick and his fancy ideas of bringing the community together, most of 'em couldn't care less about the community."

George made no secret of the fact that he just couldn't understand the Catholic faith, and their rules appeared alien to him. He had been brought up in a Protestant area of Belfast, and he remembered only too well the troubles that he had been forced to live through as a small boy. As a result of his developing mind at that time, the constant violence had been implanted on his memory for all time. He had considered that Catholics were at the heart of the troubles. It would never have crossed his mind that both sides may have been equally to blame for the unrest that was taking place. He was far too young to understand what was happening in reality, and the reason for it.

George could never understand why Catholic priests couldn't get married, and had to live a celibate life. It wouldn't make any difference to their ministry if they were married, and he was sure that it wasn't mentioned in the Bible anyway, not that George read the Bible.

At his school, all the religious teaching was aimed at Non-Catholic education. George did have some Catholic friends, however, and they seemed decent people. But, they would often speak about how Henry the Eighth changed the church to suit himself. About how he divorced two wives, and arranged a further two to be executed, because they couldn't give him a son. As far as his Catholic friends were concerned, the Protestant church had blood on its hands. This would often cause arguments between them, so they would change the subject, before fists flew. However, that was past history now, and he couldn't change it.

George looked forward to the day when the Catholic Church was built, and they could hold their services in their own place, it would certainly make his life a bit easier. He breathed a sigh and continued to get the hall ready for the social, at least there would be no alcohol on the premises tonight, so no trouble, he hoped.

*

John had been working hard, as usual. He was generally teamed up with Bill each day, one of the 'Brickies' and they worked well together. The construction project had been going well so far, the foundations had been completed, and work had commenced on the outer walls of the building. Jeff, the foreman was well pleased with the progress, and advised them that there would be a Christmas bonus in the offing. John was looking forward to the break over Christmas, and in particular, spending it with his estranged family. Especially this year, as he would have money in his pocket to buy presents. They were in the Portakabin having their lunch break. There was much friendly banter and laughing as they all took it in turns to talk about their past life experiences.

"I believe that you've had a rough time recently John?" said Arthur Mason.

"Yes I have," replied John. "I was made redundant, and this caused me to start drinking heavily. I got in with some rough mates as well, and the wife had had enough eventually. She asked me to leave."

"That must have been hard on you," said Jeff.

"It was Jeff. I was lucky to move away, and I was fortunate that I got a house here, it gave me a clean break. But then, I couldn't get a job, and so the drinking started again. I considered that I was living in a better place, but couldn't afford to buy any furniture. I lost touch with my wife, because my phone was cut off, so the result was that I was in a similar situation, but in a different place. Then Father Fenwick knocked on my door one day, and the rest is history."

"I've heard about this Father Fenwick," said Jeff. "I believe that he's made quite an impression around the estate, he seems more like a social worker than a priest."

"I think that everyone here has got some skeletons in their cupboards, and has hit hard times at some time or other," chirped up Joe Smethwick. "I was probably in a worse position than you John, it got so bad eventually that even my skeleton died." They all laughed in unison at this remark.

"How so, Joe?" enquired Jeff, laughing.

"Well I ended up in a scruffy flat, no furniture, no anything really. I had to sleep in a sleeping bag on a filthy soiled carpet. I had hardly any food, even the social wouldn't give me any money, an' it got worse."

"How could it get any worse?" asked John.

"Two bailiffs came knocking on my door one day, because I owed money for a telly that I bought on the 'never-never', when I was with the wife. They told me that they could take any possessions to the value of what I owed. They took one look around, an' could see that I 'ad nowt to take."

"What happened then?" asked John.

"I went inside for six weeks, which wasn't too bad really." They all looked at Harry and said. "You any skeletons, Harry?"

"Nothing in particular," he replied.

"How do you mean, Harry, everyone has some skeletons?" asked Jeff. "You been squeaky clean then?"

Harry simply smiled, and said nothing. When their lunchbreak ended, Jeff stood up and announced that it was time to get back to work.

"A few more days, and we can knock off for a week," he said cheerfully. They all shouted in unison at the prospect.

*

The Christmas social was hailed as a huge success. Bob had suggested to Steve, that they could go together, and Vera had offered to sit with Jen. Both of them had decided that Steve would benefit from a night out, as they thought that he was suffering from a considerable amount of stress and anxiety at the present time. Steve gratefully accepted the offer, and in particular, the suggestion of a few pints in the pub later on appealed to him. John had decided to miss the social, because he was getting himself prepared for his trip to Liverpool for the Christmas celebrations in a couple of days' time. He had contacted Father Fenwick, who confirmed that he would still be able to drive him there.

Father Fenwick was relieved that the event had gone well. There was a good crowd in attendance, and there had been many pats on the back. Father Fenwick was held in high regard by the tenants, both Catholic and Non-Catholic alike. Sam was rewarded with rapturous applause, following his renditions on both keyboard and sax, of tunes both old and new. His Christmas carols were particularly popular. He had amassed many new fans from the audience, both young and old alike, and several of the youngsters had shown interest in learning to play an instrument. The only downside in the whole proceedings in the minds of a few, was the absence of a bar, but it was not possible to sell alcohol on the school premises, so tea and coffee were the order of the day.

*

Steve and Bob went to the Dog and Duck pub after the meeting. Steve sat down at a table by the large panoramic window and made himself comfortable. Five minutes later, Bob came over with two pints of bitter.

"Well," said Bob, "I think that the meeting was very good, I particularly enjoyed Sam's music, what a musician, eh?"

"He certainly is, the way he played that saxophone, it definitely got the crowd going."

"Yes, he did," replied Bob. "I wish that I could play like that, Steve."

"It's never too late, Bob, maybe he'd give you some lessons."

"Blimey, Steve, I'd be pushing up daisies well before I could play a decent tune," replied Bob laughing.

Steve took a gulp of his pint and looked thoughtful for a moment. "I've wanted to have a chat with you for some time Bob, I feel a bit of a fool."

"Fool, how do you mean, Steve?" asked Bob.

"Well, it sounds a bit daft now, but at the time it didn't."

"You're speaking in riddles, Steve," Bob said.

"I made a confession to Father Fenwick the other day."

"Confession, what's daft about that, he is a priest after all?" answered Bob.

"I told him that I had had an affair with a lady called Sheila, and that I felt that I was being unfaithful to Jen and I regretted it."

"Good lord," replied Bob. "You have an affair? You kept that quiet."

"Yes, but the fact is that it never really happened," Steve said sheepishly. "I invented it."

"How do you mean it never happened, and who is this Sheila?"

"She's nobody in particular, I could have used any name," Steve replied.

"I'm finding it difficult to understand, Steve," said Bob.

"Well, you know with Jen being the way she is Bob, we can't get together as we once used to."

"Ah, I understand," replied Bob. "You mean sexual like?"

"That's right, Bob."

"I can understand that may be a large void in your life Steve, but why confess to Father Fenwick about something that never happened?"

"I know that it's stupid, Bob, but I used to think about what it would be like to meet someone, and it seemed so real in my mind, that I felt guilty just for thinking about it and wishing that it would happen, so I imagined that it had actually happened."

"So you confessed to ease your guilt?"

"That's right Bob, by confessing, it sort of erased it from my memory, and made me feel better about it, almost as if it had actually happened." Steve continued: "You see Bob, I have this feeling that all is lost, nothing will ever change. Jen will never be the same again, so our life is never going to be back the way it was. I feel old now, and often think back to when I was younger, I feel that I had more credibility then, I could do what I wanted and could have a life. That's why I invented Sheila, it could never happen in reality, only in my mind."

Bob felt a bit concerned about what he had just heard, although he could understand how Steve was feeling. He decided to keep an eye on him, but for the time being, he thought that it would be best to make light of it, in order to prevent causing him more anxiety.

"Ok, Steve, I understand," he said soothingly. "Now I have only imagined that you have told me about Sheila, and have erased it from my memory also."

Steve smiled and said. "Thanks for listening, Bob, you're a good friend. After a few more pints, I should feel better."

"I'll certainly drink to that," Bob replied.

CHAPTER FORTY-FIVE

It was Saturday morning, fine and dry, five days before Christmas. John was packed ready for his journey to Liverpool. After several weeks of hard work on the building site, he was ready for a break, particularly as he would be spending Christmas with his family. It was an event that he could only dream about previously.

He had packed his suitcase carefully, which contained several new outfits, which would be a big change from his tatty jeans, faded T-shirts and trainers. He was a working man again now, he had money in his pocket, and he was determined to present a different image of himself to the world. He had decided to buy presents for the kids, but wait until he got to Liverpool, most probably the first that they had got for some time, unless Malcolm had treated them of course, which was as likely as the moon being made of green cheese.

Father Fenwick knocked on his door at exactly eleven, as promised. "I really appreciate this Father, he said, as he opened the door."

"Don't mention it John, I'm only too glad to do it, anyway, I want to visit my old parish and see how things are going there." They went out of the house and got into the car, which Father Fenwick had been instructed by Bishop Larkin to make plans to hand back to the parish. Father Fenwick wondered why he had been asked to give it back, because as far as he knew, Father Jameson had his own car.

Bishop Larkin had told him, however, that they needed the car in case an emergency cropped up, and it was to be used by the parish after all.

The roads were not very busy, and so they reached John's house in about forty minutes. During the journey, John had been very quiet at first, but chirped up after about ten minutes. "I never thought that it would be possible for this to happen Father. I really messed up."

"You didn't mess up, John, you were unlucky, it wasn't your fault that you were made redundant."

"No, I suppose that you're right, Father, anyway, I'm going to make up for it now."

"Good man," replied Father Fenwick.

As they turned into John's road, he thought how grim and depressing the houses looked, after living in his new house at *New Pastures*, the sight hit him like a punch to the jaw. He was glad now that he had moved out, although the circumstances had been out of his control at that time, and his leaving wasn't out of his choosing. If he hadn't had lost his job, he may have still been living here. Although he had lost his family in the process, he had moved to a better place, and had made new friends, gaining a job in the process. He hoped now that he could move them out to his new home in *New Pastures*, every cloud has a silver lining came into his mind.

"It's just over there, Father, the third house on the right," John said enthusiastically.

Father Fenwick parked carefully at the kerb and switched the engine off.

"Right, here we are," he said.

"That's great, thanks a lot, Father, would you like to come in for a cuppa, and meet the family again?"

"I would like that, thank you, John. By the way, you can call me

James you know. Everyone seems to think that they should address me as Father all the time, but to my friends, I prefer to be called James, or Jim if you prefer."

"Ok, Jim," said John laughing. "Let's go in."

Lisa greeted them warmly at the front door, throwing her arms around John and giving him a big hug. She greeted Father Fenwick also, but with a handshake instead, and said. "Nice to see you again Father, thank you very much for bringing John, I'm sure that Malcolm will be grateful as well, you've saved him a trip. He's not very obliging unless there's something in it for him."

"I was very pleased to be of service, Lisa, I'm going on to St Matthew's to see how they're managing there, so it's fitted in very well."

"Well, have you got time for a cup of tea and a sandwich before you go?" asked Lisa.

Father Fenwick accepted the offer gratefully. George came over to him and asked if he had started John running yet, to which Father Fenwick replied.

"Well, I think that's up to your dad, don't you think, George?"

"It certainly is," John chipped in. "After a day's work at the site, I'm fit for nothing."

"It must be hard work, John, but it's very encouraging the way that you've taken it on," Father Fenwick said.

"Yes, after all the years on the dole, and the hardship, I'm very grateful for it." Molly and Sarah joined in and clung close to John. It was obvious that they had missed him, and they didn't want to lose him again. John hugged them both, and it was plain to see how happy and content that he was.

*

The wheelchair had just been delivered to Steve's house, that

Brenda and Linda had arranged for Jen. Steve viewed it as a welcome sign, as it would enable him to take Jen out, for much needed therapy for them both, and he was certain that he needed the exercise. The Occupational Therapist had rung earlier to advise him that she would call with a Physiotherapist later that day, to assess how both Jen and Steve would manage. It was essential that Jen was capable of using the chair without risk to herself, or Steve. This was an important consideration.

Steve attempted to explain to Jen what it was all about. He wasn't sure if she understood, but she smiled and nodded at the same time. He unpacked the chair, and assembled it, ready for the assessment later on.

*

Father Fenwick had enjoyed Lisa and John's hospitality. They made sure that he had a good lunch before he continued on his way, to visit St Matthew's. He was pleased that things were working out well. Lisa and the children were over the moon to have John back. Father Fenwick sincerely hoped that things would work out for them. As far as John was concerned, he hoped that they could all move to *New Pastures* with him. It was quite obvious to Father Fenwick, there was a vast difference between the house in Liverpool, and the house in *New Pastures*, which would provide a better lifestyle. Also, John had a job now on the building site, and so could not move back, even if he wished to.

Father Fenwick was looking forward to his visit to St Matthew's. Mrs Davies had told him about the so called 'mystery lady' and the suspicions that it had aroused amongst the so called 'faithful.' He was sure that the situation was quite normal, and there was a rational explanation. After all, there was nothing written down to say that priests couldn't have female friends. The dogma was due to the whole question of celibacy amongst Catholic priests.

Father Fenwick was sure that this argument would go on indefinitely, and the Vatican would not change its views concerning the subject.

Father Fenwick wished the Byrne family a Happy Christmas, and told them that he would look forward to them moving to *New Pastures* as a family unit once again. He left the house and got into the car for his drive to St Matthew's. As usual, the starter motor ground into life, and the car jerked forward with a whirring sound.

Father Fenwick was in a happy mood. He could hardly control his pleasure about the turnaround in John's life. When he had first met him, a couple of months ago, he had seen a lonely, down-beaten man, who had a huge chip on his shoulder, now the chip had been removed, bit by bit.

*

It took Father Fenwick twenty minutes to reach St Matthew's. He turned the car right into the drive and parked near the entrance to the presbytery. As he did so, he noticed a woman about to go up the steps into the presbytery.

"Ah," he said to himself. "Is this the 'mystery lady' who everyone is gossiping about?"

He was just in time to meet her, excellent timing, he thought. He could introduce himself, and have a chat with her. He would now be able to clarify the position and lay the gossiping to rest.

The lady hadn't heard the sound of his car coming up the drive. She was just about to go up the steps to the main door. So, Father Fenwick quickly got out of the car, slammed the door and walked briskly after her. He got to the top of the steps, and noticed that the door to the presbytery hadn't been closed properly. He pushed open the door further still and stepped inside. The lady was walking into the lounge, her high heels clicking on the hard floor. He noted that she was a well-dressed young woman, which enhanced her slim figure.

"Hello," he shouted in a loud voice. "I've called to see Father Jameson, I'm Father Fenwick." He almost collapsed onto the floor with shock, as Father Jameson turned around to face him. "Hello dear," he said.

*

"Now then, Mrs Farrell," Jean Fallows, the Occupational therapist said. "We're here to see if this wheelchair is suitable for you."

Maureen Burke, the Physiotherapist added to what Jean had told her.

They assisted Jen to lift herself out of her chair, using a Zimmer frame. Little effort was required, because Jen's mobility had improved, thanks to the input of the Social Services. They stood back and watched her as she moved forward slowly. When she was standing up straight, Jean told Steve to gently push the wheelchair towards Jen, until it came into contact with her posterior. This had the effect of making Jen sit down straight in the chair. Steve moved the footrests into position, and placed Jen's feet onto them. Steve then fastened the seat belt around Jen's waist, and adjusted it to ensure her comfort.

Maureen then instructed Steve to take the brakes off and push the wheelchair towards the front door, and move outside. The houses in *New Pastures* had been constructed with disability in mind, so there was a ramp outside the front and back doorways. Steve completed this task smoothly, and then pushed Jen back into the house. Finally, they watched Jen lift herself out of the wheelchair, using her Zimmer frame, with slight assistance from Steve, and assist her to sit back down in her chair.

"Mission accomplished," said Jean and Maureen in unison. "We are quite satisfied that both you and Steve are safe to use this equipment. We hope that you both enjoy the benefits and freedom that you will get out of it."

"We certainly will, won't we, Jen?" Steve said. Jen looked up, smiled, and mumbled, as was her norm.

"In fact," added Steve, "we'll go out for a spin this afternoon, for a trial run. We can take some sandwiches, and a drink. It'll be an outing."

"That's a lovely idea," Jean said. "It's a nice day out there. We'll be off now and let you get on, so if you've any questions, or doubts, you have our contact number."

A short time later, Steve made some sandwiches, and filled a flask with tea. He put Jen's coat on, to ensure that she would be warm enough. Although the day was quite warm, Steve thought that Jen may feel slightly chilled sitting in the chair not moving. He repeated the exercise that had been demonstrated earlier, and manoeuvred Jen smoothly, and without fuss, into the wheelchair. Fastened her in, footrests in place, and off they went.

Steve knew exactly where to go, somewhere that Jen had never been to, and to where he particularly wanted to go again. He wheeled her along the pavements of the estate, and into the wooded area, his favourite place. On their way, several people waved, and some stopped for a brief chat. Mrs Briggs was very glad to see Jen out. She greeted them warmly and told them how glad she was to see them, particularly Jen.

Steve felt very happy to get Jen out of the shadows of their home, and out into the bright daylight. He felt a bit puffed out at first, but he realised that he was unfit at the present time, but he hoped that would soon change.

Jen gave Steve the impression that she really loved the wooded area, and giggled gleefully when she saw all the wildlife that the woods attracted. They eventually reached Steve's '*Magic Pond*', which had been his plan all along.

"Look, Jen," he said to her. "This is my '*Magic Pond*' that I've told you about." He hadn't visited the pond for some time, and just being there once again, made him feel more at peace, his recent pain and anxiety washed away.

Steve unpacked the sandwiches, and a piece of Madeira cake for them both, he then poured two cups of tea. When they'd finished, Steve dipped his hands in the cool water, and placed Jen's hands in his own. The healing touch that he so wished for, but would never happen.

Half an hour later, Steve pushed Jen back home. This was the first of many such outings, he was sure of that.

CHAPTER FORTY-SIX

Father Fenwick struggled to compose himself. He had come face to face with the so called 'mystery lady.' He could hardly believe what he was witnessing. Father Jameson was the lady in question. He struggled to get his words out.

"What the devil," he mumbled. "I'm very glad to meet you, Father, but I wasn't expecting to meet a lady priest."

Father Jameson smiled through his make-up and said. "I'm sure that it's a surprise to you, but now that you're here, I'll try to explain."

Father Jameson, or Rita, as he called his other persona sat down at the table in the kitchen, where Father Fenwick had once eaten meals with Father Frederick.

"I realise that there has been a large amount of gossip around the area," Father Jameson began. "The gossipers thought that I was having an affair with Rita, and indeed I have, if you get my drift. It would be seen as an outrage for a Roman Catholic priest to cavort with a female, would it not?"

"It would indeed," replied Father Fenwick. "But, it does happen."

"It does. And let me tell you that I wouldn't break my vow of celibacy, no matter how tempted that I was."

Father Fenwick was interested to get to the bottom of this strangest of strange situations. He had of course, heard of transvestites, but to come face to face with one, he had never envisaged, particularly a priest in his old parish.

"Of course," continued Father Jameson, "If this became common knowledge by the hierarchy, then my position as a priest wouldn't be tenable."

"That's right, but you can be sure that your secret won't see the light of day from me," said Father Fenwick in a reassuring tone.

"Thanks for that. But, I think that an explanation is needed," said Father Jameson.

"Only if you want to tell me," said Father Fenwick. "But, you don't have to explain to me. I'm a man of the world, and I'm aware that there are people in this world who don't conform to the norm, which are set by those who consider themselves as the norm."

Father Jameson struggled to find the right words, to explain the situation.

"I know that there are men who like to dress in women's clothes, transvestites and the like. However, that's not the reason that I do it. Some people would consider me as a pervert, but that couldn't be further from the truth. Look, I'll go and change back into my normal clothes, and take this makeup off. I'll only be about ten minutes, make a cup of tea or coffee if you like, while you're waiting."

"Thanks, I will," replied Father Fenwick, thankful that he would see the real Father Jameson, what a strange and unexpected situation, he thought.

Father Fenwick made himself a cup of tea and made himself comfortable at the table, as he did so his thoughts returned to the times that he once had with Father Frederick at this very table, and all the laughs that they shared. He wondered how he was getting on, and decided that he must pay him a visit before Christmas.

Father Jameson returned after about ten minutes. How different he looked now, dressed in more dowdy clerical attire, complete with dog collar.

"That's more like it," he said with a smile. "I'll let you into my secret now."

"Shall we dispense with the formal, Father? I'm Daniel, and I've been told that you're James."

"Yes, of course, we're talking man to man now, so I'm happy to drop the Father bit, I tell my friends the same. Sometimes I hate being called Father all the time, because I'm never going to have a chance to become a father, he said."

Daniel continued with his story. "I had a sister who was called Rita. We were very close, and we had no secrets from each other, we shared all our concerns. If one of us was feeling down, the other was always there to offer support. Mum and dad doted on Rita, more than me, but I didn't mind, because she was so lovely. She was clever too, she didn't seem to have any problems with her school work, unlike me, who always had to struggle. Learning to me was like walking through treacle backwards."

Father Fenwick listened intently, but said nothing, he was interested to learn the rest of Father Jameson's story.

Father Jameson went on, "Rita got sick one day, she was taken to hospital. We were all very concerned about her. Then the biggest blow in our lives happened, she died quite suddenly. The doctors said that she a heart condition, we never knew anything about it. We were all devastated when we heard the news, she was only twenty-three. My mum was in bits, and withdrew completely from us all after her death."

"I'm very sorry to hear that, Daniel," Father Fenwick said sympathetically. "It's a terrible thing when anyone close to you dies suddenly, particularly at such a young age."

"Yes it is James, it took us all a long time to get over it. That's when I decided to become a priest. I thought that it would help me to get over Rita. It was almost as if I could be nearer to her, through my devotion to God. I felt that he was calling me through Rita's death."

"I can understand that Daniel, very often people think that they have a calling, or vocation when something bad happens in their lives. Do you think that it has helped you to come to terms with your loss?" Father Fenwick asked.

"At first I thought that it had, but now I think that I may have made a bad decision."

"Do you mean that you have lost your faith, Daniel?"

"No, not exactly. I still believe in God, and living a good life. But I don't think that you have to become a priest to do that. When you become a priest, you have to give up so much. You have to live a life of celibacy, give up your chances of marriage and having a family. You are then at the beck and call of the church. Sometimes you don't have the time to put down your roots. You're moved about at sometimes very short notice."

"I agree, Daniel," replied Father Fenwick. "I've had my doubts for some time now. Father Frederick told me to consider my position, he told me that it was too late for him. I miss all the things that you have mentioned. But, being moved to *New Pastures* has been one of the best things that could have happened. I've made some good friends there."

"That's good, James, but you don't know if you'll be moved again, when it suits the church. They won't care about the friends you'll leave behind."

Father Fenwick was quiet for a moment, as he absorbed what Daniel had said. "That's certainly something to think about, Daniel. You haven't explained why you dress up in women's clothes though."

"After Rita died, I told you that I took it really bad. I missed her so much, and I really felt for my parents. So that is why I became a priest, as a way of understanding why it happened. But, now I realise that simply becoming a priest hasn't helped me to come to terms with it at all. When we celebrate mass, we dress in fine vestments, sing hymns and preach the Gospel. But, I think that sometimes it's an empty gesture, and wonder if it's worth our sacrifices. I dress up and call myself Rita, after my sister. In a small way, I think that it almost brings her back, I wear her clothes. It's as if she lives again in me. I become Rita for a short while, it makes me feel that she is still alive. I can do this whenever I feel down."

"I see," Father Fenwick said. Although he found it difficult to imagine that dressing up in Rita's clothes helped him in such a way, but if it did, then there was no harm in it. However, the church would take a dim view of it, they simply would not understand.

"I'm trying to understand, Daniel," he said. "I've no problem with it. I deeply sympathize with what you're going through. But, we better keep this as our little secret, shall we?"

"Yes, thanks for listening, James. I agree, if this got out, it would be an end to my priesthood."

"Would that be a bad thing, Daniel? From what you have just told me, your heart isn't in it any more. Look, I'll tell you what. I'm going to visit Father Frederick in his care home tomorrow, why don't you come with me? He's a man of wisdom, and he will only be too glad to give you advice about your vocation, and the best way forward for you. They've got a bar there, so we could have a few pints, and call it our Pre-Christmas get together, you'll like Father Frederick, we'll have a few laughs together, as mates, not priests."

Daniel agreed to the plan and said it was just what he needed, he would look forward to it.

*

Sam was practising a new piece of music on his keyboard. Father Fenwick had asked him if he would play at the Christmas Day Mass, to which he readily agreed to do. He was looking forward to giving young Harold a music lesson in the afternoon also. After hearing him play at the social, Harold had expressed a wish to learn to play himself. Sam was only too happy to oblige. He decided not to charge him for the lessons. If he thought that the lad had an aptitude for music, then that would be a reward in itself. It would also give Sam the opportunity to feel useful again. Ever since his move to *New Pastures*, following his wife's death, and his part in the disastrous robbery, he had felt like a second-class citizen, thrown onto the scrap heap, and he was often on the point of despair. Music had saved him from going further down the dark road, almost to the point of no return.

Sam realised that it wouldn't be plain sailing though. It was only too easy for a beginner to become discouraged when learning to play an instrument. It was hard work, and one had to be committed to it, enduring endless hours of practice. Repetitive scales were particularly tedious, but necessary if one was to progress.

Sam certainly needed something to keep him occupied. He was missing his 'weed', which he hadn't used since his falling out with Frank. He hoped that his tutoring work with Harold would take his mind off it. If that went well, he hoped that he would eventually have more pupils. That would be the icing on the cake for Sam, his life would have some meaning.

Just as he was revelling in his new life, the phone rang. He picked the receiver up. Frank's voice chilled him to the bone.

CHAPTER FORTY-SEVEN

Five Oaks Residential Home looked very welcoming as Father Fenwick drove up the drive. There was a large Christmas tree outside the main entrance, decked out with the usual Christmas decorations, and multi-coloured lights. Father Jameson was very impressed when he saw it. "It's more like a hotel than a residential home," he said.

"It is Daniel, just wait until you see the inside," explained Father Fenwick.

They got out of the car and walked into the foyer. The sound of *'God Rest ye Merry Gentlemen'* invaded their ear drums as they went inside, which perfectly completed the Christmas atmosphere.

A female care assistant came out of the lounge, and asked who they were there to visit.

"We're here to visit Father Frederick," Father Fenwick said.

The care assistant smiled and said. "The one and only Father Frederick, he's certainly brightened the place up since he's been here, we don't need to hire a comedian with him around."

"I'm glad that he hasn't lost his touch," Father Fenwick said laughing.

"He's in the lounge at the moment, relaxing quietly for once, it makes a change from the bar," said the care assistant.

They were ushered into the lounge, which was as brightly decorated as the outside of the building. There was another large

Christmas tree in one corner, and various paper decorations around the walls, complete with a large father Christmas figure by the door.

Father Jameson nudged Father Fenwick, smiling and said, "No show without dear old Santa is there?" To which Father Fenwick agreed.

When Father Frederick saw them he came over and greeted them warmly. Father Fenwick noticed that there was something different about him. He had put on weight, and certainly looked better than last time he had seen him. Then it struck him, as Father Frederick began to speak, it was apparent that he had a new set of teeth, which stood out as bright as the Christmas decorations.

"Compliments of the season," he said brightly. "Do you like my new teeth?"

"Very nice, how's the toast doing? You look well, Father, may I introduce Father Daniel Jameson, our replacement at St Matthew's."

"Glad to meet you, Father Jameson, how are you getting on there?"

"Very well, thank you Father, Frederick, Mrs Davies looks after me well."

"She certainly will do, she's an excellent cook, her Hot Pot is to die for," replied Father Frederick, licking his lips.

They went into the rear lounge, where it was quiet, most of the residents were in the main lounge, either watching the television, or just chatting amongst themselves, some snoring away loudly.

"How are they treating you, Father Fred?" asked Father Fenwick.

"Oh, it's very comfortable here, as you can see it's like a hotel. And, there's a bar, so what more could I want?" He said winking. "No more priestly duties for me, I wish that I'd given it up years ago."

"I remember last time that I was here you advised me to consider my future in the clergy, I have been thinking about what you told me ever since."

"I did, and I told you that you were like a puppet on a string, as far as the church is concerned. They move you about without any consideration to yourself, but once you are ordained, you have to be prepared to accept it. I of all people appreciate that it is a calling, and if you have that, then you will abide by the rules. But, are the rules worth the forfeit? That is the question."

"Mm," Father Fenwick mumbled. He knew that Father Frederick knew what he was talking about, he had the years of experience under his belt.

"There's a Jehovah's Witness gentleman in here. We've had quite a few in depth discussions too. We don't realise how many of our celebrations are based on Pagan customs. Christmas, Easter, and Halloween, just to name a few. Do you know that their Elders are unpaid? No Frills Kingdom Halls, no fancy statues, no silverware, and no fancy vestments."

"You're not going to become one, are you?" asked Father Fenwick laughing.

"No, I'm a bit long in the tooth for change now, but our debates are keeping my intellectual grey cells ticking over."

"I agree with that," said Father Jameson. "One has to keep an open mind about such issues. After all, if God does exist, it doesn't matter which religion you follow, it's all manmade, one doesn't need an elaborate building to worship him, one can worship him anywhere, don't you agree Father?"

"That's correct," said Father Frederick, smiling in amusement at Father Jameson's public-school accent.

"How are you feeling about your vocation, Father Jameson? You've got years ahead of you. You've got to think seriously about your position, while you're still young. How about we retreat to the bar and have a good old discussion?"

"That's a good idea," replied Father Jameson. "As long as you're not going to teach me about the virtues of becoming a Witness."

*

Sam peered out of his lounge window, with a worried look on his face. He had been very anxious since Frank had contacted him on the telephone. Sam had not expected to hear from him again, and wished that he hadn't. Sam considered that he was a part of his past life, that had gone sour, and now, here he was again, shouting down the phone, with his usual threatening tone.

Sam was just about to engage himself in a music teaching career, something that he'd always wanted to aspire to. Then, his old demons had come back to haunt him. Ever since his wife had died, Sam had been left with an acute level of anxiety, the exclusion by his children had exacerbated this. He had become obsessive, checking and double checking everything that he did. Now Frank's harassing would not help his situation, and he felt obliged to look out of the window many times a day, to make sure that Frank wasn't outside.

Frank had told Sam that he intended to visit him, and the thought of this made him feel very insecure, and uneasy. Frank was the last person that he wanted knocking on his door. Sam tried to put his concerns out of his mind for the time being, and concentrate on Harold's first music lesson, later on in the week, but it wouldn't be easy for him to do. Frank could wreck his plans.

*

The three priests were seated in the comfortable lounge bar at *Five Oaks Residential Home*. Father Jameson was amazed that the whole décor was more like a luxury hotel, rather than a retirement home.

"Is this only for retired priests?" he asked.

"No," replied Father Frederick. "It's not. Anybody can come, as long as they can afford it of course. It's a bonus to get the church to pay for it, after all my sacrifices. It's not a permanent arrangement though. The main idea is to give me the opportunity to recuperate after my stroke. The church will only pay so much. I will get a state pension however, so I thought that I might put in for a small council flat when my time is up here."

"That would be very nice for you, Father Fred," said Father Fenwick. "You've certainly done your bit, and you deserve a rest."

"That's right, but what will I do with my time? That is the question."

"I'm sure you'll find something to do," said Father Jameson. "We can keep in touch with you and take you out in the car."

"That would be very nice, thank you. Too late to get married and have a family though," said Father Frederick gloomily.

"With your record, Father, I don't know about that," said Father Fenwick, although he realised that would be unlikely. "You could involve yourself with some voluntary work, maybe teaching children about the Bible."

"I don't know about that, I think that I've had enough religion to last me a lifetime. That is until I meet the boss, of course."

The three priests laughed loudly in unison at this remark. Father Jameson got another round of drinks in, and they continued with their varied discussion, which included Father Frederick's jokes, and loud laughter.

As the beer flowed, so did the effects of it on the three priests, and their voices became louder. They temporarily ceased to be priests, and became just three men enjoying a night out together. They were having such a good time, that Father Fenwick forgot that he was supposed to be driving home. Several hours later, and he was well beyond his driving capability.

"Ah, don't you be worrying about that," spluttered Father

Frederick, beer froth around his upper lip. "I'll have a word with Mary, she should be able to fix you both up with a bed for the night."

"Who's Mary?" asked Father Fenwick, slurring his words slightly.

"Oh she's the home manager, but I call her Matron," replied Father Frederick. "She's certainly not the Immaculate Conception," he said grinning.

He stood up shakily. "I'll be back in a few minutes lads," he said with slightly slurred speech, walking in a sort of rolling and wavering gait. He went out of the bar, almost knocking someone over on his way out. A short time later, there was the sound of a chair being knocked over. Father Frederick had come back into the bar. Father Jameson stood up, also a bit unsteadily, and grabbed hold of his arm for fear that he would collapse onto the floor.

"That's settled," Father Frederick announced. "You can both stay for the night in room thirty. I hope you're good friends because you'll have to share a double bed," he said, winking.

Later that evening, following their drinking binge, both priests made their way upstairs, and went into room thirty, after fumbling for several minutes with the key card, and giggling like schoolboys.

Father Fenwick looked at Father Jameson exclaiming. "This is a right situation, we'll have to make the best of it. I've never slept with a lady before, it's just as well that you're not dressed as Rita tonight." Father Jameson looked at Father Fenwick sheepishly, undressed, and collapsed onto the bed.

CHAPTER FORTY-EIGHT

The day before Christmas Eve dawned bright and clear. Father Fenwick and Father Jameson had woken up the following morning, feeling very groggy, following their night of heavy drinking with Father Frederick, but they had certainly slept very well. Father Fenwick was feeling unsure of his fitness to drive, but following a full English breakfast he had felt a lot better, and was sure that he was legal to drive.

They wished Father Frederick all the best before their drive back to St Matthew's. They were quite amazed that he was hardly fazed by the previous night's drinking, but he told them that he was more used to it than they were. A priest's prerogative, he said with a cheeky grin.

When they arrived back at St Matthew's, Mrs Davies was already busy with her cleaning duties at the presbytery.

"Well, you both look like something that the dog has brought in," she said laughing. "I hope that poor old Father Frederick looks better."

"Yes, he certainly does," replied Father Fenwick. "He could leave us standing, that's for sure."

"Well, I don't hold with members of the clergy engaging in the Devil's brew, but I suppose that it cheered Father Frederick up, and it is almost Christmas."

"I don't think that he needed cheering up," explained Father

Fenwick. "He's having a fine old time there."

"That's good to hear, he deserves to have an easy time now, after offering his services to the church for so many years."

"That's true enough," replied Father Fenwick. "But to listen to him now, you would doubt that he thinks that it's been worthwhile."

"Oh, I'm sure that it's just him sounding off. I've never known such a devoted man."

"That may be true enough Mrs Davies, you can be devoted to the cause, but it's the sacrifices that a priest has to make along the way. You don't have to make these sacrifices to honour God," said Father Fenwick.

"Don't you listen to this, Father Jameson, I'm sure that you will remain as devoted to the church as Father Frederick has been," advised Mrs Davies.

"Maybe," replied Father Jameson, with a wayward look in his eyes. "One has to think about it seriously. Father Frederick has been talking to a Jehovah's Witness. They have a completely different perspective to that of the Catholic Church. If one chooses to believe what they preach, it alters our thinking, and everything that the Christian church teaches us, and indeed, believes in."

"That's right," said Father Fenwick. "Nobody alive can actually prove, or discount whether God and Jesus ever existed, even the most devout person must question it at times. Jehovah's Witnesses simply study the Bible. They still believe in God and Jesus, they just have a different perspective on it, that's all. They don't rewrite the Bible, they believe that they know the truth."

"Well, that may be so, Father, but I will stick to the teaching of the Catholic Church, if you don't mind," retorted Mrs Davies sternly.

"That's fine by us, Mrs Davies," said the two priests in unison.

"Well, that's settled then, I'll make you a nice cup of tea before you go back to *New Pastures* Father Fenwick," said Mrs Davies. "I'm sure you've got a lot of preparation to do for the Christmas services."

"Yes, I have, that'll be very nice, Mrs Davies, thank you, I really miss you at *New Pastures*. I suppose a move is out of the question?"

"Don't even think about it, Mrs Davies," Father Jameson said laughing.

*

The excellent community spirit that Father Fenwick had a significant part in creating at *New Pastures*, was alive and kicking. With Christmas fast approaching, arrangements had been made to ensure that all the friends had a jolly time. Bob and Vera had invited Steve and Jen for Christmas dinner, and Father Fenwick had gratefully accepted his invitation also, which he would attend, after he celebrated Christmas mass. Mrs Davies had also asked him if he would like to join Father Jameson at St Matthew's, which he had gratefully declined, following the drinking spree the night before. There would be no midnight mass at the school, which George Chandler was very grateful for. He was very relieved that his Christmas festivities wouldn't be interrupted by such trivialities as opening and closing the school hall.

Christmas spirit was lacking as far as George was concerned, unless it was in a glass of course.

John was with his family in Liverpool, which made everyone happy, now that he was getting his life back on track.

"What about Sam?" asked Bob. "He can't be on his own for Christmas, and I don't think that his family will ask him."

"Oh, yes, I'd forgotten about Sam, you're right. Would you mind him joining us as well, Bob?" asked Father Fenwick.

"No, the more the merrier," replied Bob. "We could ask him, it would be sad if he was on his own, and he might give us a tune as well."

So it was agreed that Sam would be invited, Father Fenwick would do the honours, on Bob and Vera's behalf.

Sam was very grateful when Father Fenwick had knocked on his door. "Do come in, Father," he said. "I've just put the kettle on, would you like some tea?"

"That would be very nice," replied Father Fenwick. Why people always thought that tea was required when someone called, was a mystery to him.

Stepping inside, he noted that Sam had no Christmas tree, or decorations of any kind. The home lacked any indication that it was almost Christmas.

"I feel that I can't get in the Christmas mood this year Father. I've felt quite sad and lonely this past year. I think about my wife and children, and remember all the good times that we used to enjoy. So, to be with people like you and your friends will be a big boost for me, it'll make me feel better."

"You'll be made very welcome Sam, Bob and Vera love having people around them, they've no children of their own you see, and they only see their family on rare occasions, so the company is good for them as well."

Sam felt heartened that he had been invited to join Bob and Vera for the Christmas celebrations. He was looking forward to it already, he felt that it would fill a large void in his life, for a short time. But, the image of Frank's face, coupled with the sound of his gravelly voice filled him with dread and clouded his immediate joy somewhat. Sam's past must not be allowed to catch up with him.

CHAPTER FORTY-NINE

Christmas Day came and went. The morning mass was held in the school hall as usual, there was a large congregation, many parishioners standing at the rear of the hall, which was a huge relief for Father Fenwick. George Chandler had been given the day off, much to his relief.

All the chairs were left in place after the mass. Bob packed away Father Fenwick's altar clothing and other essentials in the suitcase, as he usually did. It was decided to leave the small crib in place over the Christmas period. There was a slight panic before the mass. Bob had unpacked the holy figures for the crib and set them in place, when they discovered that the Baby Jesus was missing.

Bob looked at Father Fenwick with a concerned look on his face and said. "We can't have a crib without the star of the show Father."

"That's quite right, Bob," said a worried Father Fenwick. "Do you think that anyone will notice?" The problem was solved, however. Following an announcement to the congregation, a small child kindly donated her small doll to replace the missing Baby Jesus.

"Do you think that Jesus will mind being a girl, Father?" she asked innocently. There was a ripple of laughter from the congregation at her question. Father Fenwick smiled broadly and told the child that Jesus wouldn't mind at all. He was warmed by the innocence of the small child.

Following the mass, Father Fenwick had got changed into his casual gear and walked around to Bob's house to join the merry crowd, who were already getting in the mood with glasses of sherry. Vera was busy in her kitchen, cooking the Christmas feast. She was determined to give everybody who were present as good a time as she possibly could. They were particularly pleased that Sam had agreed to come. Being alone at this time of year wasn't an option in their minds.

Sam sipped his glass of sherry and appeared to be relaxed, but his mind was in turmoil. The thought that Frank and his mob might pay him a visit any day soon was never far from his mind.

Bob was in and out of the kitchen, to offer any assistance to Vera, who looked quite anxious that everything was going to turn out all right.

Steve was fussing around Jen, who was in a world of her own, completely unaware of where she was, or that it was Christmas Day. He had bought Jen an extra special Christmas present, a large fluffy Teddy, which she was cuddling, with a broad smile on her face, talking to it in a whisper. Although she was happy in her own world, Steve still got very upset and agitated when he was with her. She was not the wife that he had fallen in love with, and married all those years ago. But, he still wished to care for her, and give her the best quality of life that he could. The thought that one day it may become too much for him, leading to the need for a placement in a care home, concerned him considerably; today though, he would put it to the back of his mind.

*

Meanwhile, in Liverpool. John was feeling happy, celebrating with his family. This was something that he never thought would happen again. He felt very grateful that Father Fenwick had helped him to find a job, and what better job than to be part of building a new school and church. He felt that he was playing his part in helping to build the new community. The New Year would bring in a new chapter, and John couldn't wait. For the first time in years, he had bought his three children Christmas presents. Dolls for both of the girls, Molly and Sarah, and a train set for George. Lisa received a necklace, which she asked John to put around her neck as soon as she opened it.

John had told Lisa not to bother buying him a present, because he was aware of their financial hardship recently. But, Lisa compromised, and gave him a bottle of whisky, which fitted the bill perfectly.

At St Matthew's, Father Jameson enjoyed a rather lonely Christmas Dinner, which Mrs Davies had lovingly prepared for him. After the dinner, he dressed himself as Rita and enjoyed a walk around the gardens, wishing that she was really still on this earth, she so loved Christmas. He missed her more than ever at this time of year. He was careful that nobody would see him, so he kept within the ample sized grounds of the presbytery. Mrs Davies wouldn't be back again, as she would be sipping sherry, followed by white wine chasers with her husband.

But, then, quite suddenly, a car appeared coming up the drive. With horror, Father Jameson could see the driver, it was Bishop Harris, from the Mid-Cheshire Diocese. He hadn't said that he'd be coming. Father Jameson stood rooted to the spot, unable to move an inch. The car door swung open, and Bishop Harris stepped out of the car. "What the..." he began. He looked at Father Jameson in horror, he couldn't believe what he was witnessing before his eyes.

"I think that you'd better explain yourself," he said to the horrified Father Jameson.

"Yes," he stuttered.

"We'll discuss this inside, where nobody else can see you, Bishop Harris said sharply." They both went into the presbytery, and Bishop Harris ordered Father Jameson to change out of what he called, "Those perverted clothes."

Father Jameson suddenly felt very ashamed of himself, but why should he? He wasn't hurting anyone. He felt in his own way, that he was honouring his sister's memory, and this was the only way that he could think of doing it, to be close to her, although he did realise that it was an unorthodox way of doing it. He could understand how Bishop Harris viewed it, however, he said that he thought it was perverted. Father Jameson went upstairs to change, while Bishop Harris sat seething at the kitchen table.

When Father Jameson came down, Bishop Harris glared at him and said.

"Well, what are we going to do with you, Jameson?" he dropped the father bit, as if he was ashamed to call him a priest.

"I'm afraid that I don't know," Father Jameson said sheepishly.

"You don't know," Bishop Harris snapped back. "You don't think that you can continue to be a priest here. You were moved to this parish to fill the gap that was left by Father Frederick, until another priest could be appointed. The parishioners would be aghast to think of their priest prancing around in a dress and high heels."

"I suppose so," Father Jameson bleated meekly, what else could he say?

"Does anyone else know of your sordid little secret?" Bishop Harris demanded.

"No," replied Father Jameson. He didn't wish to tarnish Father Fenwick's good name, by letting on that he knew about Rita.

"Well," Bishop Harris continued angrily. "If you wish to continue being a priest, you'll have to move to a parish that's way out of town, out of my patch. Somewhere rural, where you're not known."

This idea didn't appeal to Father Jameson at all. He was aware that the Catholic Church wouldn't tolerate any activity that was not laid down by the strict rules of the Vatican, and dressing up as a woman would certainly not feature in those rules. Father Frederick had warned both Father Fenwick and himself that the church put the strict rules of the Vatican first and those of the priests second. Once you were ordained, you had to jump to it. Father Jameson felt very uneasy now that his secret was out. He would have to think seriously about his future in the priesthood. But, Bishop Harris would certainly help him to make up his mind, he was sure of that.

CHAPTER FIFTY

Everyone was feeling low following the Christmas festivities. This was quite normal, due to the hectic build up and the highly commercialised aspect of it. The New Year was still to come, however, and this gave everyone something else to look forward to, until those celebrations were over, and the outlook became more gloomy still, when January the first loomed, together with the round of hangovers that were a normal condition of the New Year.

This particular year had been as normal as usual, and as Harold knocked on Sam's door for his music lesson, the vision of how drunk his father had been the night before, was on his mind. He was still sleeping it off in bed.

Harold knocked several times, but could get no answer. He thought that this was strange, because he had asked Sam if he could begin the new year with a music lesson. He was making progress, so much that Sam had commended him, and told him that he had promise, if he stuck to it. He wondered if Sam had drunk too much the night before like his father, but decided that that was most unlikely, unaware of Sam's past life.

Harold, as young as he was, realised that something could be wrong. He stood on tiptoe and peered through the window, but he couldn't reach high enough to see anything. He then went back to the front door and lifting the letterbox, he peered through the aperture.

Suddenly, a growling voice shouted, "Go away."

"I've come for my music lesson," Harold said, rather shakily, through the letterbox.

"Not today, thank you. In fact not any day," came Sam's reply.

Harold's young mind couldn't understand this, why was Sam like this, he sounded like a different person; was he ill? He thought to himself. This troubled his young mind, and he was worried at the situation. He decided that the best thing for him to do was call on Father Fenwick, who would surely know what to do about it, he knew what to do about everything.

Father Fenwick answered Harold's erratic knocking on the door.

"Hello, Harold," he said. "It's nice to see you, did you all have a nice Christmas, and New Year?" Father Fenwick could see that something was troubling Harold, and he feared for the worst initially.

"It's Sam Father," said Harold, struggling to speak coherently. "I went for my music lesson, an' he didn't answer the door. He told me to go away and not to come back."

"Oh, that doesn't sound like Sam," replied Father Fenwick. "I'll get my coat and we'll both go around."

They both reached Sam's house, and Father Fenwick knocked loudly on the door knocker, just as Harold had done. Father Fenwick shouted loudly through the letterbox. "Sam, it's Father Fenwick here, will you open the door?" The only reply that they got was a low moaning noise. "Are you all right Sam, Harold is very worried about you?"

"Go away, I don't want to see anybody," came the reply.

Father Fenwick was quiet for a moment, lost in thought. Sam could be ill, or he could have had a fall. His voice certainly sounded weaker than normal, as if he had suffered some sort of injury; or possibly suffered a stroke. He decided that they couldn't leave things as they were, they would have to check on him. Father Fenwick was aware that the estate caretaker held keys for any property where a vulnerable person was dwelling.

Father Fenwick told Harold to go home and leave things to him. He told him not to worry, but there was probably a simple explanation, although in his mind he doubted that it was true.

*

Mr Hughes, was the caretaker for the *New Pastures* estate, and his job was to ensure that the estate was maintained in good order. He was a keen gardener, and his main priority was to make sure that all areas of grass were kept mown, and the flowerbeds were stocked with shrubs, and flowering plants, as the season dictated. He was also responsible for keeping an eye on any resident who was deemed to be vulnerable, and take the necessary action, if there was a problem.

Father Fenwick checked on Mr Hughes' address, and made his way there immediately, he felt that there was no time to lose, as Sam might need urgent attention. He knocked on the door of number Five, Hawthorn Close. Father Fenwick couldn't fail to be impressed. The front garden was immaculate. A neat lawn, which appeared to be freshly mown; colourful flower beds, and a Magnolia tree was resplendent as a centrepiece. The garden was surrounded by a picket fence, which was painted in a dark oak stain.

The door opened, and a rather short man stood there. He was dressed in what appeared to be work clothes; as paint stains were in abundance on dark blue overalls. Father Fenwick introduced himself and explained the situation. Mr Hughes was acquainted with Father Fenwick, having attended mass regularly. "Good morning Father," he said brightly. "To what honour do I owe this call?"

Mr Hughes was well-used to Catholic priests calling, without warning. Usually, the reason behind their visit was to ask for a donation for the church. Father Fenwick was not like that. If anyone wished to donate any money, he would accept it. However, he was not in the habit of visiting with that particular reason in mind. Mr Hughes could detect by the look on his face that there was a more serious reason for his visit.

"Good morning, Mr Hughes. A happy new year to you. I'm sorry to bother you, but I need your assistance urgently."

"Yes of course, how can I be of help father?" Mr Hughes replied.

"Well," Father Fenwick began. "I'm rather concerned about an elderly gentleman, a Mr Samuel James. He lives at number Ten, The Brambles. I called to see him this morning, and he wouldn't open the door. He's definitely at home, because he told me to go away, which is quite unlike him. I believe that you hold keys for older vulnerable tenants?"

"That's right," replied Mr Hughes. "If you'd like to wait a moment, I'll get the key. I keep them locked up in a cupboard."

Father Fenwick waited patiently on the doorstep. Mr Hughes came out in a short time, and they both set off for Sam's house. Five minutes later, they reached their destination. Mr Hughes knocked on the front door first, as he didn't wish to enter right away. All they heard was a low groaning sound, just like someone was in pain.

"Right, we'd better get in now," announced Mr Hughes. He put the key in the lock and turned it. He carefully pushed the door open, and both he and Father Fenwick entered the property. The first thing that they noticed was a strong smell of urine. They went through the kitchen and into the lounge. They noticed that there was a significant amount of crockery in the sink. It was apparent that Sam hadn't done any dish washing lately.

It was a sorry sight that greeted them in the lounge. Sam was huddled in a corner. The urine smell was stronger here, so it was obvious that he had been incontinent. Father Fenwick spoke first.

"Hello, Sam, Mr Hughes, the caretaker kindly agreed to allow me to come and see you, what's happened to you, have you fallen?"

"He's coming for me," Sam bleated. "He'll get me."

"Who's coming for you, Sam?" asked Father Fenwick.

"Frank," came the reply.

Mr Hughes looked at Father Fenwick with a concerned look on his face. Sam said no more, he just shrank back into a corner.

"This looks serious, I think," said Father Fenwick. "He looks like he's suffering with some sort of paranoia, and thinks that someone is out to get him, whoever Frank is." Father Fenwick was aware that Sam was an ex Cannabis smoker, and this may have contributed to his psychotic behaviour, but wouldn't wish to declare this information to Mr Hughes.

"Yes, Frank maybe just a name that's going around in his mind, and might not exist," said Mr Hughes.

"Mm, you may be right there, Mr Hughes, but I think we'll have to get the doctor out, and get Sam assessed."

"Right, I'll leave you to it, Father, if that's all right."

"Yes, thank you for your assistance, Mr Hughes, I'll take it from here. I'll lock up and drop the key back to you later."

"Ok, if you need any more assistance, you know where I am." With that, Mr Hughes left Father Fenwick alone with Sam, to request a visit from the doctor.

Father Fenwick tried to console Sam while he waited for Dr Jones to visit, who had informed him that he would be there right away. After a few attempts, Father Fenwick managed to assist Sam to sit in a chair, who covered his face in his hands, while mumbling to himself incoherently.

Dr Jones was knocking on the door within ten minutes of Father

Fenwick's telephone call. Following a brief assessment, which provided very little information for the doctor, apart from some physical checks. He decided that an ambulance should be called to take Sam to Chester General Hospital. Once there, he could undergo further tests, and receive a psychiatric assessment, if this was deemed necessary. Dr Jones ruled out a stroke, due to no physical signs being present, but was unable to reach any other conclusion, due to psychiatry being beyond his scope.

Father Fenwick remained with Sam and Dr Jones while they awaited the arrival of the ambulance, which arrived in about twenty minutes. Sam was reluctant to move at first, but with some reassurance from Father Fenwick, and Dr Jones, he was assisted into the ambulance.

Father Fenwick advised Dr Jones, and Sam that he would contact the hospital later, to request an update on the situation. He would also contact Sam's son and advise him that his father was in hospital. Mr Hughes held next of kin details for all vulnerable tenants on the estate, so he would be pleased to provide this information to Father Fenwick. Whether Sam's son, or daughter wished to be involved, or indeed concerned, was their decision. When the ambulance had left for the hospital, Father Fenwick ensured that the property was secure, and walked back to the presbytery, wondering what the outcome would be. He felt very concerned about Sam's welfare, as he did for all the people with whom he was acquainted.

Father Fenwick hoped that things would turn out all right in the end.

*

"Mm," said Doctor Khan, as he listened to Sam's pulse. "That seems quite normal," he advised the nurse, who was preparing a hypodermic syringe, for taking a blood sample. As this was happening,

Sam was twitching, and mumbling.

"He's going to get me, go away, leave me alone."

"Who is going to get you?" asked Dr Khan. Sam didn't answer, but continued to stare ahead, with his eyes wide open. It was as if he was in a trance, quite suddenly, he began to lash out, as if an assailant was about to attack him.

"I think that we need to get the Mental Health Team on board," advised Dr Khan. "This gentleman presents as quite psychotic. In the meantime, I suggest that 5mg of Haloperidol be administered, to calm him down initially, until we can have the result of a full psychiatric assessment. We'll keep checking on him every thirty minutes." Sam was taken out of A&E, following a formal admittance procedure, and wheeled into a cubicle. The curtains were drawn around him, and a nurse was assigned to complete checks at thirty-minute intervals.

Sam soon began to calm down, as the medication began to take effect.

CHAPTER FIFTY-ONE

John was getting ready to return to *New Pastures*, following his Christmas break with his family. He was looking forward to getting back to work on the building site. Even though he considered that he was playing a small part in the construction process, he felt that this part was still important. Someone had to keep the 'Brickies' with a constant supply of cement.

Malcolm had visited several times over the Christmas period. His attitude had changed towards John. Hitherto, he had considered him to be a waste of space, and unworthy of his sister. He couldn't say that he hadn't tried to improve his life now, together with the lives of his family.

"You've made a vast effort to improve your life John, and your family," he had told him.

John was very grateful for this praise. It had been a concern for him that Malcolm had been so critical, although he did realise the reason for it. His downward trail of a deadbeat, consisting of heavy drinking, and involvement with dodgy mates was not conducive to a happy family life.

Malcolm had offered to drive John back to *New Pastures*, to save Father Fenwick the effort. Lisa and the three children had asked if they could go as well. Malcolm had agreed, as long as they didn't eat crisps in his car, as protective as always about his motor. Lisa was very keen to move to *New Pastures* if it could be arranged. John had told her that he would approach the council, and if that was accepted, their removal could be organised. Of course, it would depend on the three children being accepted at a school in the district.

They all bundled themselves into Malcolm's shiny motor and commenced their journey. The children were very excited, because it was a novelty for them to have a car journey. John had never been able to afford a car, or learn to drive. So it was rare that the children had the opportunity of being offered a lift with anyone else. Malcolm had never wanted them in his car in the past because he took a great pride in it, and didn't want it to be messed up.

The children got particularly excited when they crossed the Runcorn Bridge. George said that it was like a big blue rainbow. After slowing down over the bridge, to enable the three children to savour the view of Runcorn and the Manchester Ship Canal, Malcolm increased his speed and the car purred on towards the M56 motorway. Twenty minutes later, they arrived at *New Pastures*, and Malcolm steered the car carefully into the parking space outside John's front door. John stepped out of the car, and led the family into the house. The children rushed in as soon as the front door was open, almost as if their young lives depended on it.

"Is this going to be our new house?" asked George, in an excited voice.

Lisa looked at John, and told George that it was what they hoped for, but that would depend on how the situation developed.

"I really hope so," replied George. "This is much nicer than where we live at the moment, lovely country. I really like it here, can we move, Dad?"

"Like your mother said, this is our plan, hopefully, but we'll have to wait and see," advised John.

Lisa began to busy herself in the kitchen, moving things around, and tidying up, almost as if they had already moved in. The three children ran upstairs, shouting with excitement. "Let's see our bedrooms."

"Well, it looks like it's all settled Jonny Boy," said Malcolm smiling broadly. "Your situation is definitely on the way up for you all." Malcolm certainly meant that, his attitude was definitely changing towards John.

John nodded in agreement. He certainly hoped that he was right.

CHAPTER FIFTY-TWO

Sam opened his eyes and stared up at the ceiling. Where was he, and who were all these ghostly figures that kept appearing and disappearing, as suddenly as if they had never existed. Where was Frank? He'd told him that the robbery was going well in the bank; until.

Frank adjusted his mask, a hideous looking thing, that resembled a demon's face. The girl behind the counter trembled as she fumbled for the security alarm.

"Come on, hurry up, or I may not be as nice," Frank screamed through the mask.

Suddenly, there was panic as a customer walked in through the door.

"Get over there and be quiet," Frank ordered.

"Let's get out while we can," Sam bleated, he was getting quite panicky now. "You said that it would be easy. The cashier would hand over the cash, and we'd be off, richer than we've been in a long time."

"Shut your noise," growled Frank. "Get the engine in the motor running, this won't take long, hurry up woman, hand the cash over."

Sam couldn't get out quick enough, he was really panicking now. This wasn't how he thought it would be. Edna had mentioned only that morning that she yearned for a holiday, as they hadn't had one in years. Sam was always off playing in a gig somewhere. Sam couldn't afford a holiday, as he was always short of cash. He had promised Edna that he would try to earn some extra money, and they could go off to the Lake District for a week. Frank had said that this would be easy, a piece of cake.

Out of the corner of his eye, Sam noticed a swift moving figure. Then he heard a loud bang, and much screaming. The man lay on the floor, blood streaming from his chest. Frank's gun had gone off and downed a customer.

"Get out now," Frank ordered. Another shot, another man down.

"It's all over," Sam shrieked. "We're done for."

There was a further loud shot. Sam fell to the floor. Blackness overtook him.

*

Dr Khan stood at the foot of Sam's bed reading the observation chart. The Haloperidol had sedated Sam, and he had slept for two hours.

"How are you feeling, Mr James?" asked Dr Khan.

"Those men who were shot by Frank, how are they? Are they dead? That wasn't supposed to happen," Sam gasped out the words, as if much effort was needed.

"What men?" Dr Khan asked.

"The men who Frank shot. He didn't mean to shoot them, it must've been an accident, didn't you hear the shots?"

Dr Khan looked at Nurse Rogers and told her that Sam had been suffering with delirium, due to the effect of the medication.

He then addressed Sam. "Mr James, try not to get yourself distressed, you're quite safe here. Another doctor is coming to see you in a short while. You've been sleeping peacefully. I can assure you that nobody has been shot."

Dr Khan addressed Nurse Rogers again, "I've spoken to Dr

Stevens. He will make an assessment of Mr James' condition today. He may recommend transfer to Woodley Hospital, on the Acute Psychiatric Admission Ward, most probably on a Section Two of the Mental Health Act. He could be detained for up to twenty-eight days, to allow for full assessment and treatment. I've read his notes. Evidently, this poor chap has gone through a rough patch recently. I believe that he was a musician. His wife died, and his son and daughter disowned him for some reason, very sad state of affairs, if you ask me; it doesn't take much to tip one over the edge."

Dr Stevens made his assessment later that day. His diagnosis was of the opinion, that Sam was suffering with Acute Paranoia. He believed that he was being persecuted, by a man called Frank. He also believed that he had been involved in a bank robbery, where several people had been shot and killed. However, the latter was the result of the medication that he had been given, while in the hospital. Nurses would later file in the nursing report that Sam had been shouting, "No, No; don't do it," while he was under the influence of the drug.

It was arranged that Sam would be transferred to Woodley Hospital the following day, under a Section Two Order, of the Mental Health Act, where he would undergo further assessment and treatment.

*

Clive Roberts was a nursing assistant at Woodley Hospital. He was forty years of age. He had always nurtured a desire to be a qualified nurse. Unfortunately, he lacked the necessary qualifications to be accepted for training. He had been unemployed for two years before working at the hospital. He was offered the chance to complete a one-year course, by the employment service. The course consisted of instruction in such areas as IT, Sociology, and a varied number of other day courses, at the local College of Further Education. The idea was to prepare him for employment.

Clive had jumped at the chance that had been offered to him, and hoped that it would lead to something worthwhile. The course lasted for twelve months, and during this time, Clive took advantage of everything that was available to him. He attended one-day courses on a wide variety of subjects, which included First Aid training, and care work.

Towards the end of the course, Clive considered where his future would lie, and he was determined to make the best use of any chances that came his way. One day, he noticed that there was a vacancy at Woodley Hospital, for a mini-bus driver. The word hospital appealed to him, and he decided that there was no time to waste, and he should apply immediately.

Clive decided that he should present his best possible image, if he was to stand any chance of being successful at the interview, which was conducted by Charge Nurse, Jeffrey O'Donovan.

"Why have you applied for this position?" Mr O'Donovan asked him.

Clive thought about this for a moment, and decided to play it safe, and present the best possible answer. Simply to say that he had been unemployed for two years, and he needed a job, was not the most enduring answer.

"Well, Mr O'Donovan," he began. "I love everything about hospital life. I always wanted to become a nurse, but I lack the necessary entry qualifications."

"So you think that driving a mini-bus will fill that gap?"

Clive thought about this question and once again he decided to play it safe with his answer. "I realise that it's hardly nursing, but I would still feel that I would be an important part of the team, after all driving patients around is still a vital part of the care regime."

"Mm, that's a good answer, Mr Roberts," replied Mr O'Donovan. "But, you wouldn't only drive patients around, although that would be part of the post. The job would also involve ferrying staff as well. For example, taking night staff home after their shift, and collecting the day staff. As you are aware, this hospital is hardly on a main bus route, it's very rural. Many of the staff members don't own a car, or even drive, in some cases."

Mr O'Donovan was lost in thought for a moment. "I'm sure that you would be very good at the job Mr Roberts. However, I can see that you have a caring nature. How would you like to become an auxiliary nurse here, there is a vacancy at present, as it happens?"

Clive's mouth dropped. He could hardly believe it. An auxiliary nurse, surely it would be the next best thing to being a qualified one.

"Thank you, Mr O'Donovan, I'd welcome the opportunity," Clive stuttered.

"Right, Mr Roberts. You'll be working on the Acute Psychiatric Admission Ward. Patients who are diagnosed with the more serious illnesses, such as Schizophrenia, and Bi-Polar disorder, for example are placed there. How do you feel about that?"

"I'd welcome the chance," Clive replied. "Thank you for giving me the opportunity, Mr O'Donovan."

Clive started the following Monday, and underwent an induction period, which lasted for one week, which he enjoyed very much.

He was sitting in Sister Beth Warner's office at the present time, on Ward Two. Sister Beth was a large, imposing woman, and many of the staff were wary, and feared her. This was particularly true of the kitchen staff. At mealtimes, the kitchen porters would open the ward doors, and swiftly push the meal trolley in, disappearing in a flash. However, as regards the staff on her own ward, she was an excellent boss, and would support them to the hilt, if ever there was a problem.

Sister Beth was very impressed with Clive. She considered that he was so caring, and the patients on the ward warmed to him, he was just what the ward needed. Whenever a new patient was admitted onto the ward, she would place them in Clive's care for a couple of hours. This would give him the opportunity to glean any information from them, which would appear less formal for the patient, as he would chat to them in a friendly manner. He would then discuss this information with Sister Beth afterwards. He had the skill of gaining a person's confidence, and soothing their anxiety. Sam would soon be his next challenge.

CHAPTER FIFTY-THREE

Father Fenwick had received a telephone call from Bishop Larkin. "I wonder if I could visit you Father Fenwick? I wish to discuss a matter with you of some urgency," he had told him. Father Fenwick had no choice, he couldn't refuse the bishop. He wondered what it may be about. It must be important for Bishop Larkin to visit him in *New Pastures*. Normally he would be summoned to his plush office, in Chester.

Bishop Larkin arrived at three in the afternoon. Father Fenwick peered out of his window, as his car parked outside. He greeted him warmly at the front door, and invited him inside. It would be the first time that he had visited the presbytery. Father Fenwick invited the bishop into the kitchen. He had hurriedly been tidying up, not that the place was in a mess, but it wasn't every day that he would have a visit from a bishop.

After Father Fenwick had made a pot of tea, and placed some chocolate digestive biscuits on a plate, Bishop Larkin cleared his throat and began to speak. "I wish to speak to you about a rather delicate matter, Father," he began. "I have been in dialogue with Bishop Harris. As you are aware, he is the presiding bishop over the Warrington Diocese."

Father Fenwick was becoming a little concerned now. He had a feeling what Bishop Larkin was about to tell him.

"Bishop Harris has informed me that Father Jameson should be removed from his post at St Matthew's. Of course, this will leave us in an awkward position. It would mean that you would have to fill the gap, as you did before, until a replacement could be found."

"Oh, I see," said Father Fenwick. "May I ask why should Father Jameson be removed? I have found him to be an admirable priest, and the parishioners love him. Indeed, Father Frederick is very impressed with the way that he has taken over the running of St Matthew's."

Bishop Larkin coughed nervously. "I'd rather not divulge the reason Father. It is rather a delicate matter," he said.

"If I may interject Bishop, I think that I may be aware of this concern."

"What, I hardly think so, Father, how could you know what this is about?"

"Well, I think, at least, that I should be made aware of any reason why you decide that Father Jameson should be dismissed from the parish. I may be able to assist with the situation."

Father Fenwick realised that the concern in question was most probably about Father Jameson's dressing up as Rita routine. However, he felt that he was on shaky ground, and it was obvious that Bishop Larkin had no idea that he was aware of it, and would be very angry if he knew that he was. He decided that he would speak to Father Jameson first, to verify that this was the reason of the visit. He would then be in a position to offer support if it was needed. If he told Bishop Larkin now that he was aware of the issue, and he was wrong, it would place Father Jameson in an awkward position.

That settled, Bishop Larkin prepared to leave.

"I'll keep you informed about the situation, Father Fenwick," he said. "I noticed that the school and chapel building is progressing very well. They are on target, and the opening and consecration of the chapel should be complete in about six months' time. Your objective will have then been achieved. I'll be in touch, good afternoon, Father Fenwick."

Father Fenwick thought about Bishop Larkin's closing statement for a moment, after he'd gone, regarding his 'objective.' He had a worrying feeling that he would be moved on as soon as the parish was up and running, just as Father Frederick had told him was likely to happen. He quickly changed into his running gear, and went out for a run. This was always his way of relieving his tension and anxiety. Then he would ring Father Jameson and discuss this major issue.

*

Father Jameson sounded tense as he answered the phone. Father Fenwick gathered the reason why.

"Hi, Daniel," he said. "How are you doing?"

Father Fenwick thought that he would give Father Jameson a bit of breathing space, rather than diving in too soon.

"Have you heard the news?" Bishop Harris saw me dressed up as Rita, and he went mad. He told me that the church would take a dim view of it. He told me that I will have to move away from St Matthew's, and be sent to some parish in the middle of nowhere."

"Well, Daniel," Father Fenwick began. "I've had a visit from Bishop Larkin. He told me that you'll have to move, and I may have to step in again to fill the gap."

"Did he give you a reason?" asked Father Jameson.

"No, he was very professional about it, and retained your confidentiality."

"Very good of him," said Father Jameson sharply. "What do you think about the situation?"

"I'm not happy about it, in fact I think that it's a disgrace, it's pandering to the Vatican hierarchy. It shouldn't matter what a priest does in his free time, as long as it's legal of course. What you are doing in no way compromises your duty as a priest. In fact, I don't think that the parishioners would give two hoots."

"I wish that I shared your optimism James," said Father Jameson. "You didn't mention that you knew about it then?"

"No, I wanted to be sure that that was the reason for the bishop's visit. But, I will speak out on your behalf, if you wish."

"It wouldn't be a good idea James. Why blot your own copy book on my account?"

"My copy book has got more than a few blots on it already, Daniel. Another one won't matter. I can't stand by while a good priest, and a friend is hung out to dry."

"That's very commendable of you James. I'll leave that to your own judgement, if you think that it will do any good, I'm happy about it."

"Whether it will do any good or not, is not the question. It's more about loyalty and decency to a good friend."

Father Fenwick rung off, and decided how he would approach his phone call to Bishop Larkin, and what his answer would be. He was soon to find out.

*

"What, you knew about it?" Bishop Larkin shouted down the phone.

"Yes, I was aware of it Bishop Larkin. I came upon Father Jameson one day when I visited St Matthew's."

"And you decided to keep this to yourself, did you not?" Replied an angry Bishop Larkin.

"I did. After Father Jameson had explained the reason why he dresses up in a woman's clothes, I sympathised with him about it. I don't think that he is doing any harm actually."

"I see." Another sharp exclamation from Bishop Larkin. "Would you care to explain to me?"

"Yes, I would Bishop Larkin. But I would rather that we had a meeting about it, with Bishop Harris, and Father Jameson present. I don't think it would be good policy to discuss it over the phone."

"Mm," grunted Bishop Larkin. I'll have to contact Bishop Harris, and see if he's interested in making himself available."

Father Fenwick left Bishop Larkin to arrange the meeting. Bishop Harris has got to be interested, he thought, it's his duty, as Father Jameson's bishop, and a human being.

CHAPTER FIFTY-FOUR

Clive was aware of a loud grunting sound, which was emanating from the female unit, on Ward 2. That'll be Barbara, he thought to himself. Barbara was a fifty-five-year-old woman, who was suffering from Schizophrenia. She very often used to shout out in a loud voice, and sometimes, like now, she grunted like a wild bear. She had been a patient on Ward 2 for a couple of years. She was one of the patients who would be considered as at risk in the community, and so she would remain on the ward, until a secure placement could be located for her elsewhere.

Barbara was very keen on knitting, and she would sit for hours, completely absorbed in it. Clive wasn't sure what she was knitting, possibly jumpers, or baby clothes. Whatever it was, it kept her occupied, unlike many of the other patients, who would constantly amble up and down the ward, or just sit staring out of the window.

Barbara was quite a character, and Clive was very fond of her. He remembered one particular day, her brother, who also suffered with Schizophrenia, visited her. He came up on his motorbike, and asked Barbara if she would like to go for a spin. Barbara didn't need to be asked twice. She got on the back of the motorbike, and with a loud scream, like a Banshee, they roared off. Neither of them wore crash helmets. Clive knew better than to attempt to stop them. The ward staff were aware of her comings and goings, as it was a regular occurrence. She always came back safely. The objective of Ward 2 was not to keep patients locked away, as if they were living in an institution, but to assist them to live as normal a life as possible, until such a time when it was deemed safe for discharge.

Ward 2 was an assessment ward, where patients were assessed by a consultant psychiatrist. It was meant to be short term. However, care in a community setting was not an option for some patients, and Barbara was one of those patients, she was long term on the ward, and she felt quite at home there.

"What's all this noise about Barbara?" asked Clive.

"Oh, I felt a bit bored, and thought that I'd make a bit of noise," was her answer.

"That's no problem," was Clive's reply. "You know that when I'm on duty, you can always talk to me, if you feel a bit out of it, that's what I'm here for."

"You're a very caring person, Clive," she said.

"Well I do try, so remember, I'm here for you all." Barbara gave Clive a broad smile, and carried on with her knitting, with a much quieter grunt.

Ray was another interesting patient. He was seventy-six years of age. He had a past life of alcohol abuse, and dependency on prescription drugs. His family had disowned him. He once told Clive that he hadn't seen his family for years.

"You know Clive," he had told him. "I've walked along in the past, with a bottle of whisky in one hand, and a bottle of paracetamol in the other."

Clive felt very sad when he heard this.

"That's one hell of a night out, Ray," he said making light of it.

Clive knew when to make light of any remark that he might hear. Ray would see the funny side. But, knowledge was needed. On one occasion Clive had cracked a joke to another patient, who immediately grabbed him by the tie, nearly throttling him.

"When I want a funny man, I'll ask for one," he had growled. Clive never forgot that experience.

Ray was another of his favourites, just like Barbara. He didn't have a violent bone in his body, a lovely man, and this is how he ended up. Clive very often went home after his twelve-hour shift, and thought long and hard about such patients.

Many of the patients wouldn't open up to the psychiatrist, or the nursing staff. They would consider them as the enemy within. So Clive was allowed to take a few patients out into the woods. Sometimes they would be out for several hours. As one male patient once said to Clive. "This is better than all your drugs." This made Clive feel good about himself. He wasn't a trained nurse, but he could interact well with many of them, and then pass the information onto Sister Beth, and Dr Morrell, the consultant psychiatrist. This made Clive feel more important, needed, as he had hitherto held little confidence towards his ability, and nothing much had gone right in his life. He hadn't even had success with girlfriends, and was still single as a result.

Sam was his latest patient. Clive thought that he wasn't totally unlike Ray. He had lost touch with his family, through the passing of his wife, and then his children disowning him.

Sam was engaging well with his medication. Initially, he had been uncooperative, and he was living in a trance like state. Chlorpromazine had been prescribed by Dr Morrell. This had a positive effect on Sam, and had reduced his delusions. When questioned, he had told Dr Morrell about his past life, as a musician, his Cannabis addiction, and his part in the robbery. He had thought that Frank was out to get him, and this had become an obsession.

Dr Morrell had come to the conclusion that this event, coupled with his addiction to Cannabis had produced a traumatic effect on his perception of life.

Sam was later to discover, through his sessions with Dr Morrell, that Frank had been 'banged up' for the last six months. He couldn't possibly have contacted Sam. The phone calls were all part of his psychotic state of mind. When Sam had been given this information, the effect on him was amazing. He began to return to reality. He felt like a new man.

Dr Morrell was pleased with his progress, and told Sam that he could be discharged in a week or two, as long as he maintained his medication regime, and continued to be in a stable condition.

"That's great news Sam," Clive had told him. "You'll be able to pick up the pieces of your life again." Sam felt much better than he had in a long time when he had been told this news.

Clive asked him if he would like to go out for one of his forest walks to celebrate the good news. After checking with Sister Beth, to ensure that it was ok, they both set off. They breathed in the fresh forest air, it felt so good. Clive had always considered that this was not like work, he enjoyed every minute of it. The only downside was that he would miss Sam when he had been discharged, as he had got so attached to him. This was the same as many other patients who he helped to care for.

Unfortunately, Ray would be a long-term patient. Dr Morrell considered that he would be at risk if he returned to the community. Ray didn't mind one little bit. He found that institutional life suited him. He felt safe on the ward. On the other hand Sam couldn't wait to get back home. Father Fenwick paid him a visit, accompanied by Bob. The three of them talked for a couple of hours, and Father Fenwick made arrangements to take Sam home when the time came for his discharge. To a more peaceful, settled life, that was free of the ghost of Frank.

CHAPTER FIFTY-FIVE

Father Fenwick was on his way to St Matthew's for the meeting. Bishop Larkin had advised him that the meeting that he had requested had been arranged for that afternoon. Bishop Harris had considered the proposition carefully, and felt that he had no option. As far as he was concerned, he wished to get the 'unsavoury' business over as soon as possible. Father Jameson, in his opinion, had crossed the line that was expected of him as a Roman Catholic priest. He felt that if the news that Father Jameson dressed in women's clothes was made public, the church would be a laughing stock.

As far as Father Fenwick was concerned, he was determined to clear the situation up in Father Jameson's favour. He hadn't done anything wrong in his mind, and he wished to clear his name if he could. If it went against Father Jameson, he was willing to resign from the priesthood.

When he arrived at the presbytery, the three men were sitting around the table. Father Jameson looked anxious. Bishop Harris was looking grim, with Bishop Larkin slightly less so.

Bishop Harris looked up as Father Fenwick was ushered in.

"Good afternoon, Father Fenwick," he said with a sour note to his tone. "Shall we begin? I'm very busy today, and can't spare much time."

Father Fenwick felt quite angry at the bishop's remark. This was a serious issue, and it could lead to a good man, and priest being made a scapegoat. He was certain that there had been much worse conduct by Catholic priests. There had been many scandals in the news about child abuse, involving Catholic priests, and the church had always attempted to cover these cases up. Priests hadn't been 'defrocked', but had simply disappeared into the 'woodwork', to some obscure diocese, out of range of the flack that it would have caused. Father Jameson simply dressed up in Rita's clothing, in memory of his deceased sister. It was a sad situation, unusual to say the least, but he couldn't see any harm in it. It was his way of coping.

Bishop Harris spoke first. "Well, Father Jameson, would you like to explain yourself?"

"I don't think that I've anything to explain," Father Jameson said in reply.

Bishop Harris coloured slightly at this remark. Father Fenwick was also taken aback by Father Jameson's attitude. He wasn't endearing himself to Bishop Harris, but was more likely falling on his sword.

The room went quiet for a short time, while Bishop Harris struggled to contain himself.

Father Fenwick felt extremely uncomfortable, and he felt that he should say something. "I think..." he began.

"Silence," boomed Bishop Harris. "Enough."

Father Fenwick shrank back, at the severity of Bishop Harris's outburst.

"I certainly do think that an explanation is needed Father Jameson," Bishop Harris said in a slightly less severe tone.

Father Jameson thought about the situation for a moment, and he regretted his blunt reply. It was necessary to explain himself, he couldn't leave things as they were at the present time. He hadn't done anything wrong in his estimation, but he still needed to put his case forward. Furthermore, Father Fenwick had been good enough to attend the meeting and support him. He could be putting his own reputation on the line. He was willing to do this for him, so his cavalier attitude to Bishop Harris looked as if he wasn't grateful for his support.

"I'm sorry," he said. "I would like to apologise for my attitude, and an explanation is necessary. The reason that I dress up in female clothing, is not because I'm perverted in any way, or do it for kicks, or anything like that. Not that transvestites are necessarily perverted, in my opinion, they may have their reasons also. But, my sister died recently. We were very close. Her name was Rita. I struggled to cope at first, but I found a way of keeping her memory alive, by dressing up in her clothes. I understand that it may seem a strange way of remembering her, but it's my way. When Father Fenwick discovered my secret, he felt as you do now. But, when I explained the reason for it, he was sympathetic, and offered to support me."

"Mm," replied Bishop Harris. He suddenly felt a pang of guilt about the way he was treating Father Jameson. He was reminded of his own past, he was hardly squeaky clean. As a young priest of twenty-seven years of age, he had an affair with a married woman. Her name was Josephine, and she was thirty-six. She was a regular at mass each Sunday. She always took communion, and the young Father Harris couldn't fail to notice how attractive she was. One day he got talking to her after mass.

That was the beginning of the relationship. Josephine was lonely. Her husband didn't take any notice of her any more, and he had had several affairs. She warmed to Father Harris, he was everything that her husband was not, young and handsome. Father Harris ignored the fact that he was a priest, and was supposed to observe strict celibacy. They had a sexual relationship, which lasted several months.

As a result of their affair, Josephine became pregnant. Her husband never found out who the father was, and divorce was the result.

Josephine vowed to keep her secret, and young Father Harris kept his guilty secret also.

Bishop Harris suddenly leapt out of his past. He certainly wouldn't want that skeleton coming out of his cupboard. How could he penalise Father Jameson after what he'd done? All Father Jameson had done, was dress up in a woman's clothes.

"I thank you for your honesty, and accept your explanation, even if we did have to go around the houses somewhat. I can understand that it must have been very difficult for you to 'come out of the closet,' so to speak. I also commend Father Fenwick, for his Christian support, and his observing of your privacy. Under the circumstances, I suppose that we could overlook it. I realise how difficult it has been for you, but I would ask if you can possibly find another way to remember your sister, by a more conventional method. I am deeply sorry for your loss. If only you could have approached me, or Bishop Larkin, we could have offered you some counselling and support. After all, the church is not a completely harsh institution."

Father Jameson was deep in thought for a few moments. "Thank you for your understanding, but I don't think that you should concern yourself Bishop Harris, it won't happen again."

"That's good. If we can be of any help to you, we will always be here, and Father Fenwick, of course." Said Bishop Harris, much more empathetic now.

"Thank you," Father Jameson said. "I feel such a fool now."

"Nothing of the sort, Father Jameson," replied Bishop Larkin. "We are only sorry that you felt that you couldn't approach us earlier."

"So I can remain at St Matthew's?"

"Of course, if you wish to do so," said Bishops Larkin and Harris, in unison.

Father Jameson breathed a deep sigh of relief when both bishops had gone. "I feel like a gay man who's just come out," he said to Father Fenwick. "I feel much better for it now." He looked at Father Fenwick, and said. "I think that it's time to let Rita go now, to put her to rest, James."

Father Fenwick smiled, and patted him on the back. "We'll both say a mass for her, Daniel."

CHAPTER FIFTY-SIX

John was in an extremely good mood. He was back at work, which was like winning the pools for him. He'd enjoyed celebrating Christmas with his family, and welcoming in a new, better year. As he shovelled a load of sand and aggregate into the mixer, Bill shouted over to him. "So you had a good Christmas then John?"

"I did Bill, spent it with the family. They want to move over here and live with me. I've approached the council, and the local school. St Edward's could take all three of them."

"But you're Catholic, aren't you John, St Edward's is Church of England isn't it?"

"That's right," John replied. "But under the circumstances, it doesn't really matter much. The kids could transfer to this Catholic school when it's finished."

Bill laughed. "Well, we'd better get a move on then, hadn't we? Keep that mix going." John did just that, heaving another load of sand into the mixer.

*

John may have been happy, but Steve, on the other hand, certainly was not. Jen had been getting progressively worse. Her level of mobility, although much reduced, had now reached the level where she could barely stand. This had a severe effect on Steve's level of anxiety.

He now found it an impossible task to get Jen into the wheelchair unaided.

When it was first delivered, Jen could stand with the help of a Zimmer frame for support. Steve would take her out of the house for fresh air, and much needed exercise for himself. He would take her through the woods, and visit his '*Magic Pond.*' He found these little excursions very therapeutic for himself and Jen. Just to breathe in the fresh air, and be amongst the wildlife, helped Steve to relive the things that they used to do years ago.

Now, he felt almost like a prisoner in his own home. Carers would come in four times a day, but these calls were always cut short. The carers would complete the basic tasks and then would disappear, as suddenly as they had arrived. Steve was aware that care agencies placed a great deal of work onto their carers, and so they felt the need to complete their tasks in the shortest time as possible. One carer explained to him that they weren't paid travelling time. They were only paid for the time that they spent with clients. So if they had a twenty-minute journey to the next client, they would need to reduce the time that they would spend with the previous one.

This can't be right, Steve thought to himself. The service was geared to the requirements of the agency, and not for the clients. This made Steve feel very angry, and he would very often fly into fits of temper, and would lash out. He would never aim any aggression towards Jen of course, he would never harm her, although he did get impatient with her at times. The target of his temper would often be aimed at the furniture. On one occasion, he kicked the sofa so hard that he tumbled to the floor, it was as if the sofa had given him a backlash, and fought back.

He lay there for a few moments, feeling quite anxious. Then he got up, pulled himself together, and laughed at his behaviour. Rant over.

Steve was made aware that quite soon he may need to make a difficult decision. Whether to let Jen remain at home, leaving him to struggle on. On the other hand, there was the question of residential care. The latter choice was not the one that Steve wished to take, but possibly one that he felt that he must consider in the future. If Jen was in a residential home, she would receive the best possible care. She would have companionship also, whereas she only had Steve for company at the present time. He decided to ask Brenda to visit him, to discuss the implications. Finance was not a concern. Their capital was below the threshold that was allowed by the council, and they didn't own their own home. A means test would be completed, to establish how much would need to be paid towards the care, however.

Although, as far as Steve was concerned, he would pay any amount that was necessary if Jen received the care that she so richly deserved.

He rang the Social Services number, and went through the usual list of selections, press this to go there, or that to go somewhere else. When he eventually got through to the correct department, he was informed that Brenda was on holiday for two weeks. However, Linda would arrange to call in her place. Steve grimaced a bit when he was told this, because he thought that Linda was a bit severe, he remembered her from the last time she visited with Brenda. An appointment was made for two days' time, so Steve held his breath. No need to get anxious now, as he had two days to prepare for the visit.

*

The time soon passed, and on the day in question Steve heard a loud honking of a car horn. He peered out of the window anxiously, and was just in time to witness Linda narrowly failing to take his neighbour's wing mirror off as she swerved into the car park. There was a brief exchange of loud voices, Linda's, as usual boomed out the loudest.

"Get a life," she shouted, as a fist was shaken at her furiously out of the other car window. Steve gritted his teeth, in anticipation of the visit. How did she ever pass her driving test, he thought to himself?

"Hello again, Mr Farrell." Linda boomed as she was ushered inside by Steve. "How are you today?"

"Well," Steve began, shakily. "I've not been too good lately. I don't think that I'm coping very well looking after Jen."

"Nonsense," replied Linda, in a reassuring voice. "You've managed to keep her out of one of those money-making care homes so far. This was one of Linda's remarks that was supposed to reassure the clients. It wasn't very reassuring to Steve at the present time, however. Linda had made it known more than once about her feelings regarding private care. She was one of the 'Old School.' She was passionate about care being provided by the state, which would have happened widely before the NHS and Community Care Act came into being. As far as Linda was concerned, she followed the ideology of William Beveridge, when he had stated that the state had a duty to bring an individual back to health, above all else.

She had crossed swords with many care home managers on this point. She would say that she had seen too many care home owners become rich at the expense of clients in their care homes. However, this was strictly Linda's personal view, and was open to argument. Linda loved a good argument, and would always take the opportunity to be involved in one.

"Well then, Mr Farrell, let's see how we can help you." As she said this, there was a loud knocking at Steve's front door.

Steve opened it, wondering who it could be, as he wasn't expecting anyone else to call. Mr Roberts, Steve's next-door neighbour was standing there, with a face as red as a beetroot.

"Hello, Dave," Steve said meekly.

"I'd like to have a word with that woman, who almost crashed into my car. She was on the wrong side of the road," Mr Roberts spluttered, stumbling over his words.

Mr Roberts was a rather small man. Normally, he was very calm, but now he was having one of his 'funny turns,' which he did get on a regular basis, when someone upset him.

He heard loud footsteps coming to the door, and was suddenly faced with Linda, who looked menacing, as usual, in her tweed attire, and heavy brogue shoes.

"Yes," she shouted. "Have you got a complaint?"

"Er..." Mr Roberts appeared to have suddenly calmed down, the wind having been taken out of his sails, when faced with Linda. He stuttered to get his words out. "Well..." he began. "You almost crashed into my car earlier."

"Well, almost, but I didn't," Linda spat the words out. "It was only nearly, so what are you complaining about?"

"Um..." Poor Mr Roberts was made speechless, by Linda's attack, he could offer no answer. He turned rather swiftly, and walked back to his front door, without a further word, muttering to himself as he went.

"Now where were we?" asked Linda, completely unaffected by the proceedings, as she shut the door with her usual bang. Steve gulped, and decided that he would have to apologise to Mr Roberts later. This episode had done nothing to quell his anxiety.

CHAPTER FIFTY-SEVEN

"It sounds like a good idea, James," said Father Jameson, when Father Fenwick had suggested that he join him for a walk in the Yorkshire Dales. He wasn't a strong walker, but the idea of raising some funds for a window in the church did appeal to him. He also thought that it would be a good idea for both of them to get away for a few days break. *The Three Peaks* walk did appeal to him, but twenty odd miles, he felt tired just thinking about it.

The chance to get away, and have a few nights in the pub appealed to him more though. He was still reeling following his meeting with Bishop Harris and Bishop Larkin, a few days earlier. He definitely needed a break, and a few nights drinking some good Yorkshire ale definitely appealed to him. He relished the opportunity of stepping out of his priestly role for a short time also.

"That sounds great James," he said enthusiastically. "When were you thinking of going?"

"How about a week on Wednesday, Daniel? Obviously, we can't go at the weekend. We could travel up on Wednesday, have a few pints in the pub, do the walk on the Thursday; another few pints in the pub Thursday night, to celebrate our achievement, and come back on Friday, job done. What do you think?"

"Sounds good," replied Father Jameson, although he felt doubtful about his ability of finishing the walk. "I'll tell Mrs Davies that I'll be away for a few days, I'm sure she can hold the fort while I'm away. We'll go in my car, shall I pick you up at ten, we can have a leisurely drive up. Where are we staying by the way?"

"I thought that we'd stay in a guest house, within about a twenty-minute drive from Horton in Ribblesdale, where we start the walk. I'll check up and see if I can book one. I'll announce it at Sunday mass. I'm sure that the parishioners will be generous when I tell them what it's for."

"OK, I'll leave you to make the arrangements, James," replied Father Jameson pensively. He had a feeling about this venture, what could possibly go wrong?

*

Father Fenwick consulted his map of *The Three Peaks* area and then googled guest houses in the vicinity. His initial search yielded no results, they were all booked up. One or two even told him that they were open for families only, not for single young men on their own.

Obviously, they had had bad experiences in the past. On the fifth call, he got lucky. '*Fellside View*,' sounded ideal. Just two miles outside Hawes, about ten minute drive to Horton.

"Hello, *Fellside View*," came the response, "how may I help you?"

"Oh, hello," replied Father Fenwick. "Have you got a double room available for two nights, a week on Wednesday please?"

"Let me see," came the reply. Father Fenwick could hear the sound of rustling as the proprietor turned the pages of her diary.

"Yes, I have those two nights free. What's the name please?"

"Mr Fenwick and Mr Jameson," Father Fenwick replied. He decided to use the titles Mr and not Father, just in case.

"Right, that's booked for you. My name is Mrs Jollie, with an ie, not a y. It's eighty pounds a night each, but I make sure that you get a proper Yorkshire breakfast. Are you coming for the walking?"

"Yes, we're planning to walk *The Three Peaks*, hopefully," replied Father Fenwick.

"Well, I hope the weather keeps for you, it can get very wet up here at this time of year.

Only last week, one of my clients went up to his knees in a bog."

"Well I hope that doesn't happen to us," Father Fenwick thought to himself, Father Jameson wouldn't like that.

*

Mrs Jollie looked anything but jolly, as she opened the door. She presented as a rather stout woman. Her hair was pulled back in a bun, rather severe looking, Father Fenwick thought. She was wearing an apron, and by the look of the amount of flour on her hands, it looked as if she was doing some baking; altogether, she didn't look in a good mood.

"Ah, Mr Fenwick and Mr Jameson," she said, sternly.

"That's right," replied Father Fenwick. "Good afternoon to you."

Both he and Father Jameson were ushered inside, humping large rucksacks over their shoulders. The guest house was at the end of a block of houses, with excellent views of the fells to the rear. It was constructed of stonework that was typical of Yorkshire and Cumbria, very solid looking. The inside looked quite gloomy, as they entered the hallway. There was a desk by the entrance with a large diary on it, behind which was hung a huge mirror. There was also a shelf containing leaflets of local attractions. "If you'd like to sign in, I'll show you to your room," advised Mrs Jollie.

Father Fenwick couldn't help noticing a notice, entitled, 'Rules of the House' on the wall. He grimaced as he read what was written on it. When he reached the last three lines, he was particularly concerned. No swearing, no raucous behaviour, consumption of alcohol is not encouraged in this house.

Mrs Jollie noticed him reading the rules and grunted. "I've had a few rough un's here. Coming in late at night as drunk as skunks. I like to think that I keep a Godly house here, I encourage daily reading of the Bible, and strong drink gets in the way of that, Teetotalism is the only way, keeps a clear mind for the service of the Lord."

"Exactly," replied Father Fenwick, rather sheepishly, as Father Jameson covered his mouth, to stifle a snort, as he struggled to contain his amusement. If only she knew that they were both Catholic priests. They'd have to be careful to make no noise when they came in from the pub though, no schoolboy behaviour in this establishment.

Mrs Jollie showed them to their room. It was quite a comfortable looking room, but basic. Twin beds, each with a bedside cabinet and reading light. A built-in wardrobe, which would be well large enough for their clothes, not that they had much with them, just walking attire, and a change for the evenings. On each bedside table, there was the usual Gideon Bible.

Father Jameson smiled and said. "I don't think we'll be bothering with that, not exactly good bedtime reading."

Father Fenwick laughed and said. "Don't let Mrs Jollie hear you say that."

*

After a hearty meal of fish and chips that evening, complete with the usual mushy peas, washed down with two pints of *Black Sheep Ale*, Father Fenwick got his map out and laid it on the table.

"Here's where we'll start, Daniel. It's a short drive to Horton, we'll park there, past the Crown Pub, and up the track to the summit of Pen-y-Ghent."

He'd decided that it wouldn't be wise to attempt the whole Three Peaks walk now, due to the time of year, coupled with the possibility of bad weather, also Father Jameson's lack of experience, and stamina could create a problem. Mrs Jollie's words echoed in his mind. To complete the whole walk in the normal time of twelve hours would be a push, the days were still rather short. Father Jameson was not a seasoned walker, and they could be stranded in the dark, Father Jameson breathed a sigh of relief at this news.

"We'll walk from Horton, up over Pen-y-Ghent, and then over to Ribbleshead, then we can walk back to Horton along the road. What do you think?" Father Jameson agreed with this change of plan, although he wasn't sure what he was agreeing to.

"I'm sure that our 'benefactors' won't mind if we take the short-cut, they'll be happy to contribute to the cause. We'll take photographs to prove that we've actually been here," said Father Fenwick.

"Does that include a photo of Mrs Jollie?" asked Father Jameson laughing.

"Heaven's no, I value my camera lens," replied Father Fenwick.

*

The next morning both priests rose at seven thirty, for breakfast at eight, "I'm famished," declared Father Jameson. "That *Black Sheep Ale* certainly hits the spot."

"It sure does," Father Fenwick replied.

The dining room was a small affair, containing one large dining table, six chairs and a large dresser. There was the usual array of jams and marmalade, and pots of tea and coffee. The aroma of bacon and eggs cooking was a very welcoming sign. They were not disappointed. As Mrs Jollie had told them, the breakfast was fit for a king.

"The weather looks a bit rough today," she said, as she placed their breakfasts on the table. "Well, it's just as well that we've reduced our walk today then, we're not doing *The Three Peaks* now, my friend is not a regular walker, and it's rather a long way. I wouldn't want to get into difficulties."

"Very wise," replied Mrs Jollie. "There's too many people getting lost on the fells, and they have to rely on the volunteer mountain rescuers to bring them down, anyway, have a nice walk."

"We certainly will," they both replied.

*

That evening, the two priests were sat in the pub, after a hearty meal and two pints down, two to go. Father Jameson was struggling to sit comfortably, and kept wriggling from side to side.

"The walk went well, we didn't fall into any bogs," said Father Fenwick. He advised his friend that they had walked about twelve miles.

"Oh, is that all? It feels like I've done about fifty," groaned Father Jameson. "I feel like I've been battered by a baseball bat, I can hardly stand up."

"You'll soon recover," Father Fenwick told him sympathetically. "You've done very well. Now let's have another two pints, or maybe three. Then back home tomorrow."

But, before then, they had to risk the wrath of Mrs Jollie when they got back to '*Fellside View*.' They would be walking on eggshells.

Apart from the glare of disapproval from Mrs Jollie when the two priests got back to the guest house, there was no problem.

"We'll bid you goodnight Mrs Jollie," they said, and staggered upstairs.

"There's a Bible for each of you both in your room," she said. "But, I don't suppose that you're in a fit state to read it, with the drink in you."

*

They both laughed during the drive back home.

"She wasn't a bad old stick really," said Father Jameson, as Father Fenwick chuckled to himself. He suddenly became more serious. "I hope Steve's ok, he's been very stressed lately about Jen. He had the social worker out the other day, I think he's considering putting her into a home."

"That will be sad," replied Father Jameson. "I understand how difficult it is caring for a loved one with Dementia."

"Yes it is, Daniel. But it's not solely the caring. It's heart-breaking seeing them deteriorating day by day. I'll pay him a visit tomorrow and see how he is. I realise that we are not experts, and can't make decisions, but, we can offer as much support as possible. Nothing's impossible though. John Byrne for example. With support from us, he has turned his life around. There's Sam as well, I think that he's coming out of hospital in a few days, he'll need good friends around him."

"Yes, isn't that the musician chap?" asked Father Jameson.

"He is, and a good one at that. He used to play in a band. I'm thinking of asking him if he'd like to be our church organist."

"That will be a good idea, James, and it will be beneficial for his mental health."

"I think so too. I'll discuss it with him when I collect him from the hospital." He chewed on this thought as the car ate up the miles.

CHAPTER FIFTY-EIGHT

Following Linda's visit a few days earlier, Steve had been deep in thought, he had to make the most important decision of his life. As far as Linda was concerned, she was adamant that Jen could be kept at home, with ongoing support.

"It's her right," Linda had told him sternly. "To take someone out of their home goes against all of my principles as a social worker. You can see how her care is handled in your own home. In a care home, you don't know what goes on behind closed doors."

"I think that I understand what you're saying," replied Steve meekly. "But, seeing her every day getting worse is terribly distressing for me."

"Yes, I can certainly understand that Mr Farrell, it's the worst thing possible to witness what this terrible disease does to people. It has got to be your decision, I can only guide you. If you do decide to place her in a home, and it doesn't work out, you can have her back home again."

So Steve had finally made the difficult decision to have Jen placed in a care home. She had received a temporary placement in *Happy Days* a while ago, but Steve considered that it was too far for him to visit. He didn't drive, so he would need to rely on somebody else to take him on visits, and these needed to be on a regular basis, he couldn't survive for long without seeing his beloved Jen. Linda advised him that Brenda would locate a suitable place where she could go. Steve didn't feel too confident in himself that one could be found, after listening to Linda's negative perspective.

Father Fenwick paid Steve a visit, a short time later, when he returned from his trek in deepest Yorkshire, with Father Jameson. He assured Steve that he would provide him with as much support as possible. This would include taking him to see Jen several times a week, so there was no problem with transport, as he still had the use of the car from his old parish at St Matthew's.

Following further discussion with Linda, who assured him that there was a current vacancy in *Happy Days,* Steve decided that this was the best place possible for Jen, and he made a decision. As Jen had been there before, he was aware that the care was excellent, and he had no concerns. Linda arranged this without delay, in Brenda's absence, in case the vacancy was lost, and Jen was transferred three days later.

"I feel so guilty," Steve had told Father Fenwick. Who assured him that he had supported Jen for as long as was possible, he had done a good job, and now was the time to step back. There was no doubt that Jen would receive the best level of care that could be provided.

Furthermore, Steve would still be in her life, and could enjoy a lifestyle of his own, that had been bereft of him for so long.

CHAPTER FIFTY-NINE

The day had started much the same as usual on Ward 2. Patients constantly walking up and down the corridor, to the accompaniment of a chorus of shouting in the background. Clive had commenced his twelve-hour shift at eight on this particular morning. It was the day that Sam was expected to be discharged. As usual, a ward round was to be convened at ten thirty sharp. Dr Morrell timed his appointments, and meetings to the second; the staff joked that he had a stopwatch in his pocket. Sam's discharge would depend on whether Dr Morrell was satisfied that he was ready to return to his home, and could take his place in the community, without risk. His medication would control the symptoms of his Paranoia, but the intake of this medication would need to be strictly monitored by the Community Psychiatric Nursing Team, to prevent a relapse.

Sister Beth had prepared well in advance for the ward round, as she had always done, she was so efficient; indeed, she was aware of Dr Morrell's obsession with timing, and everything else for that matter. She arranged the case notes in precise order on her desk. Sam's report was the first on the list.

"How's Mr James been sister?" Asked Dr Morrell, in his usual sharp manner, as he took his place in the same chair that he always sat in; there were several chairs in the office, but he always chose the same one. Before he sat down, he brushed imaginary dust and particles from the chair cushion. He suffered from an obsessive disorder, like many of his patients that he treated.

"There haven't been any problems," replied Sister Beth. Clive has been working with him. His mood is much better, and his Paranoia has much reduced."

"That's encouraging," replied Dr Morrell. "Clive seems to have settled in here very well, he's an asset to the ward, he should consider training."

"Yes, I'm intending to discuss it with him," advised Sister Beth.

"With support in the community, Mr James should be all right. I believe that he has a good friend in Father Fenwick."

"Yes he has," replied Sister Beth. "Father Fenwick is coming to drive him home. He's made several visits here, and the patients have really taken to him. He's more like a social worker than a Catholic priest."

"Maybe he missed his vocation," replied Dr Morrell, who had made it quite obvious in the past, that he had no time for religion of any sort; his beliefs were in the here and now. "Maybe he should think about training to be a social worker."

"Or, a nurse," added Sister Beth. "In fact, I've asked him if he'd consider becoming the ward Chaplain. The patients really like his visits. It would be good for them to talk to a clergyman, he and Clive would make a good team."

"Mm," was the reply, as Dr Morrell wiped imaginary dust from his trousers. "If you think that it's a good idea, it's ok with me; it certainly can't do any harm. Right then sister, we'll get the paperwork sorted out, and get Mr James on his way back home. One less to worry about, eh? Now who's next on the list?"

Later that day Sam packed his bag, assisted by Clive.

"I'll miss you around here," he told Sam. "I think that we've got time for the last walk in the forest, if you fancy it?"

Sam didn't need to be asked twice. They both enjoyed their walk. Sam was able to tell Clive how much better he was feeling, and was more positive about the future. He opened up about how much of a mess he considered that he had made of his life. Although, Clive reassured him that the death of his wife was on no account his own fault. Furthermore, his part in the bungled robbery was not his fault either. He was at a low ebb, very vulnerable at the time, and under pressure to give his wife the holiday that she desired.

"You know Clive," uttered Sam. "You've done more for me here than all your fancy doctors. You should train to be a qualified nurse."

This sounded very encouraging to Clive's ears. It made the job worthwhile to get praise, which was not expected in this job.

When they returned to the ward, Father Fenwick was waiting for them. Clive said his goodbye to Sam, and wished him luck for the future.

"Anytime you're around *New Pastures*, feel free to call in, I'll leave my address," said Sam. To which Clive readily agreed.

Later on that day, Father Fenwick had arranged to take Sam home to take his place in the community once again. With the help of Father Fenwick and friends, the future would be much brighter; but close monitoring would be imperative, to ensure that there was to be no relapse.

As for Clive, he was determined to return to studies and get some qualifications, which would help him to reach his ambition of becoming a qualified nurse. Sister Beth agreed that she would support him in this venture. Sam wished him all the best, and assured him, that in his opinion, he would make a fine nurse.

"Thanks, Sam," he replied. "I'm really going to work at it. Mental health nursing really interests me, rather than general nursing."

"You could do both," replied Sam. "Whichever way you choose to go, you'll be good at it." With that, he said good bye to Clive, handing him his address on a piece of notepaper.

Father Fenwick started his engine and drove Sam back home. "I'll call around later Sam," he told him. "I'll go back to the presbytery first and see if there are any messages for me."

As soon as Father Fenwick was back inside the presbytery, he noticed that the answerphone was flashing. There were three messages. The first two were from parishioners, enquiring about various matters that were connected with the church. The third message surprised him somewhat, it was from Julie Bingham.

"Hi Father," she said. "I'm sorry that I couldn't come to any of your masses. I do miss you around, and I intended to visit. Will it be all right if I call sometime?"

"Sure," Father Fenwick replied. "It will be good to see you again Julie."

He was wondering why the impending visit made him feel so excited, stirring emotions that priesthood had withheld from him for so long.

CHAPTER SIXTY

SIX MONTHS LATER

It was a warm and sunny September morning. The day had finally dawned, when the first mass was to be celebrated in the new church, the parish of St Michael. Everyone was full of expectation, and were looking forward to the proceedings. Father Fenwick could hardly believe that it was about to happen.

His mind drifted back to the day in October, the previous year, when Bishop Larkin had told him that he was going to be moved to *New Pastures*, which was a new estate, in the heart of Cheshire, to assist in the formation of a new parish. When he had heard the news at first, he had dreaded it, his heart had sunk. The expectation that he would be capable of making a success of it was far from his mind. And yet, it was now about to happen, he could hardly believe it. Not only was the church about to be consecrated and the first mass to be celebrated therein. But, he had made a new life here. His new friends were very dear to him. The thought that he may now be moved elsewhere concerned him.

He had witnessed the improvement in John's life, the family being reunited, and all happily living in *New Pastures*. The three children would be starting in the new school when the autumn term arrived.

Bob and Vera had become firm friends, and had been a great comfort to Steve, when Jen had been placed in a care home. Steve had decided that he would become a volunteer, working with those individuals who were suffering with the effects of Dementia, and their carers, who were supporting those who were dear to them. He would have the time now that Jen was in a care home. He could still visit her every couple of days, and be involved in her care.

Steve had been particularly supportive to Sam following his discharge from hospital. He was aware that he had never really recovered from his grief, following the death of his wife.

He had been led along a down trodden path, getting involved in drug addiction, and petty crime with Frank, which had led eventually to alienation from his son and daughter.

Father Fenwick had offered to provide Steve with all the support that he would need in his new venture. He suggested that the presbytery could be utilised for carer's meetings. This could provide a place where issues could be discussed in a private setting, and also present the individuals with the opportunity to allay their fears, and anxiety. Bob had also offered his support and encouragement in this venture.

Indeed, Father Fenwick remembered how supportive Bob had been to him when he had arrived at *New Pastures*, as a young, and very insecure priest, who had grave doubts about his own ability to succeed. Without Bob's support, Father Fenwick was sure that he would have struggled to carry on, and he would have failed.

It was because of all these memories, that Father Fenwick was so worried about being moved elsewhere by Bishop Larkin. The words and advice of Father Frederick echoed in his mind. His success at *New Pastures* could be replicated elsewhere. He would resist any effort to be moved though, from his new home, even if the future of his priesthood depended on it.

As he was sitting in the church, these thoughts and memories spun around in the whirlpool of his mind. He digested his surroundings. Although the church would double up as a school hall, there was a proper altar, which would be closed off when the school required its use.

Father Fenwick was particularly proud of the stained glass window that was resplendent behind the altar. The original plan had been to fit ordinary plain frosted glass, but his sponsored walk, coupled with the kind donations from all the local folk, had provided sufficient funds for this beautiful window. Steve had been particularly generous with his donation, he said that it would be what Jen would have suggested, and it would remind him of her.

In another couple of hours the church would be full to capacity. Bishop Larkin and Father Fenwick would join together to celebrate the first mass in the new church. The parish of Saint Michael was open for business.

It had a pleasant ring to Father Fenwick's ears. Following the mass, there would be a short reception to officially welcome everyone. He couldn't help feeling more nervous than he had ever been before. Today was the culmination of his work here. This had been his mission.

He had been full of doubt at the outset, but it had all worked out in the end, thanks to the support he had received. He thought of Steve, and felt sad that Jen had needed to be placed in a care home. He wasn't alone however, he had Bob, who was a pillar of strength to him. Sam and John had also become good friends.

Father Fenwick decided that he would go for a run to soothe his nerves, before the service began. He went back to the presbytery and changed into his running clothes. His T-shirt sported the logo, 'The

Three Just Men', a name that Steve had coined many months ago, when they had decided to help John in his time of need. He had thought that it was so poignant a name, and decided that it would describe the three of them perfectly, and what they hoped to achieve in the future. So when he had decided to complete his sponsored walk, the name seemed to echo his thoughts, and feelings.

Today, his run would be quite short, as he wouldn't want to appear too drained for the mass. A couple of miles would fit the bill. He ran through the woods, his favourite retreat, stopping briefly at the '*Magic Pond*', which had given him such a boost in confidence all those months ago, when he doubted his ability and confidence to reach his objective. Once again, the pond provided him with the boost that he needed so much now.

After his run, he had a shower, which made him feel better. He was now ready for the day before him. He made his way to St Michael's and changed into his cassock, and vestment, there was no need for Bob to bring a suitcase any more. Shortly after, Bishop Larkin arrived, and to Father Fenwick's surprise, and pleasure, he was accompanied by Father Frederick, who told him how proud he was of his success, and wished him well for the future, winking as he did so.

"Well, Father Fenwick, you've done it, I always knew that you were the man for the job," Bishop Larkin told him.

At exactly twelve noon, Father Fenwick and Bishop Larkin welcomed the parishioners into the new church, which was full to capacity. Sam took his place at the organ. There was never any doubt who would have the privilege of becoming the church organist. Unfortunately, a pipe organ was deemed out of the question, due to the expense and the work that it would entail. However, through the very kind donations from many of the parishioners, plus money left over from Father Fenwick's sponsored walk, there was enough left to purchase a digital church organ, which provided an authentic church sound. Sam was over the moon when he had seen it for the first time. As he had explained. "I'll be givin' it plenty of welly," and he certainly did just that. Before the mass Sam had given a short organ recital, to demonstrate his prowess, which had taken everyone's breath away, at the level of his virtuosity. There were tears in people's eyes when he played, 'You'll Never Walk Alone.'

After the mass, which was a joyous experience for all who were present, the congregation assembled at the back of the hall for the reception. Father Fenwick was praised for his work, which made him feel very humble. He explained to them all that it was not his work alone that had made the venture a success. He praised everybody who had helped him to settle into the community, and achieve what he had been sent to do, and this day was the culmination of the work.

Bob and Steve had been like a rock to him, not just because he was their priest, but because he was also their friend. He thanked them for that. In particular, he thanked Steve, who had continued to support him, even through his anxiety, when Jen had been placed in the care home.

Steve had told him that Jen's move to the care home had made him into a stronger person, and he was determined to use his experience, as sad as it was, to offer help and support to others who were in a similar situation. Bob, and Father Fenwick had offered their support in this venture as well. One possible idea was to set up a support service, for all those in need in the community, and especially for those individuals who were suffering from the ravages of illnesses, such as Dementia, and their carers, who gave up so much of their own lives in the service of others.

Bob and Vera had invited Steve, Sam, and Father Fenwick for Sunday lunch after the mass, as an extra celebration. As they were preparing to leave the church, Steve turned to Father Fenwick and drew his attention to the window above the altar. The sun had started to pour through it, bathing it in all the colours of the spectrum, just like a rainbow.

"I feel confident for the future," Steve said. "I think that everything is going to be all right."

Bob and Father Fenwick smiled and nodded in agreement. Then, the 'Three Just Men', walked out of the church, the future had just begun.

ABOUT THE AUTHOR

Born and bred in Liverpool.

Moved to North Wales in 1993.

Studied Sociology, Social Policy and Social Work, at University of Wales, Bangor.

Now retired.

Printed in Great Britain
by Amazon